PRAISE FOR
— Manflu —

"A lethal pandemic.
Governmental abuse.
A dramatic shift in power.
And motherhood, but to an infant of the wrong gender!

"In a powerful novel easily ripped from contemporary headlines,
author Simone de Muñoz explores shattered boundaries,
power grabbing politicos, the scientific quest for a vaccine and the
survival of humankind in the aftermath of the global pandemic known
as MANFLU. To complicate things even further, will infant males
born into this new cultural climate even be permitted to thrive?
Thought-provoking and compelling!"

—LAURA TAYLOR,
6-Time Romantic Times Award Winner

MANFLU

by

Simone de Muñoz

FROM THE TINY ACORN ...
GROWS THE MIGHTY OAK

Manflu

Copyright © 2021 Simone de Muñoz. All rights reserved.

Printed in the United States of America.

For information, address Acorn Publishing, LLC, 3943 Irvine Blvd. Ste. 218, Irvine, CA 92602
www.acornpublishingllc.com

Cover design by Damonza.

Author photo by Steven Siebold.

Interior design and digital formatting by Debra Cranfield Kennedy.

ISBN—978-1-952112-30-0 (paperback)
ISBN—978-1-952112-32-4 (hardcover)
Library of Congress Control Number: 2020919856

For the many women

who blazed the trails

down which I stride

and for those who will follow.

■ ■ ■

MANFLU

...

CHAPTER 1

. . .

Morgan Digby woke up groggy from her usual nap as her self-driving, electric car pulled into the driveway of her small suburban house. She had dreamt that her husband Jonas was walking toward her on a crowded sidewalk, cradling a baby in his arms. If only any small part of that dream had the remotest possibility of coming true, Morgan could be happy.

She stretched and brushed her black bangs out of her eyes, feeling the hollow spaces beneath them with her fingertips. Tired from a busy day working at the lab on the manflu vaccine, the nap prepared her for the long evening of caretaking that lay ahead. Her husband Jonas was mostly bedridden after his bout with the pandemic ten years ago. His body no longer actively fought an infection, but he would never be the same.

Morgan was about to enter her house when she saw her neighbor put down her garden rake and cross the street to chat. Sarah, like many women nowadays, no longer bothered with a bra. Her full, bouncing breasts, barely covered by a thin, V-neck t-shirt, drew the eye. An image quickly flashed through Morgan's mind of a time years before when Sarah had pressed those breasts against her and leaned over to kiss her on the lips. Morgan quickly shook her head to clear the thought.

"Morgan, big news!" said Sarah when she was within gossip range. "Beth's nephew came to stay with her. He's a Vulny. I got a glimpse of him through the curtains, and he is a hunk and a half. Pale, obviously. About 5'10" with black, curly hair and surprisingly muscular. He must spend a lot of time lifting weights. I'm charging my vibro3000 as we speak."

Wow, a Vulny! Morgan had never seen one before. Vulnies were the men who had never gotten manflu and were therefore still vulnerable to it. These men could not go out in public for fear of being infected, thus the pale skin. Women could be infected as well as transmit the virus to others; however, they experienced very mild cold-like symptoms and quickly recovered. Both men and women who had previously been infected could not contract the virus again; however, men with post-manflu viral syndrome were immuno-compromised and at high risk of contracting other infections.

Morgan immediately thought of the vaccine she was working on, and she wondered if this man could be a test subject for it when it was completed. She wanted to rush over to Beth's house right away to meet him and find out more, but she couldn't. Jonas waited inside for her to make his dinner, bathe him, and keep him company. She was accustomed to putting aside her own desires to care for her husband, but she still felt a sting of disappointment each time.

Sarah pressed on. "He came here to escape the outbreak happening right now in Colorado. He and his mother drove straight here. Rumor has it that the government is putting manflu on public surfaces to purposely spread it."

"That seems a bit far-fetched to me. Why would the government want to spread manflu? Outbreaks are bound to happen periodically.

That doesn't mean the government is behind them."

"That's what Beth said when she told me her nephew was here. But you're the scientist. You're probably right," said Sarah, taking off her gardening gloves.

"So, how's Robert doing?" Morgan asked, changing the subject. It made her uncomfortable when people thought she knew everything because of her job. Ever since childhood, she had been "the smart one," which she absolutely hated for placing her at a distance from everyone else. Talking about Sarah's husband was safer because it was common ground.

Robert also had been afflicted with manflu during the pandemic. "Same as always," said Sarah, sighing. Like most men who had survived manflu, Robert—like Jonas—was impotent, sterile and mostly bedridden. Sarah, along with many others, made liberal use of her vibro3000 to compensate. Morgan preferred the Bunny Ears Model 5 but still felt shy discussing the topic with the other women in the neighborhood.

Morgan put her hand on Sarah's arm. "Robert should join Jonas's online support group for those suffering from long-term manflu complications. The men find it so useful to talk to others in the same situation. They share information about medical care and vent sometimes."

Jonas found meaning in helping others. When he was first dealing with the aftermath of manflu, he became very depressed. He had lost a number of close friends to the disease, and his life had changed dramatically and quickly. He could no longer play soccer and drink beer with friends, nor was he able to participate in previously very enjoyable marital activities. But he had adjusted to his new life and had become passionate about helping others do the same.

"I've mentioned it to him before, but he doesn't seem interested. He's very bitter about the situation he's in. Luckily, he's still able to work a bit from home. Otherwise, I'm not sure how he would survive." Sarah shook her head, causing her honey-colored hair to shift around her face. "It's been difficult for both of us."

Morgan understood how hopeless and lonely her friend felt since she struggled with those feelings, too. "I know it's been hard, Sarah. I admire how you've stuck with Robert through it all."

"Well," Sarah paused as if considering her words carefully. "Love doesn't always look how you think it will."

Morgan said goodbye to Sarah and stepped into her outdoor disinfecting shower. She needed to wash off the germs from the outside world before entering the house to protect Jonas from anything she might bring home on her clothing from her lab work. She was frequently tested for viruses at work, so the risk of person-to-person transmission of any illnesses was low; however, the shower added another layer of protection. The lemony, chemical smell of the disinfectant soap was an unwelcome intruder in her nose. She put on clean house clothes and went inside.

She first stopped by the laundry room to make sure that the laundrybot was working correctly. Years ago, the first wave of majority-female politicians implemented contests with big cash prizes for inventing robots that could take over household tasks. The lab next door to Morgan's won the prize for the laundrybot, and Morgan had them build her a replica so she wouldn't have to wait for it to become commercially available. She was still waiting for a kitchenbot, which had a waitlist of over a year! After she verified the laundrybot was not putting any of her wool sweaters into the dryer, she went in to Jonas.

Jonas lay in bed, wearing his typical outfit of button-down old man pajamas. Of Scandinavian ancestry, Jonas had been paper-white prior to becoming ill. His skin now displayed a yellowish hue. He watched the news on TV, his head propped up with pillows and his thin legs and concave torso covered in a stack of worn, faded blankets.

An ad advertised SquirmySpermy, the best sperm bank in the region. The few men who were not rendered impotent and sterile by manflu received exorbitant fees for their donations. Some women were desperate to have babies at any cost. Most wanted female babies not at risk of contracting the virus.

Morgan had thought about having a baby but did not see how to make it work between her job at the lab and her sick husband. Recently having turned forty, Morgan was all-too aware that she was running out of time. The topic was painful to both Morgan and Jonas, so they avoided discussing it. Jonas turned off the TV as Morgan sat on the bed.

"How was work, sweetheart?" Jonas asked, his voice reedy sounding.

"Actually, we hit a very important milestone today," replied Morgan. "We completed the testing on mice, and we're ready to begin the primate trials." Her heart beat quickly as she shared this new development.

"That's fantastic!" Jonas exclaimed, his voice cracking with the effort of speaking.

Morgan twisted her wedding band around her finger. "It is good news, but we're under a lot of pressure. The lab's license to conduct testing on primates is about to expire. We have to finish the research in the next few months."

"Can't you renew the license?" Jonas asked, taking her hands in his.

"I think we could, but I'm not sure. Animal activists have been protesting our use of primates to test vaccines. They could get the lab shut down." Morgan sighed. She loved animals but had long ago made peace with the necessity of sacrificing some in the name of scientific advances that would save the lives of millions of humans. Without a vaccine, far fewer male human babies were being born. Humanity itself was at risk without a new infusion of men.

"Would they really shut the lab down?" Jonas asked.

"I don't think the government would let that happen. It's a government-funded lab after all." Morgan's voice sounded unsteady. She wasn't sure if she was trying to convince Jonas or herself.

"Any news about funding? I know that's been a struggle."

Morgan loved how engaged Jonas was with her work. His questions made her feel cared for. They connected deeply on an intellectual and emotional level, and her love for him had never wavered, despite the change in their circumstances. "We've had so many challenges with funding. Nothing new has come through. We're trying to make do with the limited amounts we've received so far."

"That's too bad. I know things would go faster for you with more resources."

"The bottom line is that no one's in a rush to find a vaccine. Everyone likes things this way, with women in charge. I don't blame them—men had been making a mess of things. But there are men out there, Vulnies, who really need this vaccine. And it isn't sustainable to have mostly female babies forever. Society will need more men eventually." Morgan rested her head on Jonas's pillow.

"The women *are* running things much better." said Jonas. "On the news just now, they mentioned President Álvarez's signature initiative, which is turning yet another defunct federal prison into a community center. Locally, they're building several new roads and bridges with state-of-the-art technology. Plus, the stock market is up. We should've put you ladies in charge a long time ago. Too bad it took this horrible illness for us to get here. I wish we could've figured this out without all the suffering." He slowly raised a weak hand to Morgan's face and gently stroked her cheek.

The couple continued to talk as Morgan gave Jonas a sponge bath and changed the sheets on the bed. Her arms were wiry and strong from years of caretaking. She noticed, as she did every time she bathed him, how little remaining muscle tone he had. She gently and lovingly trimmed his beard, witnessing up-close how sunken and deeply wrinkled his cheeks were.

He appeared far older than how Morgan had pictured he would look at forty-two. It was ironic how thin he was because *before*, Jonas was a big social drinker who sported a jiggly beer belly. He had thought nothing of eating a whole pizza or an 18-ounce steak in one sitting.

Morgan preferred Asian-style meals heavy on vegetables and rice like those she had grown up eating. Now, however, Jonas could barely keep down the hospital-style meals that Morgan prepared for him while hardly eating anything more substantial herself. On the menu tonight: chicken noodle soup and strawberry Jell-O for two.

CHAPTER 2

...

"**G**ood morning, Gena," said Morgan as she came upon her best friend parking her bike in the rack outside their workplace the next day. Nearly identical to all the commercial buildings in their bio-technology-focused suburb, the lab was a box-like structure.

"Hey, Morgan," said Gena, looking up, "I barely made it on time today. I fit in a run before I rode my bike over." She took off her helmet and smoothed her curly brown hair, pulled up in a ponytail so it would stay out of her way in the lab.

Morgan was always impressed by Gena's commitment to fitness—Morgan was more of a "lounge around and read a book" type of person, although she didn't have much time for that between her job and her responsibilities at home.

"Did you get Patty to run with you this time?" asked Morgan.

Patty was Gena's partner. She wasn't big on fitness either, but Gena could occasionally convince her to do a workout together. Morgan was ashamed to admit it to herself, but she sometimes felt jealous that Gena had a partner capable of going for a run. She was so lucky to be a lesbian! Unlike other women who had become more open to the same gender since the pandemic narrowed their options, Morgan was not interested in women in that way. When her neighbor Sarah had tried to make out with her after a few glasses of wine that one night, the whole thing felt awkward. Jonas had said he didn't mind if she needed some extracurricular activity, but she just couldn't get turned on by a curvy blonde.

"No, she was busy preparing for class," said Gena, holding the door open for Morgan and walking in after her. Patty was a philosophy professor. Morgan nodded to Andrea, the office manager/receptionist, who greeted her briefly, and returned to the phone conversation she was having in Spanish. Andrea carried herself with the bearing of someone who had enjoyed a private school education. Her graying brown hair was always styled in an updo that revealed a rotating variety of cat earrings seemingly at odds with her elegant persona.

"Good morning, Andrea. Did the cell culture material come in yet?" Gena asked.

Andrea pressed a button to put her call on hold. "No, we had to wait until the start of the new quarter to put the order in because funds were not available. The material should be in next week."

"All right, thanks," said Gena, groaning softly. She turned to Morgan with an exasperated look that said, *How am I supposed to make vaccine samples without cell culture material?*

Morgan gave Gena a sympathetic nod. Last quarter, she had had to argue that food for the monkeys was not something that could wait for a new budget cycle. The women walked past the reception area farther into the building. As they passed, Andrea continued talking on the phone, glaring at them.

"She keeps 'forgetting' that I speak Spanish," Gena whispered to Morgan. "She just called us a name that I won't bother translating for you."

"I wonder what her problem is," said Morgan. Gena shrugged.

Morgan could only speculate that Andrea resented the fact that the scientists were paid much better than the support staff. Money was a tricky topic because, over the past decade, many women had been forced to adjust to managing household expenditures without a male partner to share the burden.

Morgan looked back as the lobby door closed loudly. Her boss, Charlotte, had come in. As Morgan and Gena watched, Andrea seemed to transform into a completely different person. She immediately ended her phone call, stood to greet Charlotte, and offered to make her a cup of coffee. Her voice took on a simpering tone. Charlotte smiled broadly in response.

Morgan turned away in disgust. How could Charlotte not see through Andrea's brown-nosing? She and Gena continued walking toward their desks.

"I heard Gavin is coming in today," Gena said with a slight frown. "I wonder if the entourage will be joining us." She sat at her desk and turned on the computer.

"Luckily, I'll be busy prepping the primates for the vaccine testing and won't have to deal with them." Morgan, sitting at her own computer next to Gena's, pulled up her work plan for the day.

Gavin was one of the lucky few who had survived manflu unharmed and with usable sperm. He was a test subject helping researchers determine why he had been spared the ill effects of the virus and use that knowledge to develop treatments for those still suffering the lingering effects of manflu. To Gavin, manflu had been no worse than a mild cold. The researchers still had not figured it out.

What Morgan did know was that Gavin was making money hand over fist with his frequent donations. He usually rolled up to the lab in a very fancy sports car, a rare commodity given the mechanic shortage despite the fact that more women had eventually entered the field following the pandemic.

From what Morgan had observed in the lab, she found Gavin to be very full of himself. To be fair, it would be hard not to develop an ego with women fawning all over you everywhere you went because you were one of the few fertile and virile men on earth. Still, Morgan thought he could tone it down a bit. If she were in his shoes, she would surely act with more decorum.

At that moment, Gavin, looking like the IT nerd he was *before*, with his mud-colored messy hair and thick black-framed glasses, entered the building surrounded by women of the type you usually didn't see anymore. With few men to impress, most women wore flat shoes, elastic-waist or yoga pants, baggy t-shirts, no make-up or fancy jewelry, and casual hair, much of it gray. These three ladies were a blast from the past with stiletto heels, tight skirts, low-cut tops, and full hair and makeup. Every time Morgan saw them, she felt relieved she didn't have to dress like that ever.

Gena had made up nicknames for them—Eeny, Meany and Miny, and Gavin was Mo. Miny was short and curvy with freckles and a blonde bob; Meany had jet-black, long hair and a permanent look on her face like she had just eaten a lemon; and Eeny was the other one, a conventionally attractive Caucasian brunette.

Morgan reflexively sucked in her stomach and sat up straight with her small chest angled out until she caught herself and relaxed. Who was she trying to impress? She didn't even like Gavin. Her willingness to work with him showed how devoted she was to identifying treatments for manflu and finding the vaccine. Nothing about the research process was easy. The lab had been working on manflu for nearly ten years now. They had developed only a few moderately effective treatments. Morgan finally felt like they were getting close to a vaccine and she was willing to do whatever it took to complete it.

Morgan and Gena's supervisor, Charlotte, a middle-aged curvy Black woman with short gray hair, approached them, barely making a sound in her squishy black ballet flats and pajama-style black clothing. She carried the coffee that Andrea had made for her. Charlotte, a motherly type, wore her red glasses on a chain long enough for them to fall past her chest. She often organized office potlucks and meal trains for those whose husbands had taken a turn for the worse.

"Gena, come on. We're about to start our meeting," said Charlotte.

Gena rolled her eyes to Morgan behind Charlotte's back before walking off in the direction of the conference room. Their office was heavy on meetings. It was impossible to get anything done without near consensus.

Morgan knew Gena constantly had to check her tendency to steamroll in order to accomplish what could be done a lot faster if she were in charge. They had both seen what had happened to others frustrated with the office dynamics. They were pushed out, and nothing changed.

"And Morgan, I need you to do Gavin's exam. Shoshana is off today taking care of her husband," said Charlotte, handing Morgan a HERO, an electronic clipboard-style device whose acronym stood for Health Electronic Record Object, pre-loaded with the interview questions.

As Charlotte walked toward the conference room, Morgan said, "Charlotte, wait. I need to prep the primates for the vaccine testing."

Charlotte paused to look at Morgan. "This is the priority right now, Morgan. Either find a way to do both, or the primates will have to wait until tomorrow." She did not wait for a response but continued on.

As Morgan always did, she went along with what she was told. She mentally re-arranged her schedule to make sure she could still complete her critical work with the primates later that day.

She glanced over the questions on the HERO, her eyes widening, and she bit her lip.

First of all, she didn't even usually work with human subjects. Her specialty was studying the effects of potential vaccines on primates. Her days typically began with visiting the monkeys the lab kept for vaccine trials and, if any trials were in progress, assessing the monkeys' symptoms. She also analyzed data that resulted from these trials. Interviewing actual humans, however, made her uneasy, though she was always willing to help a colleague in need. People were often out caring for ill husbands, fathers, or sons. Many had covered for her when Jonas's condition flared up.

When she looked at the interview questions, she noticed she would need to ask Gavin all kinds of personal questions about his sex life. Talking to strange men about sex, especially one as full of himself as Gavin, made her uncomfortable. She looked around to see if there was anyone nearby who might be able to take over, but there was not. Morgan sighed. She would have to do the interview.

Morgan approached Gavin and the women, who were sitting in the lobby. She took a deep breath and said in her most professional voice, "Hi Gavin, I'm Dr. Digby. Are you ready for your exam? Please come with me."

The lovely Eeny, Meany, and Miny made a move to tag along, but he shook them off and followed Morgan to an exam room. The entourage remained in the lobby to wait for their virile, if slightly nerdy, Prince Charming. Morgan couldn't believe these women had nothing better to do than follow Gavin around all day.

When Morgan and Gavin entered the exam room, Morgan motioned for him to sit. "I'm going to ask you some questions. They are a bit personal in nature this time." From reviewing the information on the HERO, Morgan knew that Gavin's previous exams had been more general. This time they would focus on his sexual behavior and fertility.

"It's fine. I understand you need the information for your research," Gavin said.

Morgan was glad he wasn't going to be difficult about it. With his technical background, she assumed he understood the value of science.

"All right, let's begin. How many times a day do you typically ejaculate?" Morgan jumped right in with the hard question. She blushed quite easily and willed her flushed face and neck to cool off.

"Around three or four," replied Gavin.

Morgan swallowed nervously as she took notes. "Are those occasions, um, with partners or alone?" She tried to maintain a scientific detachment, but a profound sense of embarrassment continued to creep over her, making her skin prickle.

Gavin took a deep breath. He sat on the exam table, kicking his legs like an overgrown child. Morgan thought he must have felt awkward, too.

"I usually start off with a partner, er, some partners, and I make sure to finish in a sample cup."

"Every time?" Morgan coughed.

"Yes, they pay me thousands for each sample. I don't want to waste a drop," Gavin said. "Also, I wouldn't want to get anyone pregnant. Becoming a father would definitely cramp my style, if you know what I mean." Gavin winked at Morgan, who blushed even deeper.

"And how do you transport the sample to the sperm bank?" Morgan asked when she could squeak out a few words. Her embarrassment was turning to anger at Charlotte for putting her in this position.

"I send my self-driving Maserati. Gets there real fast—still warm," he offered casually. Morgan got a mental picture of a sports car filled with sperm samples. She blinked rapidly to clear her mind.

"Do you or your partners use some sort of birth control? In case of any, erm, unexpected situations?" Morgan asked.

"Birth control?" Gavin seemed surprised. "I haven't seen birth control in years. Do they even make it anymore? Nah, if they get pregnant, they'll either keep it or have an abortion, up to them. Unless it was a boy—no one in their right mind would keep a boy."

Morgan noted to herself how casually he spoke about a potential baby of his own while his sperm donations had resulted in untold numbers of new lives.

"All right, thanks for this. You've been very helpful," said Morgan. She double-checked her HERO to make sure that she had captured all the necessary information. This had better be sufficient because she was more than done. "Now we will need to collect a sample. You can use the room over there," Morgan said, pointing to the door.

"Can I invite some of my friends to, uh, lend a helping hand?" asked Gavin, smirking.

Morgan was sure she had gone beyond flushing red. She felt full-on purple from her hairline to her toes at the thought of some kind of orgy happening at her place of work. She paused briefly. "Ummm, absolutely not. We prefer to keep the environment professional." She raced out of the room as quickly as possible, leaving Gavin to chuckle as he jumped off the table and went to complete the task at hand.

Morgan escaped to the break room, where she put her head down on her arms like a kindergartner taking a nap at school. She thought about when she was a child and had asked her parents where babies came from. Her conservative Chinese parents couldn't bear to have this type of conversation with her, but because they knew she was growing up in a different world than they did and she needed the information, they always had a book ready for her. Still, she had absorbed from them a deep sense of shame.

She couldn't understand how Gavin could discuss these topics so blithely. His casual attitude rubbed her the wrong way. She vowed never to conduct interviews with him again. Charlotte would have to find someone else to replace Shoshanna next time.

She powered through the rest of her workday, feeling the heat rise in her cheeks whenever her thoughts turned to Gavin, which they did surprisingly often. She wondered what he looked like without his glasses. Images flashed in her mind of the entourage helping Gavin with his "work." She was relieved when it was time to go home. Taking care of Jonas would consume all of her thoughts and leave no room for these unwelcome distractions. She spent her Friday night like any other, feeding Jonas dinner, giving him a sponge bath, and reading aloud to him from one of their favorite poetry books.

CHAPTER 3

...

The next morning, as she frequently did on Saturdays, Morgan walked over to her neighbor Beth's house for a chat. Strolling on the well-maintained sidewalk, she took a moment to tilt her head up and savor the sunshine that already warmed the leafy suburban block. Morgan usually didn't notice the beautiful California weather because she spent most of her time in her lab or at home.

Morgan always struggled with leaving Jonas on his own for a few hours but felt an obligation to check in on Beth. Like Morgan, Beth had no children. Morgan worried that the older woman might grow lonely even though she would never admit it nor ask for anything. Morgan had always enjoyed spending time with Beth, but she made more of an effort to keep tabs on her since her husband had died in the pandemic.

Beth, a nurse at the local hospital, was very no-nonsense. She wore sensible shoes to parties *before* as well as now. Even her hobbies were productive—knitting and baking. Morgan could count on something fresh out of the oven every time she visited.

Morgan thought about whether there would be chocolate chip cookies or apple strudel on offer when she walked up to the house.

Beth opened the door. "Hi, Morgan. You can come in the house, but please disinfect in the outdoor shower unit first because my nephew is visiting. I have a robe you can use."

Morgan had completely forgotten that Beth's supposedly gorgeous nephew was in town. She couldn't wait to get a look at him. While she showered, she looked down at the exposed white skin of her legs sparingly sprinkled with dark hair that she no longer bothered to shave. Now, she felt self-conscious.

As the water washed over her, Morgan closed her eyes and thought about how she would get ready to meet a man in her younger days, when she wouldn't meet in person until she had chatted with him online for weeks first, building anticipation. She recalled the hours spent selecting the perfect outfit, often in consultation with a girlfriend over video chat. And the long showers she would take, washing her hair with flower-scented shampoo and shaving her legs with foaming-peach shaving cream and a pink plastic razor. Fruity body lotion, shimmery makeup, and gooey hair products would follow. So many different creams, powders, and potions packed with feminine scents.

At the time she had her first date with Jonas in the 2020s, jumpsuits were in fashion. She had carefully selected a black body-skimming jumpsuit with a halter top; her hair, cut at a trendy sharp angle, stopped right before the tie at the back of her neck. The outfit showed off her shoulders, the creamy skin flawless. Jonas hadn't been able to take his eyes off of her. She remembered feeling pretty and desirable as they spent hours eating, drinking, and chatting in a beer garden.

The harsh lemon scent of the disinfectant soap brought Morgan back to the present. She must have been in the shower for a while because her fingers were wrinkled. Beth and her nephew would wonder where she was. Morgan finished her shower and shrugged into the clean white robe Beth kept on hand for guests, then glanced at a shoulder no longer creamy white but marked with a spattering of age spots.

The nephew was in the living room, playing classical music on the piano with long, thin, elegant fingers. Morgan's neighbor Sarah was not wrong. He was a hunk and a half. With his curly, medium-length black hair, pale skin, sparkly blue eyes, dimples, and compact, muscular frame, he was movie-star, drop-dead gorgeous. When he finished what he was playing, he turned to smile at Morgan, who promptly forgot how to breathe. She was very aware of her thin body, completely nude under the robe. She perched on the edge of a high-backed chair, not daring to sit on the couch where she might sink in and expose even more flesh.

"This is my neighbor, Morgan. She plays the piano, too," Beth said, breaking the awkward silence.

Morgan nodded mutely.

"Nice to meet you, Morgan, I'm Nate," said the younger man in a deep, friendly voice that completed the perfect package. He bounced up off the piano bench and flopped on the couch near Morgan's chair like a teenager might, even though he was in his early twenties.

"Nice to meet you," said Morgan, who could think of literally nothing else to say. She felt as if her tongue were swollen to ten times its normal size. The blood drained out of her brain, leaving her incapable of rational thought. She caught Beth looking at her oddly and flushed.

"Nate's visiting from Colorado," said Beth, rescuing them again. "There's a very severe outbreak there right now, and he's a Vulny. I'm sure his mother and sisters—my sister and nieces—are missing him something awful right now. He's such good company, playing piano for me and fixing my computer." She smiled at Nate. "Morgan is researching a vaccine. She's so smart. I know she will make it work. Maybe someday you will be vaccinated and live a normal life."

Morgan prayed Beth was right. She wanted nothing more than to help people like Nate live full lives. She only hoped that Beth wasn't over-promising.

"Please tell me about your job, Morgan. I want to hear about this vaccine you're working on," said Nate, leaning forward and fixing his blue eyes on her.

She wanted to swim in them like one might take a dip in the ocean. "I would love to tell you about my work," said Morgan. "How much do you know about the science of manflu? I don't want to tell you what you already know."

She felt a little distracted by his gaze, but her love of science kicked in, and she was excited to share her knowledge. She rarely had the opportunity to discuss her work with people outside of the lab, and she always enjoyed it. Conversations like these were also a way to connect with the memory of her father, who had been a science professor and loved sharing his knowledge with others.

"Start from the beginning. I learned a little about it from my high school online biology class, but to be honest, I was playing a video game while I was supposed to be paying attention, so I'm sure I missed a lot." Nate chuckled.

Wow, high school biology. Morgan must have taken that class twenty-five years ago. She looked at Nate with his unlined face and bright eyes and felt every one of her forty years. "Great. Well, not great that you missed out on biology, but great that I get to explain it all to you," said Morgan, going back to the science, where she felt comfortable. "What's known commonly as 'manflu' is actually a novel paramyxovirus. This family of viruses causes familiar diseases such as measles and mumps."

"Yup, I remember that. And everyone gets the MMR vaccine as a kid, right?" asked Nate.

"That's exactly the problem. Most people get that shot, which is for measles, mumps, and rubella; however, about fifteen to twenty years ago, there was a growing cluster of people who refused to vaccinate their children, and measles outbreaks became more common."

"I don't know how some people can be so stupid," said Beth, who had been quiet up to that point. She shook her head angrily. Morgan knew Beth, a nurse, was very science-minded. She had even volunteered with a nonprofit whose mission was vaccinating children.

"Researchers believe a particularly virulent strain of measles mutated into manflu, but it acts similar to mumps, which among other things causes orchitis. Manflu disproportionately impacts men."

"What's orchitis?" asked Nate.

"Swelling of the testicles," said Morgan. "The vaccine we're working on for manflu mimics an inactivated vaccine that was the first vaccine used against mumps. The current mumps vaccine is from an attenuated virus, but manflu is so deadly, we don't want to take the risk of using live virus, even if it has been weakened."

"Wow, that's fascinating," said Nate. "Sign me up for the next study."

"Would you really be willing to help test the vaccine?"

"Absolutely! What've I got to lose?"

"Nate has always been so brave," piped up Beth, who stood behind him and affectionately patted his shoulder.

"That's very kind of you. I'll definitely take you up on your offer," said Morgan. She was excited by the thought of having more contact with Nate through her work.

"Nate, have you ever been tested for manflu antibodies?" asked Morgan. She assumed that he had been, and had tested negative, but wanted to make sure. If he somehow did have antibodies, that would mean he had already been exposed to the virus and had immunity and therefore could live a normal life.

"I was as a kid, but they said the test wasn't very accurate. It came back inconclusive. Why do you ask?"

"They're developing a new test that is rapid and super accurate," said Morgan. "Would you want to take it?"

"Definitely. If I had antibodies, that would change everything," said Nate. "I could go out in the world and live. I could travel and meet people and so much more."

Of course Nate longed to go out and live his life, Morgan thought. What young man his age wanted to hang out with his middle-aged aunt forever, as lovely as she was.

"I'll let you know when it becomes available," said Morgan. "I should have access to it at work. We're expecting development to be completed soon."

Beth served fresh scones, and the conversation moved on to piano and Nate's love of classical music, especially Beethoven. Their situations were different, but Nate said he felt inspired by how Beethoven overcame challenges with his hearing to compose his famous symphonies. As a social person, Nate had to fight to overcome his isolation since fear of manflu kept him homebound.

Morgan thought about how she had been forced to play piano for years by her parents, who believed that learning a musical instrument helped with brain development. At first, she resisted as any teen resists the things that seem important to their parents. She eventually came to love music, too, especially classical. She was now very glad she had an interest in common with Nate.

"Morgan, will you come play piano with me sometime?" asked Nate.

She would love to play piano with Nate. She was nearly drooling at the possibility. However, should she put herself in a tempting situation like that? Visiting a handsome younger man to play piano did not seem consistent with the wedding vows she had made to Jonas. But she was so lonely and in need of some fun adult contact. She could come over once and see how it went. That wouldn't cause any harm. Anyway, what trouble could they get into with Beth around?

"Sure, Nate, I would like that." She kept her voice calm so as not to reveal her excitement at the prospect of sitting next to this handsome young man on a small piano bench.

Back at home later that evening, Morgan slipped into the guest bedroom, the one that had been meant for a baby someday, and took her Bunny Ears Model 5 out of the nightstand drawer. She got into bed and lost herself in a fantasy of taking charge with Nate, grabbing his hand and leading him to his bedroom, where she would direct him to caress every part of her body with his long fingers. In her fantasy, she didn't feel shy or reluctant to take what she wanted.

The guest room shared a wall with the master bedroom, and Morgan knew Jonas could hear what she was doing, but they never talked about it. Jonas tried to bring it up one time in a gentle way, encouraging Morgan to let him watch, but she couldn't.

She had been raised in the type of home where the word "divorce" was whispered and no one was allowed to date until they turned eighteen. The conversations she had about the birds and the bees were of the "don't do it" variety. If her parents had ever seen a vibrator, they would have fainted from shock.

The building physical sensations eventually pushed all thoughts of Jonas and her parents out of her mind until she climaxed, biting down on the pillow to keep herself from crying out.

CHAPTER 4

· · ·

few days later, Andrea stopped Morgan as she walked
through the front of the office. "Charlotte's looking for you,"
Andrea said with a smile, as if Morgan were in trouble and
she was happy about it.

As Andrea spoke, Morgan noticed her desk area covered with
framed pictures of her daughter at different ages, nature posters, and
various cat-themed decorations. *What was it with those cats?* She
waited to see if Andrea would say more, but she just crossed her arms
over her chest smugly.

Morgan proceeded to her own desk, which was devoid of any
personal items, and had barely settled into her seat when Charlotte
approached carrying the gleaming HERO. Her pajama-like outfit was
dark gray instead of black for a change. Gena sat at the next computer
but remained engrossed in her work and did not even look up.

"Good morning, Morgan. Hello, Gena. I hope you're both well.
Morgan, Shoshanna is out for an extended period, and I'll need you
to take over the research with Gavin permanently," said Charlotte,
attempting to hand over the HERO.

Morgan sucked in her breath. She had been dreading this moment. She stood and put out a hand in the universal "stop" gesture. "Charlotte, I'm not sure if I can do this. I'm very busy with the primates right now."

"Look, Morgan, everyone needs to help out. This research is top priority. And Gavin has specifically asked for you."

Could it be true? Why would Gavin ask for her? They barely knew each other, and she had nearly died of embarrassment when she last interacted with him. She didn't know what to say. She couldn't exactly tell Charlotte that she couldn't handle a research subject.

"What about the primates, Charlotte?"

"You're so efficient, I'm sure you can handle both. I'm counting on you, Morgan." Charlotte stood with a hand on one hip, tapping her foot impatiently.

There was no way Morgan could say no to her boss. She would have to make it work. Maybe she could increase the hours of the caregiver service she used so she could work longer hours. If Charlotte was asking, it must be important.

"He asked for me . . ." Morgan mused aloud.

"I'm not sure if you're aware, but Gavin is a major financial supporter of this lab in addition to being a research subject. Whatever he asks for, within reason, he's going to get. So please take this HERO and go meet him in the lobby. I don't want him kept waiting. I'll trust you to work out any remaining details at a later time."

Charlotte handed over the HERO and walked away without even looking back as if certain Morgan would do as she had asked.

Morgan took a moment to read over the questions. Her hands were already shaking and sweaty from the conversation with Charlotte. The thought of speaking to Gavin again was making her even more agitated.

Gena stood up from her own computer and went over to Morgan.

"What's the research topic?" Gena asked gently.

"It looks like the questions are all about nutrition, at least for today," said Morgan, blowing out a breath and giving herself a silent mini pep talk.

"Nutrition. How bad could that be?" said Gena shrugging.

"Thanks a lot, Gena! You probably jinxed me by saying that," said Morgan.

She and Gena both laughed, Morgan's giggles higher pitched while Gena's were throatier. Gena returned to her computer, and Morgan went into the lobby to greet Gavin. He smiled and looked pleased to see her, which made her chest tighten and her hands start to tremble again.

"Good morning, Gavin. I'll be conducting your research studies from now on," said Morgan as she led him through the lab and into the exam room. She kept her face neutral and professional so he wouldn't realize she would rather be anywhere else doing anything else.

"That's great news," said Gavin, rubbing his hands together excitedly. "Shoshanna was kind of boring."

Morgan's eyebrows shot up before she could stop them. How dare he criticize her colleague so flippantly? Shoshanna was a very nice person and an excellent researcher. She was not boring! Morgan had spent hours analyzing the white blood cells' immune response to manflu with Shoshanna and thought she was brilliant. However, Morgan was not about to get drawn into discussions with Gavin that did not relate to the research, so she said nothing to defend Shoshanna.

Morgan instead introduced the topic of the day. "Gavin, today we're going to discuss nutrition. We will be looking at whether anything in your diet contributes to your immunity to manflu. This information is critical to developing potential therapeutics for the virus. Please begin by telling me what you eat in a typical day."

"Do you mean food only, or are you interested in other things that go into my mouth as well, Dr. Digby?" asked Gavin with a smirk.

"What?" Morgan frowned. She was not prepared for this—she had been expecting a conversation about nutrition! This would be even worse than she had thought. She was furious with Charlotte for making her do this.

Gavin stared at her. He blinked rapidly behind thick glasses and smiled subtly with surprisingly red, sensual lips.

"Just food, please," said Morgan, recovering herself. She glanced over Gavin's head at the exit, tempted to escape to the breakroom.

"All right. I start the day with a smoothie that one of the ladies concocts for me. She makes sure to add lots of fruits and veggies to keep me at peak performance. I have an omelet on the side for some protein. I drink plenty of water to keep up my fluids. Lunch, I go a little crazy. I like to relive the old days studying computer science and working in tech—I usually have a burger and fries or some pizza. Don't worry. I burn it all off in the afternoons," he said with a wink. "Dinner is whatever the ladies are eating. Usually a salad. I like to keep things light before turning in for the night." He winked again.

Jeez, this guy could make anything sexual, even a salad. He was cute, but being so obvious was a major turn-off, at least for her. She felt so embarrassed by these conversations. Her mind flicked over to Nate's more subtle sexuality, his gorgeous body and the way it moved. She forced herself to re-focus on the interview.

"What about snacks? Do you typically snack throughout the day?" Morgan asked.

"No, I don't have much time for snacks with all my *activity*," Gavin said suggestively. "Plus, I try to stay trim for the ladies." He patted what Morgan noticed was an extremely fit midsection.

Morgan continued without comment. "Are there any desserts

you typically enjoy?" She braced herself for whipped cream-covered body parts or edible underwear, but Gavin didn't go there for once.

"I do have a weakness for chocolate. Thank goodness those researchers developed that low-cal version. It's delicious!"

"What about alcohol consumption?" Once again, Morgan mentally prepared herself for a description of wild, cocktail-fueled, sex parties.

"I have a few beers now and then. To be honest, drinking sometimes gets me down." Morgan looked up suddenly, surprised that Gavin had said something serious and non-sexual.

"Do you suffer from depression?" she asked.

"I wouldn't say depression, but the world is a lonely place without any guys to hang out with. Sometimes after a few beers, I start reminiscing about having drinks with the guys *before*. I think about the dive bar that we used to hit up after work. It's sad not to be able to do that anymore, you know?"

Morgan nodded silently. Was she supposed to feel sorry for him because he couldn't go bar hopping with the guys? Her whole family had died, and her husband was bedridden. She glanced back at the HERO and quickly asked the rest of her nutrition questions with half of her mind on other things. Why hadn't she stood up to Charlotte? Surely there was someone else who could conduct these interviews? Aparna must have some free time now that the mice testing was complete. Had Gavin really asked for her personally? She found herself strangely flattered at the thought.

"So, what do you like to do when you're not asking me personal questions?" asked Gavin as the session wrapped up.

"Well, the primary focus of my research is testing vaccines on primates," replied Morgan.

"That's great, but I mean, what do you like to do for fun?"

"Um . . ." Morgan stammered and fell silent. She thought about the hours she spent feeding and bathing Jonas. It's not like she had time for a hobby.

"What, too personal of a question?" asked Gavin.

"No, it's not that. It's just that I don't have time for fun."

"Oh? Why is that?" Gavin looked at her intensely. She wasn't used to anyone focusing on her like that. She looked down at her HERO.

"I'm married, and my husband is . . . you know . . ." Even after all this time, she couldn't easily put Jonas's condition into words. "He needs a high level of care," she finally said. "He has suffered greatly from the aftereffects of manflu."

"I didn't realize. I understand now. That must be so hard for you both," said Gavin.

Morgan was surprised by his empathy. She looked into his eyes and found a more serious expression than she ever remembered seeing before.

"It's important to me that we overcome this terrible disease. I mean, we as a society," said Gavin. "I got lucky. It could've been me in that situation. Instead, I live in a mansion surrounded by beautiful ladies. It's not fair. I feel a responsibility to help others now."

Morgan considered that she might have underestimated Gavin. Obviously, he liked to have fun, but it now seemed there was another side to him.

"We appreciate your help, Gavin. We really do," said Morgan.

"Sure, anytime."

As she walked Gavin out, she felt less angry at Charlotte for assigning her to do these interviews but also confused about her feelings. She never would have guessed that Gavin was actually a caring person. Oddly, he was both raunchy and nice. Morgan had never before encountered this combination in one person, and she did not know what to make of it.

CHAPTER 5

. . .

Morgan was exhausted when her alarm went off the next morning. She longed to remain in bed just a few extra moments but couldn't. She had stayed at work late, completing some of the tasks she had been unable to do in the morning because of her session with Gavin. She still had more to do. She turned on the TV at a low volume, taking care not to wake the still-sleeping Jonas as she bustled around the bedroom.

The morning news came on. The anchor said, "As we do every year on this date, we are observing a moment of silence in remembrance of men lost during the manflu pandemic ten years ago and those who continue to be affected." Morgan felt as if she had been punched in the stomach. She had completely forgotten about Manflu Remembrance Day.

She stood still for a moment with her eyes closed. She thought of her dear father and younger brother, who had passed away quickly, before anyone had identified the virus. And of her mother, who had succumbed to heart trouble only a year later, literally dying of a broken heart. She mourned the strong, robust man her husband used to be and the babies they would never have. And of other family members, friends, and neighbors who had passed on or were bed-bound, dependent on the women in their lives for care.

Her thoughts turned to those women, busy keeping the world spinning. So many had stepped up to take over jobs previously done for the most part by men. The younger generation didn't know any different, but Morgan was still surprised when she saw a female plumber or mechanic. Many of those women did the hard labor and then went home to work another shift, caring for men who could do very little for themselves.

"Good morning, dear," said Jonas softly.

Morgan opened her eyes and looked over at him lying in bed. She went to him and bent down, draping an arm over his thin body. He weakly returned her embrace. She sat next to him, and they held hands for a moment. Morgan languished in her own sad thoughts, just like Jonas. There was nothing left to say. Her eyes burned with the weight of ten years of tears. She felt so sad, she didn't know how she would make it through the day.

CHAPTER 6

...

Morgan left work a little early, drained from the painful reminders she encountered during a day filled with colleagues becoming emotional as they remembered loved ones who had passed away. Morgan decided to stop by Beth's house. She wanted to see how her friend was holding up on Manflu Remembrance Day. And, if she was being honest with herself, she needed to unburden herself of some of the grief she felt.

When she walked up to Beth's house, she was surprised to find Nate in the front yard, his dimpled face turned to the waning afternoon sun, free of any mask.

"Nate?" she called out. She kept her distance, having not yet taken a disinfecting shower.

"Oh, hi, Morgan," said Nate. "I just wanted to get some fresh air. Are you coming in? I'll meet you inside after you shower." She nodded as he turned and stepped inside before she could say anything. She thought about admonishing him to stay inside and be safe, but it wasn't really her place.

Morgan paused on her way to the shower. If Nate was outside, that meant Beth wasn't home. Beth would have told him to stay inside. Morgan didn't know what to do—should she risk the temptation of being alone with Nate when her attraction was so strong? Well, she reasoned, just because she liked him didn't mean he liked her back.

She went through the shower, thoroughly disinfecting herself, and put on the waiting short, white robe. Her legs were smooth— recently shaved. Those memories of getting ready for dates when she was in her twenties had inspired her to dig through her bathroom cabinets, looking for a long-neglected plastic razor. She couldn't find one, so she borrowed the shaver she used to keep Jonas's beard neat.

"I'm glad you're here. I could use a partner," said Nate.

"What?" exclaimed Morgan. She couldn't imagine what he might need a partner for. Well, she could imagine, but would not.

"Someone to throw a football with," said Nate, reaching to grab a ball and bouncing from one foot to the other with an excess of energy like a Labrador retriever, ready to play fetch.

"I'm not very sporty," said Morgan, "but I can try." *He must miss his sisters.* She imagined him throwing a football around a leafy backyard with two young, equally athletic women.

Morgan and Nate tossed a ball back and forth. Morgan tried not to stare, but she was drawn to the way his long, thin fingers expertly gripped the ball. And every time he cocked his arm back, his white t-shirt lifted, exposing a muscled, pale belly covered in dark hair. Before she could stop the thought, she wondered what it would be like to lick him all the way up to his mouth and all the way down to his . . . She wondered if the hair tasted of salty sweat.

"Do you want some water?" asked Nate.

Oh dear, had she been licking her lips? The heat rose to her cheeks.

"No, thank you. I'm fine. How's it going with that piano piece you were working on?" she asked. It was hard to talk to someone who never went outside. Especially when all your thoughts when around them were about *indoor* activities.

"I hit a bit of a wall with my composing," he said. "Maybe I need a muse."

Morgan bit back a gasp. Her body felt warm and melty. Was he flirting? Could he be attracted to her? She was too busy trying not to be obvious about her attraction to him. She reminded herself once again that she was at least fifteen years older.

"My middle name is Muse," she found herself saying with a smile. Really? Was that the best she could come up with? She could kick herself.

Nate lifted one thick, dark eyebrow and smiled. "Well, Ms. Morgan Muse, come over by the piano and let's see what we can do." He worked on his piece for a while, and Morgan helped when she could.

"What were things like for you *before*?" Nate asked Morgan as they sat at the piano bench together, close but not touching.

"I had an ordinary life. I worked at a lab that was seeking science-based solutions to fight climate change," Morgan started to explain.

"What's climate change?" asked Nate.

"Oh, gosh. Sometimes I forget how quickly everything changed and how young you are. Humans were polluting the air through manufacturing and agriculture and through the use of fuel in cars before electric vehicles took over. All the carbon in the atmosphere led to strange weather patterns, including significant temperature increases in many regions across the globe. The lab I worked for was developing technology to sequester carbon," said Morgan.

"What happened with that?" Nate asked.

"Well, as the men died or were weakened, transportation and manufacturing needs decreased. People traveled less because they were either home sick or caring for sick loved ones. Fewer products were purchased because there was less disposable income, and as men started dying, there were fewer people to use the products. Also, agricultural production decreased, particularly livestock. Once again, fewer people to eat all that meat. Basically, air pollution went way down, and the climate issues reversed themselves. So the lab I was working for shut down, and I came to work on the manflu vaccine," Morgan continued.

"Wow," said Nate. "Go on." He leaned forward and fixed his blue eyes on her.

"Right, so going back a bit. I was working long hours on climate change, which made it hard to meet men, so I got on a dating app and met the man who would become my husband, Jonas. He was a therapist at the time. Obviously, he couldn't date his patients, so he also struggled with meeting people to date. We clicked right away. We complement each other. At least, we used to. He loves being with people and is so good at focusing on achieving goals. I'm more introverted—typical for a scientist, I guess. I'm also a bit of a dreamer."

Morgan stood and walked around the room, stopping by the window and staring out.

"We loved learning about each other's backgrounds, too. While it would seem that we were raised very differently—me by immigrant Chinese parents and him in an all-American family—the underlying values were the same. The focus was on achieving in school so we could have a good future and the ability to support a family and help others.

"Anyway, we got married and were thinking about having a baby, and then everyone started getting sick. At first, we assumed it was simply a bad flu season, but people noticed eventually that the women recovered and the men did not."

"I remember watching bits of the news on TV as a kid," said Nate, abandoning the piano bench and going to the window to stand behind Morgan. "Especially when the president died, and then the vice president, and then more than half of Congress evaporated. But I was too young to really understand."

"Yes. Around that time, my dad and my brother got sick . . . and then Jonas did, too." Morgan paused, her eyes filling with tears. "I couldn't go to see my dad and my brother because I had to take care of Jonas. I never got to say goodbye," she cried softly, her head in her hands.

"I'm sorry to bring this up. It must be so painful for you," said Nate.

Morgan saw him out of the corner of her eye, moving to place a hand on her shoulder and stopping himself. She regained her composure. They barely knew each other, and it wasn't his job to comfort her.

"No, it's all right. It's good to talk about it, to remember them. My dad was a science professor, who loved to mentor young students." She brushed the tears out of her eyes and turned away from the window to look at Nate. "We always had people over to the house for dinner. My mom made sure to have a big pot of something cooking every night and rice going in the rice cooker. Dad passed along his passion for science to me. My favorite memory is going to work with him as a young kid and looking through the microscope at specimens while he asked me what I thought they were.

"My brother was the total opposite. He was a class clown who liked nothing more than a good practical joke. He played on people's expectations and used the element of surprise in his humor—no one ever thought the Asian kid would be such a trickster. When I helped my mom clean out his room after he died, we kept finding whoopie cushions and rubber chickens.

"After they both died, my mom couldn't go on. She was in so

much pain. The house was too quiet. She was soft-spoken herself, but she thrived on all the energy—like me with Jonas, I guess. I miss being able to call and talk to her. She was such a good listener, you know?"

Nate nodded sympathetically.

"What about you, Nate?" Morgan asked. "You were so young." Morgan sat on the edge of the couch with her legs close together, bare feet crossed at the ankles, short robe modestly arranged.

Nate sat on the opposite couch, leaning back into the cushions. "Well, obviously it was hard when my dad died," he said. "But my parents had been divorced. I was living with my mom and my sisters anyway, so it was sad, but it didn't change a lot for me on a day-to-day basis. After people realized it was a pandemic, my mom, sisters and I stayed home eating whatever was in the house for weeks. Lots of tuna and frozen burritos. But eventually, they figured out it was only the boys getting really sick. My sisters went back to school, but I couldn't go. My mom home-schooled me when she wasn't working. The Internet was my connection to the outside world. I spent a lot of time alone and taught myself a lot. That's when I started getting into piano."

"Your parents got divorced." said Morgan, shaking her head. "That must have been hard for you and your sisters. It seems like everyone was getting divorced back then. Except for my parents. They were married for decades, and they still got along so well. I promised myself that I would have a marriage like theirs."

She bit her lip. "I have to go home to Jonas." She did not want to leave, but she felt this conversation was becoming too intimate and thus, somehow disloyal to her husband. She stood.

Nate gave her a look that made her really want to stay. It was a shy glance that took in her whole body, then asked for more.

Morgan brushed past him and ran out through the shower, hurriedly putting on her clothes in a rush to escape. Her face felt hot, and she worried Jonas would instantly know she had been emotionally, if not physically, intimate with someone else.

CHAPTER 7

...

M organ had always been told her face was an open book. She came home and did everything she could to avoid Jonas so he would not be able to read her thoughts. She cleaned up the house, checked on the laundrybot, and even cooked an elaborate late-night dinner. Eventually she brought the tray in to him, her gaze fixed on his meal.

"Morgan, sweetheart, this meal looks lovely. Where have you been today if I may ask?"

"I've been at Beth's place," Morgan hesitated, "with her nephew."

"Is that the Vulny who's visiting?"

"Yes, there's an outbreak where he's from, so he's staying here." Her throat felt tight, and it was hard for her to get the words out.

"Poor young fellow, probably gets pretty bored and lonely." He had been through a very lonely period himself when he'd first gotten sick. He had adjusted to his circumstances and was relatively happy now, finding satisfaction in helping others online.

Morgan's heart was heavy with guilt. She looked up and met his eyes. She saw understanding and love, along with a small twinge of regret.

"It would be a kindness to keep him company sometimes," said Jonas.

Morgan knew what Jonas was doing. He was giving her permission. She didn't know if she could accept it. When she married Jonas, she had made a commitment till death. Not till an illness leaves one person weak. She was human, though. There were things she needed for survival: food, water, shelter, and . . .

"Of course, I'll go over to visit. I will keep things appropriate, Jonas. I wouldn't want to do anything to disrespect what we have."

"I know what we have, Morgan. Whatever happens won't tarnish that. I trust you."

Morgan stroked Jonas's cheek. "You should eat, dear," she said, pointing to the food growing cold on the tray.

"What about your dinner, Morgan?"

"I'm not hungry," she said. "I'm going to go lie down in the other room for a while."

Morgan went into the guest room and pulled her vibrator out of the side table. She settled into bed and tried to empty her mind of Jonas. She thought about Nate's abundant chest hairs and beautiful hands. Bunny Ears wasn't doing the trick today though. She usually felt satisfied afterward, but this time, she didn't.

She wanted more—a real person to touch her, not a machine. And her vibrator didn't have those long fingers and hard abs that she could feel in her fantasy. It would be so much better in real life. She was left with an uncomfortable longing. Even though Jonas had given her tacit permission, her sense of guilt oppressed her on a grand scale. She didn't know what to do.

CHAPTER 8

. . .

The next day at work, Morgan wrapped up her email at the same time Gena shut down her computer and grabbed her messenger bag. "Want to go for a drink?" Gena asked.

"Sounds great! I have a lot to tell you. Also, you totally jinxed me when you said nutrition was a safe topic. Anyway, should we do Art Bar or Foot Bar?" asked Morgan.

Now that women were the major customers, bars had been revamped. A place only for drinking was not going to work—women required multi-tasking. Bars were combined with car washes, laundromats, painting studios, and nail salons. There was actually one bar where you could do all of the above. Morgan and Gena most often went for either paint on a canvas or on their toes. Sometimes Gena's partner Patty joined them. The walls of the lab office space were covered with slightly sloppy looking paintings of flowers and landscapes they had painted while drinking cocktails.

"Wait a minute, how did I jinx you on nutrition?" asked Gena as she and Morgan walked out of the building together and into another cloudless California afternoon.

How do I put this? "The first question was about what he eats in a typical day, and he asked if I was only talking about food! It went downhill from there."

"Ugg," said Gena. "He seems a little creepy."

"Well, he is, but he's also empathetic. He's invested in finding a vaccine and treatments for manflu, and he's more complicated than he seems." Morgan picked up her pace to keep up with Gena.

"I guess we'll take the help where we can get it with funding levels so low," Gena mused. "We didn't decide on the bar, did we? I could use a pedicure. I shredded my toenails running a 10K this morning. I need to get new shoes. Let's go to the Foot Bar. Oh! And I have a lot to tell you, too."

"Foot Bar, it is! I'm excited. Do you want to call Patty and see if she can make it?" asked Morgan as the two women turned down the side street toward the bar. The lab was conveniently located near the downtown of the suburb, packed with eateries ranging from casual to elegant, which made grabbing lunch or drinks after work easy.

"No, she's got plans with her knitting group. The knitting channel on TV is having a special on Christmas sweaters, and they're all going to watch and follow along," said Gena.

"I guess you know what you're getting for Christmas," said Morgan. She quickly messaged the Caregiver on Call service to have them bring dinner to Jonas, and she texted him to see if he needed anything else while she was out. He responded that he did not.

"I get so overheated, but I have to play along and pretend like I love them. By the end of Christmas day, I'll be nothing but a puddle of sweat," said Gena. "We live in California, for heaven's sake!"

"Patty is so sweet, it must be worth it," said Morgan.

They entered the bar/nail salon where they selected nail polish colors and drinks. Morgan went with a classic red nail and a full-bodied chianti to match. Gena chose a sophisticated purple polish and a Manhattan. They had to wear closed-toed shoes at work for safety, but both lived in sandals on weekends.

As they removed their shoes and sat in the spa chairs, Gena said, "I'm a very lucky lady. Patty is definitely worth a hot, itchy sweater once a year. And how are things going with Jonas these days?"

"Same as always," said Morgan, "but there's something else going on." The attendant placed the nail-painting machines on each of their feet, made sure they were comfortable, and hit the "on" buttons. The light, efficient machines whirred away, sensing where the nails stopped and the skin began and painting neatly and efficiently. Morgan barely felt a tickle.

"Something new? You haven't said anything. What is it?" Gena asked.

"There's a gorgeous Vulny staying with my neighbor. His name is Nate. He's young and fit, and I can barely control myself. I've gone over there to play piano with him. Nothing has happened yet, but it's only a matter of time." Morgan felt better after getting all that off her chest. The machines beeped and the attendant removed them. She left Morgan and Gena to relax in the comfy chairs.

"That's why you've had a glow lately! Now it's starting to make sense. I have so many questions, I don't even know where to start," said Gena. "Most obvious, I guess, would be, does Jonas know?"

"He suspects, but I haven't said anything to him. He's always said he would be fine with me going elsewhere to, uh, get my needs met. It's hard to actually go through with it, though."

"Sure. That would be tough," said Gena, nodding in agreement. "What about the infection risk?"

"I haven't talked to Nate about it. As long as I take the disinfecting shower, the risk should be minimal, but that's for him to decide. If I did give him manflu, the guilt would be overwhelming. Chances are small, but it's possible I could even bring something from the lab that could hurt him inadvertently." Morgan played with the stem of her wine glass.

"You're trained in disinfection, and we get tested all the time at work. I don't think you would get him sick," said Gena, finishing her cocktail and signaling for another.

"Are you saying I should go through with it? Do you think it's wrong morally, though?" Morgan stared into her wine, not daring to look at Gena.

"I'm not saying that. I can't tell you what's allowed or not allowed in your marriage. That's between you and Jonas. I'll support you either way."

Morgan wished that Gena would tell her what to do. Decisions were so hard. Maybe she would actually go through with this. It hadn't felt real before. It was all just a fantasy. But the more she thought about overcoming the obstacles, the more she felt compelled to press on. She did appreciate Gena's support, though. Sometimes, she felt like Gena was the only person in the world she could count on.

"Meeting him has reinforced for me the importance of the work we are doing. There are people like him out there who can't leave their houses. They should be able to live normal lives. If we succeed, the world will open up for them," said Morgan.

"Can you imagine if men were strong again? Would they try to take back the power women have now? I guess people would choose to have male children again if they couldn't get manflu. I bet the government would put a cap on the number of males born. Women don't want to go back to the time *before*. Everything is so safe and peaceful now. We could walk out of here at three in the morning naked and nothing would happen to us. That still amazes me every day," said Gena. "Do you remember what things were like when we were in college? You couldn't set down your drink at a party. Women carried rape whistles. You could never feel safe walking around at night. And not to mention all the harassment at work. Remember those assholes who would talk right over us in meetings at the climate lab?"

"I remember. I don't want to go back to all those horrible things either. I mean, I wish I could go back to when the men I loved were strong, but nothing is going to bring my parents and my brother back to life or restore Jonas to how he used to be. No, I want to move forward to a world where everyone is safe and valued, even the Vulnies," said Morgan.

"I agree one-hundred percent. You know how I feel. We talk about this all the time." Their nails done, they moved to a different section of the bar where people could dine. Gena ordered a snack platter.

"Gena, you said you had news, too. I'm so sorry I've been going on about me this entire time," said Morgan, putting her hand on Gena's arm.

"That's okay, Morgan. My news is not nearly as exciting as yours. You know Gavin's friend Eeny?" Morgan nodded. "She was caught in a restricted area at the lab while Gavin was in that session with you. She said she was looking for a bathroom, but she's been to the bathroom before and it's nowhere near where she was."

"That's weird," said Morgan. "What do you think she was doing?"

"I'm not sure. Maybe she's secretly a journalist trying to get the scoop on the vaccine status?" The waitress appeared with a plate piled high with cheese, crackers, potato chips, and chocolate. Gena went straight for the cheese. Morgan popped a piece of magic low-calorie chocolate in her mouth.

"I'm sure that if a journalist requested information, we would give it to her. Aparna recently sat for an interview with CNN about the mice trials," said Morgan. "Charlotte has done some press, too."

"Well, who else would want to poke around? I don't think the German lab also working on the vaccine has the time and resources to embed a spy over here," replied Gena.

"Maybe she did get lost going to the bathroom. The women who follow Gavin around are probably not the sharpest knives in the drawer. Please excuse the cliché," said Morgan.

"Well, the simplest explanation usually is correct," said Gena.

Morgan and Gena caught up on some other lab gossip, finished their drinks and snacks, and left the bar together, both heading home to their partners. When they parted ways, Morgan didn't look up and down the street or hold her keys in her hands like a weapon even though the sun had set and the area was quite dark. Morgan had enjoyed spending time with her dear friend, but she still didn't know what she was going to do about Nate.

CHAPTER 9

...

That weekend, Morgan popped over to Beth's house again. She walked up and down the block, waiting until Beth's car was gone before she rang the bell. The entire time she walked, she questioned herself on the morality of what she was doing. Beads of sweat formed at her hairline, and she wasn't sure if it was from the warmth of the day or the stress of doubting herself. Why not go in while Beth was still there? Obviously, she wanted to be alone with Nate. As a married woman, she knew what she was doing was wrong, but she couldn't bear to go in when Beth would take one look at her face and know she wanted to be alone with Nate. Was it so wrong, though? All she wanted to do was flirt a little. And stare a tiny bit.

When Morgan rang the bell, Nate told her to enter through the shower, as usual. After she was disinfected and wearing the short white robe, she sat with Nate by the piano. "Nate, have you ever dated anyone?" Morgan asked after they had fooled around with the piano for a while. She had surprised herself by asking him such a bold question.

Nate looked at her questioningly for a moment. This was a topic they had never discussed. He took a deep breath before he said, "There have been some girls I've talked to online, but no one in person."

"Are you scared?" Morgan asked. She was scared.

"Of getting sick? Not really. I understand the risks, and I know they're low if the person I'm with disinfects properly." Morgan was unnerved by the jumble of emotions she felt, and she thought Nate might be, too.

"You're scared of something else?" Morgan's peeked at Nate from under her dark eyelashes. He stared at her intensely, his eyes bluer than ever. Her voice was a little hoarse, and the tips of her fingers tingled. She could tell he felt something, too, but she didn't know what, exactly. She feared that she was in way deeper than he was.

"I'm scared of getting hurt. I can't be in a relationship with someone—I can't even leave the house. Any woman is going to get tired of me. They would want to be out in the world, living their life. I can't even take someone on a date to McDonald's."

Morgan started to see things from Nate's point of view. Her life must seem exciting to him—working in a lab, having drinks with friends, speaking to neighbors outside. Even simple things like grocery shopping were beyond his reach. But her life felt ordinary to her. He provided most of the spice.

"Nate, you have so much to offer. You're easy to talk to, you play piano beautifully, you're able to work from home and contribute professionally, and, um, you're nice-looking. Any woman would be lucky to have you even if you can't go out. And maybe someday you will be able to live a full life. We're working so hard on the vaccine. And don't forget about the antibody testing. A normal life might come sooner than you think."

Morgan's body flooded with warmth as she pondered Nate walking out his front door, free and unencumbered. In her excitement, she reached over and grabbed his hand. It was the first time the two had ever touched. His skin was so smooth and pale. He closed his fingers around her smaller hand, and she felt how long and strong they were. The two sat on the piano bench quietly, and Morgan looked down at their clasped hands. She thought about the chasm they had already leaped over and what might come next.

What if the antibody test came back positive, and Nate could go out in the world and live his life? What if he was free to travel and date any of the millions of lonely, eligible women in the world? He certainly wouldn't choose to spend his time fooling around on the piano with her, an older married scientist with a pretty boring life. Why had she even brought up the antibody testing? She felt a heaviness in her chest. She regretted having said anything.

She took a long look at Nate, memorizing his hair, face, body, and hands for her late-night solo fantasies because she was sure that was as close as she would come to having him. Then she stood to leave, pulling the robe tightly around herself like a shield.

"I have to go," she said.

"So soon?" He looked hurt. They had been speaking quite intimately, and her departure was abrupt.

"I'll see you soon, Nate." She didn't intend to explain her train of thought. She shouldn't even be here anyway.

CHAPTER 10

. . .

A few days later, Morgan escorted Gavin into an exam room. She passed Gena and Andrea, the office manager, as they walked down the hall together to the large conference room.

"You're not coming? I thought you would be in this meeting, Morgan," Gena said, obviously surprised.

"What meeting? I'm supposed to conduct an interview right now," said Morgan, nodding at Gavin.

"It's a workshop on the new rapid antibody testing that recently became available," said Gena.

Morgan was shocked no one had informed her. She had been following antibody testing research closely and was more interested now than ever since meeting Nate.

Morgan looked at Gavin and back at Gena and Andrea. "Andrea, is there any way I could attend? Maybe I could find someone else to do the interview?" Morgan noticed that Gavin was frowning at her petulantly.

"Absolutely not, registration was completed last week," said Andrea, her cat earrings swinging as she shook her head. "The room's full." Morgan couldn't believe what she was hearing. It shouldn't be difficult to squeeze in one extra chair. And surely someone who had signed up would end up not going. She glared at Andrea.

"Don't worry, Morgan, I'll take notes for you," said Gena.

"All right. Thanks, Gena," said Morgan. She still couldn't understand why she hadn't been informed about the workshop. She had been busy with the primates, but she always made sure to stay on top of her emails and calendar invitations.

"Shall we, Gavin?" Morgan motioned for him to continue walking down the hall into the exam room. She tried not to let him see the depth of her annoyance with Andrea.

"What's the topic of the day, Doc?" Gavin asked.

That was a good question. Morgan had not had the chance to review the questions prior to their session. She looked down at her HERO.

"The questions today are about family health history." Morgan couldn't wait to see how Gavin would turn the conversation to sex. However, the naughty grin Gavin usually sported was replaced with a scowl. He barely spoke, let alone attempted any dirty comments.

"You don't seem like yourself today, Gavin. Is everything okay?" asked Morgan.

"I'm fine. I had to pay taxes this week—always makes me cranky," Gavin said.

"But taxes have gone down by forty percent since women took over and got rid of most of the military spending," Morgan said, shocked.

Taxes were not among most people's complaints about the new regime. There had been a fair amount of upheaval when women had first taken over as government leaders. The first congress *after* went on a shopping spree, funding universal healthcare, universal parental leave, several food programs, clean water projects, and essential jobs programs required to train women to do jobs that were now vacant due to the loss of so many men.

However, costs reduced in other areas generated more than enough savings to offset the new benefits. The near-dismantling of the military saved hundreds of billions of dollars each year. Once the budget was balanced by a handful of responsible women, another few hundred billion were saved annually on debt-service costs. Every time a prison closed, the government saved tens of millions of dollars. The examples of savings were endless.

Recently, under the Ximena Álvarez administration, more funds had been approved to help women choosing to have babies. Caregiving assistance was also a new benefit. Álvarez had ramped up spending to butter up the electorate for the upcoming election. She was running for her second term as president.

But that was all a drop in the bucket compared to the decline in spending that occurred once a fully equipped military complex was no longer needed. Spending was way down compared to what it had been with men in charge. Mostly, people complained that it took forever for anything to get done because consensus had to be reached.

"I'm sure your taxes went down, but mine went way up because they tax the shit out of sperm donation earnings!" said Gavin. "Maybe I should go back to IT. This is no way to make a living. I hope Álvarez loses the election."

Ah, Morgan had forgotten about some of those targeted taxes. Well, they didn't seem to be hurting Gavin too much. He lived in a mansion with a Maserati and was surrounded by several gorgeous women at his beck and call at all times.

"That must be frustrating," said Morgan, looking down at the HERO. "Let's get back to the research, if you don't mind. In the forms you filled out, you mentioned no serious health conditions in your family history. I want to go carefully through the list to make sure nothing was missed."

Morgan asked about diabetes, heart disease, and cancer.

Everything was a no. She finally got down the list to serious viruses.

"I do remember having a pretty serious virus once as a child."

"Please tell me more."

"Well, I was quite young, so I don't remember much, but I know that it was on a summer trip to Korea to visit my mother's family. My father and I both got sick with high fevers, but my mother was fine. Her relatives said it was because our Western diet was lacking in some important components. My dad is white."

"Interesting," said Morgan, taking notes. "What happened next?"

"They gave us some herbs, which did seem to help, although my dad didn't buy it. My mom put them in his food so he wouldn't argue."

"Do you know what the herbs were?"

"No, but I can bring some in. My mom still sends them to me all the time and reminds me to make a tea from them if I'm not feeling well. Do you think this is important?" If Morgan's mom were still alive, she would probably send her own blend of herbs to an ill child. Morgan regretted that she had lost this small slice of traditional knowledge with the passing of her parents.

"I don't know. We have to look at everything in your history to find a possible connection to why you have immunity." Morgan tapped the stylus against the HERO. "You didn't mention herbs when I asked about your dietary habits?"

"I didn't think about it. They're not something I take on a regular basis. I didn't mention taking ibuprofen for a headache, either," he said sarcastically.

"How is your family's health now?"

"Totally fine. My parents are retired. My mom taught elementary school, and my dad was a lawyer. They play golf and tennis in the retirement community where they live."

"Do you have any information on your father's fertility or, um . . . sexual health?" asked Morgan.

"He doesn't donate sperm, if that's what you're asking," he said as he laughed.

Morgan looked away, not responding to his comment. She tried not to picture an older version of Gavin donating sperm.

"Dad mentioned having been in for a checkup recently, and he doesn't have any health issues. I'm not sure about his fertility, but he and my mom seem very happy, if you know what I mean." Gavin winked. "I'm pretty sure they're still doing it."

"Yes, I didn't need that spelled out, but thank you," said Morgan. It was amazing that Gavin's father seemed unaffected by manflu, too.

Morgan found herself fascinated listening to Gavin speak about his family. Despite being frustrated with his habit of making everything sexual, she admitted to herself that she enjoyed his masculine energy. In fact, she had accidentally on-purpose neglected to mention to Gavin that some of the research sessions could be conducted via video-conference.

Later that afternoon after Gavin left, Morgan checked in with Gena. "How was the antibody workshop?"

"It was great. It's easy to check for antibodies now, using the new test that has been developed and shipped out to labs around the country. In fact, there are already supplies here in this lab that you can use for testing."

"Wow! I had no idea that development was completed. I can't wait to test Nate," said Morgan. She hadn't expected such quick availability. She was thrilled at the progress that was being made. Even though she had mixed feelings personally, she wanted the best for Nate and hoped that he did have the antibodies.

"Does he want to be tested?"

"Yes. I already spoke to him about it."

"Perfect. Come on. I'll walk you through how to do it."

CHAPTER 11

. . .

The next time Morgan visited Nate, it was with one purpose in mind—getting his blood for the antibody test. He had agreed and seemed excited, but approaching him with a giant needle might trigger a different response. This new test provided instantaneous results, which claimed to be one-hundred percent accurate.

For this visit, she had brought sterile scrubs in her kit to change into after her disinfecting shower. She didn't want to draw blood while wearing a short robe. She entered the living room in her fitted, pale green scrubs, which contrasted nicely with her dark hair, and greeted Nate. They stood several feet apart, neither speaking. Piano usually smoothed things between them, but now wasn't the right time.

"Should we get right to it and take the sample?" Morgan asked. She spread out her gear on the kitchen table and sat down, test tubes ready, needle prepared, and gloves on. Nate sat and pushed up the sleeve on his t-shirt, exposing a pale, muscular bicep covered in dark hair.

"Morgan, I never talked to you about why I left Colorado," said Nate.

Morgan gently took his arm and positioned it. Goosebumps appeared on his skin, cold, or perhaps unaccustomed to the touch of a woman who wasn't part of his family. She tied a tourniquet on his upper arm and asked him to make a fist, watching how the muscles in his arm moved and his veins popped out. No matter how sexy she found those arms, she refused to let her mind wander to unprofessional territory.

"There was an outbreak where you lived, right?" Morgan asked as she swabbed the spot on his arm with alcohol as gently as if she were caressing him with her bare hand. She inserted the needle, watching as the blood quickly entered the barrel of the syringe.

"It's more than that. The government there is spreading manflu on purpose, so the pandemic doesn't end, and the men are either killed or stay at home and out of the way. The outbreak where my family lives was traced to agents spreading the virus in mall food courts. Video that would show who did it mysteriously disappeared, and this isn't the first time something like this has happened," Nate explained.

She had heard rumors like this about the government before, but she'd never given them any credence.

While Nate talked, Morgan took eight vials of blood. Into one vial, she dipped a white test strip that was marked with one dark blue line for comparison purposes. If an identical line appeared beside it, the patient had antibodies. She set a timer for three minutes. While she awaited the result, she untied the tourniquet and placed gauze over the spot, pushing down to stop the bleeding. She placed a bandage there. Next, she prepared the other vials for testing back at the laboratory, labeling them all with the patient's information and the date of the draw.

"Nate, I heard about that, but it's hard to believe that the government would be trying to hurt men. I know there are a lot of women who don't want things to go back to the way they were *before,* and I can't say I blame them. That's no reason to hurt anyone, though. It's not your fault that many men behaved badly when they were in charge," said Morgan.

"Morgan, it's not a theory. I'm telling you the government is spreading manflu," Nate insisted. "I read about it on a ton of websites."

"I'm not sure, Nate. I don't believe the government could do something like that," said Morgan. "You can't believe everything you read on the Internet."

She remained calm even as Nate became more agitated. She cleaned up as they talked. Soon, the timer beeped. The antibody test was complete.

"Are you ready, Nate?" Morgan asked. "This will tell you what your level of immunity is to manflu."

The beeping triggered excitement in her that she had kept at bay while focusing on mundane tasks. Her heart pounded, and her palms felt instantly damp. If this was how nervous she was, she couldn't imagine what Nate was feeling.

"Yes, I want to know." Nate squeezed his eyes shut, as if willing the results to turn out positively.

Morgan pulled the test strip out of the vial. It was stained with blood but otherwise unchanged. She looked Nate in the eyes. "You have no immunity at all. I'm sorry." She felt her pounding heart crash down all the way into her stomach.

Nate looked disappointed but not surprised. He stood up. "Thank you for telling me," he said. "If you don't mind, I'd like to be alone now."

Morgan approached him, but he nimbly avoided her touch. He turned away from her, his head hanging down.

"Nate . . ." she began, but didn't know how to finish the sentence. Without a word, Nate walked through the door in the living room that led to a bedroom and closed it behind him. Morgan understood that he didn't want to be with her right now. From his perspective, she was someone who didn't know what it was like to be at risk for something because of who she was. She left the house and drove the samples over to the lab for further analysis while they were still fresh.

CHAPTER 12

...

Morgan felt as though she had spent one endless day at the lab because she was so busy with the primate vaccine trials. In fact, the weeks were ticking by. She had contacted Nate multiple times, but her messages had gone unanswered. She had agonized about what to say. Each time she called, she grew slightly more desperate starting with, "Hi there..." and then "How's everything?" and finally, "I'm here if you need to talk." The spark that Nate had brought out in her dimmed a little more each time he ignored her.

The only time she allowed herself to think about him was when she commuted to or from work in her self-driving car. She would play piano concertos through the sound system, close her eyes, and picture Nate playing the pieces, his curly dark hair flopping adorably as his head swayed with the music. His body was like the piano keys, pale white with black accents, hair setting off the shape of the muscles on his arms.

It was a beautiful afternoon after a productive day, during which Morgan had enjoyed a research session with Gavin at the lab, and for once, she sat in the car and listened to a piano concerto without thinking of Nate.

Her phone rang. It was him.

"I want to show you something. Can you come over?" he asked, bypassing any awkward small talk caused by his lack of response to her messages. A warmth traveled through her body as she heard his voice. She wondered what he wanted.

"Now?" she whispered.

Please say now, she prayed. His voice instantly transported her body to how it felt sitting on the piano bench and almost touching him.

"Now," Nate said with a depth to his voice that Morgan had not heard before. She hung up the phone and instructed her car to drive to his house. She felt tingles all over as she anticipated seeing him.

Morgan strode purposefully into the outdoor shower. She disinfected her whole body more carefully than she ever had before. The water was scorching hot, and the soap smelled like lemons masking chemicals. She scrubbed under her nails. She cleaned each and every orifice. At last, she stepped out, dried off, and slipped into the bleached white robe. It seemed to have gotten even shorter since the last time she wore it. She tied the attached belt into a bow, artfully arranging the robe so that a hint of her small breasts was revealed.

Finally, she approached the piano where Nate sat. He was playing a beautiful piece. It was in a minor chord and sounded melancholy, like it was capturing the pain of a lonely time and releasing it into the world so that its owner could be free. She sat next to him and felt the music connect them, flowing first through one and then the other person.

"Thanks for coming, Morgan," said Nate.

"Of course! I've been concerned about you." In no universe could she have decided not to come. At that moment, her desire for him dominated everything.

"I needed some space after getting the antibody results. And I was upset that you didn't believe what I said about the government spreading manflu."

Morgan didn't know what to say. She still struggled to believe the government was capable of an attack on its own citizens. "I work for a government-funded lab. The government is supporting research to prevent and treat manflu. Why would the government try to hurt its own citizens? It doesn't make sense to me."

"Come with me. I want to show you something." Nate took Morgan's hand and led her to his bedroom. Were they still talking about manflu or was there something else he wanted to show her? She didn't know what to expect. Her heart pounded at the thought of being alone with him in his bedroom.

When they were inside the room, he closed the door, motioned for her to sit on the bed, and pulled up a split-screen video on his computer. On one side, it showed what looked like a janitor wearing heavy gloves pouring a substance from a bottle marked with the "poison" symbol onto a table at a busy food court and spreading it around with a cloth. On the other side, there was an ID picture of the janitor along with her name and other details, including the name of the government agency where she supposedly worked. The video was dated several months prior, around the time Nate had left Colorado.

"Do you believe me now, Morgan?" asked Nate, stopping the video. He sat next to her on the bed and looked at her expectantly.

"Nate, I don't know what to say," Morgan sputtered. "Where did you find this? Is this video public?" She stood and paced the room, not knowing what to think.

"A friend of mine sent it to me. He did some digging to find it. It's not exactly a secret, but the media won't publish it. There are other videos going back several years. They match up with the dates of some of the bigger outbreaks." He stood, too, as Morgan paced.

"Wouldn't the media be all over something like this?" Morgan asked, stopping to look at him.

"The government's covering it up, and the media's going along with it," said Nate. "Don't you see?"

Morgan couldn't believe what she was hearing and seeing. The government attacking its own citizens? This went against everything she believed in. The government was supposed to help people. She had to think that was still true. Maybe this was some rogue group or a faked video. Maybe it wasn't even manflu that was being poured onto the table. She couldn't share these thoughts with Nate, though. She needed to support him.

"I'm sorry I doubted you, Nate. You're right," she said, taking his hand. "The video does seem to show the government putting something dangerous where it could easily be picked up by anyone and spread. It certainly could be manflu."

She thought about how Nate must feel, under attack, at least in his own mind, from the very institution meant to protect him. "Is there anything I can do to help?" She gently squeezed his hand and looked into his worried eyes.

"Morgan, it could be very dangerous to get involved. You're already helping to develop the vaccine. Keep working on that, and you'll save the lives of many men. It means so much to me that you're out there fighting to protect us." He looked at her with admiration. At that moment, she would have done anything for him: scrub tables at a food court, fight the government, develop a thousand vaccines, or . . .

He licked his lips, pink tongue quickly darting out and then back into his mouth. She wouldn't have noticed if she hadn't been staring, thinking about what it would feel like to kiss him. Did he want that as much as she did? His lips parted again, and she heard his rough breathing.

She stepped forward and lifted up onto her toes. She had never been one to make the first move, and she worried about whether he wanted her to. When she placed her lips gently against his, her fears were quickly allayed as he responded with equally soft pressure. She felt herself sinking into the kiss and reached up to steady herself, gripping his sculpted shoulders in her hands. The muscles rippled against her palms as he moved his hands to her slim waist, cradling her at her narrowest point.

Breathing in, she inhaled his musky scent and wanted to bask in all of his flavors. She parted her lips and sent her tongue exploring, soon finding his minty mouth open for her. Her wet tongue stroked his for minutes, or maybe hours, until the rest of her body demanded to join in. She felt him hard against her and knew that his body wanted more, too.

She pulled back slightly and looked at him, eyes closed and lips still pursed in a kiss, hard inside his sweatpants. She waited for him to open his eyes, and when he did, she instantly let her robe fall to the floor. He gasped, eyes running up and down her nude body. One word escaped his lips, "Amazing."

She looked at him from under her dark eyelashes and gently snapped the waistband of his sweatpants. He took the hint and first pulled off his t-shirt, grabbing it from the back of his neck and pulling it over his head with one hand. Gosh, she loved how men undressed, careless of clothes and bodies. She had missed this. His torso was stunningly masculine—pale, muscled, and covered with dark hair that she longed to tug. As she watched, he slipped off his sweatpants and underwear and stepped out of them, kicking them out of the way. He stood in front of her, totally nude, ready for her to guide.

She resolved to go slowly with him since she knew he was inexperienced. She stepped forward, intending to kiss him again. But she had forgotten that they were nude now, and kissing put their bodies in intimate contact. Every point at which their skin met tingled on her body. His hair tickled her, and she felt him hard against her belly. She fought the urge to reach down and slip him inside her. Instead, she stared into his blue eyes, soft-focused with desire.

She picked up his hand, lovely long fingers at rest, but not for long. She placed it against her breast. His thumb found the tip, pressed against it and then slowly rolled it. She moaned with pleasure. He seemed to gain confidence and moved his hands more deliberately over both of her breasts, cupping and then stroking them as he kissed her mouth deeply.

Oh God, those long fingers. She wanted to feel them inside her, in the place that was begging for more. She took his hand and placed it on her stomach below her navel, fingertips pointed down. He responded by lowering his hand and rubbing her with his fingers until she couldn't take the teasing anymore.

She took his hand in hers and led him to the bed, where he lay back against the pillows. She climbed up, straddling him on her knees. The beauty and youth of his eyes, skin, hair, and muscles dazzled her. It was as if she were looking at a piece of art in a museum. She guided him into her body with one hand and moved down to envelop him, savoring every sensation along the way.

He moaned deeply, reminding her that he was an active participant in this fantasy come to life. She ran her hands through the hair on his body as she lowered herself down onto him again and again. He rose up and met her with his own thrusts, his face contorting with pleasure as they found a rhythm and moved faster toward its peak. She didn't want it to end, but she couldn't hold back much longer, and she could tell from his twisted mouth that the same was true for him.

He let go first, rocking his hips quickly, which set her off, and she bit her lip so she wouldn't scream. She must have bitten hard, because she tasted blood. He groaned and gripped her against him. She cried out, unable to stop herself. Waves of pleasure sizzled through her, one after another in a seemingly endless current of sensation. Her mind was completely, pleasantly blank. And then they were lying side by side, sweaty and satiated.

"Are you okay?" she whispered, not daring to look at him. She was overwhelmed with the sensations her body had experienced and couldn't imagine what he was feeling.

"More than okay," he responded.

She felt better when she heard the smile in his voice. As she stretched her arms and rolled over, she happened to glance at a bedside clock. She realized Jonas had been waiting for her arrival for at least an hour. She scrambled out of bed, then said a hurried goodbye to Nate, who slowly propped himself up on one arm to watch her go. She exited the house through the shower in order to throw her clothes on before rushing home.

When she reached the house, Morgan went through her own disinfecting shower, glad for the built-in excuse to wash off the sex smells before seeing Jonas. She should have used the time to gather her thoughts, but her mind stayed empty. She dried off and dressed in house clothes and went through to the kitchen to get Jonas's dinner for him. She walked into the bedroom, carrying his dinner on a tray.

"Hi, dear, did you have plans this evening?" Jonas asked.

"I stopped by to see a friend," Morgan said. "Sorry to arrive late without letting you know." She caught a glimpse of herself in the mirror over their dresser and saw that her normally pale skin was flushed.

"Do you feel ill, love?" Jonas asked. "You look warm."

"No, I'm fine. The shower I took just now was really hot," Morgan said smoothly. "Here's your dinner." She handed over his tray. "I'm going to catch up on a few things." She couldn't bear to be around sweet Jonas right now. He hadn't seemed to have caught on yet, but if she kept talking to him, he would soon figure things out.

CHAPTER 13

...

The next day at work, Morgan furiously whispered to Gena while they sat at their respective computers typing.

"You, me, lunch!"

Gena whispered back, "Training run today."

Morgan whispered, "S-E-X."

Gena replied, "Run canceled!"

When it was finally lunch time, Morgan nudged Gena. They grabbed their lunches from the cafeteria then quickly ducked into one of the small conference rooms, locking the door.

"Go!" said Gena, wasting no time.

"I had sex with the Vulny, Nate," said Morgan. There was no use beating around the bush.

"Oh, my God! How was it? Was he a virgin? Was it any good?"

"He's not very experienced, but it was amazing. It's been so long, Gena, I can't even explain how badly my body needed that release. We have amazing chemistry."

Gena was rapt. She leaned forward, failing to notice that her shirt was dangerously close to her plate of pasta. "Please continue. I'm very into hearing about hot sex. Doesn't matter to me that you all are straight."

"You remember those movies from *before* where the man and the woman would come simultaneously and everyone always made fun of that and said it was impossible?" Morgan asked.

Gena nodded.

"Well, it's possible." Smiling broadly at the memory, Morgan paused for a bite of food. She didn't even notice what she was eating.

"Wow! Good for you. Good for both of you," said Gena, ever the supportive friend.

"We didn't have any time for cuddling. I jumped up and ran home like Cinderella leaving the ball. I hope he's okay. I should probably call him, but I don't know what to say," said Morgan.

"You'll figure it out," said Gena. "Hey, what did you guys do about birth control?" Gena finally looked at her lunch and her shirt's proximity to it, tucked in the garment, and started to eat.

Oh, no! "That thought didn't even cross my mind. Birth control. Oh my goodness." Morgan froze, the blood draining out of her face.

"Didn't you take health class *before*? Didn't you and Jonas use birth control? What the fuck, Morgan?" Gena slammed her fork down.

"Gena, it's been over 10 years! I forgot about it. I wasn't using birth control with Jonas. We'd been trying to have a baby when everything happened." Morgan rested her head on her hands.

"I'm sorry, sweetie. I didn't know that," said Gena, gently rubbing Morgan's arm.

"What am I going to do?" Morgan asked.

"Don't panic. You can take the morning after pill. This was yesterday, right? You've got plenty of time," said Gena calmly.

"The morning after pill? Do they still make that? Why would anyone need that now? Where could I find it?" Morgan asked.

"You don't need the official morning after pill. All you have to do is take a few birth control pills within seventy-two hours. You can get them at any pharmacy. You don't even need a prescription anymore," said Gena.

"Why do you know this?" asked Morgan.

"Patty used to get painful cramps. She started taking birth control pills and hasn't had a period for years," Gena explained.

"All right, I'll stop by the pharmacy after work," said Morgan. "Thank you so much. I can't believe I forgot about the possibility of pregnancy. I guess the sex shut down all rational thought for a moment. It was like being a teenager."

"Do you think you guys are going to get together again?" asked Gena.

"I don't know. I definitely want to, but I'm worried Jonas will find out. The attraction is so powerful, though. I don't think I'll be able to stay away. I don't know what's going to happen."

"I thought Jonas was okay with extracurricular activity," said Gena.

"He's said so, but the reality of it is different. I think knowing about it would crush him. He already feels so powerless stuck in that bed all day. Gena, what would you do if Patty were unable to, um, you know . . .?" asked Morgan.

"Oh, we talked about it and made our plans. We have a detailed list of what is and is not acceptable in a number of circumstances. The list is in our safe with our birth certificates, will, and other important documents. Basically, in that kind of situation, we're both all right with the other person getting her needs met as long as we never find out. So, I understand where you're coming from with Jonas."

A page came through the work phone system and interrupted them. "Dr. Digby to the primate area," said the disembodied voice.

Morgan stood and tossed the remainder of her lunch into the

trash bin. "Oh my, that doesn't sound good. There must be an emergency. Sorry to eat and run, Gena."

Gena waved her off. "No problem. Go take care of those monkeys! I'll go do part of that training run."

Morgan speed-walked through the building to the primate area where an assistant met her and told her that one of the adult monkeys had a fever and seemed quite ill. It wasn't clear if this was a reaction to the manflu vaccine the monkey had been given, or if it was an unrelated sickness. Morgan spent the afternoon caring for the ill monkey and carefully examining the other animals to see if they showed any signs of the same condition.

Around dinner time, Morgan's stomach grumbled. Pausing her work, she called the caregiver service to bring over a meal to Jonas. As she was eating a protein bar that she kept with her for these situations, she realized she would need to leave work right away if she wanted to make it to the pharmacy before it closed to pick up the morning after pill. Gena had said she could take it within a few days, though. She was sure it would be fine if she took it tomorrow. She wasn't done examining all of the monkeys yet.

CHAPTER 14

...

Morgan did pick up the pills the next day, and she took several according to directions she found on the Internet. The next few weeks passed quickly. Morgan cared for the ill monkey and completed other vaccine-related tasks at work and cared for Jonas at home, and, any rare chance she got, she fantasized about Nate. She would slip into the guest room to satisfy herself, images of his pale, hairy body flashing in her mind. In her dreams, his bright blue eyes gazed lovingly at her. But she held back from contacting him. He didn't contact her either. Morgan guessed that Nate, both younger and less experienced than she, and aware of the complexities of her situation with Jonas, was waiting for her to make the next move.

One morning, Morgan was at work checking her email when Gena walked in carrying two coffees. She handed one to Morgan, who thanked her. Morgan removed the lid to cool it off and bent her head to breathe in the scent. She loved coffee. Except not this kind—it smelled terrible. She suppressed a gag. Maybe it was burnt. She didn't say anything because she didn't want to be rude to Gena. She shrugged it off and went back to reading her email as Gena logged onto her own computer.

"Oh, no!" Morgan shouted. She felt the muscles in her face tense, and she froze like an animal about to play dead.

"What is it?" asked Gena when Morgan didn't say anything for a full minute.

"The renewal of our license to test the vaccine on primates was denied!" Morgan couldn't believe it. They were a government-funded lab researching a deadly virus. Primates were critical to their work. How could this have happened?

"Denied? That's impossible!" said Gena. "Who submitted the paperwork?"

"Andrea must have. This doesn't make any sense. Should I have Andrea call and check?" Her brain felt like it was spinning in circles as she ran through all possible explanations.

"Andrea seems like she has it in for you lately. Remember how she wouldn't let you in the antibody workshop? You better call yourself," said Gena.

Morgan got on the phone to the licensing office right away. The entire time she talked, Gena stared at her.

"So?" asked Gena as soon as she hung up.

"There was an error in the paperwork. They're granting us a temporary extension, but it's going to take time to get the mistake sorted out. I'm going to be up to my eyeballs in paperwork for a while." This was just what Morgan needed! She was already doing double duty by interviewing Gavin and taking care of the primates. Now, she would need to add correcting paperwork to her to do list. She felt exhausted just thinking about the tasks ahead.

"That stinks, Morgan. Let me know if I can help in any way," said Gena. Once again, Morgan was glad that there was one person in the world she could rely on during what was certain to be a difficult time.

CHAPTER 15

...

Morgan fell into another work abyss of a couple of weeks spent getting the licensing paperwork straightened out to the best of her abilities, emerging when she checked her calendar one morning to find Gavin scheduled for that day. Charlotte had sent the questions Morgan was to go through with Gavin earlier that day. Morgan, busy with the primates, hadn't looked at the HERO until she reached the exam room with him.

Well, finally a topic that Gavin couldn't get sexual about. Bathroom habits. Morgan went through the list, and Gavin answered the questions very professionally. Morgan started to feel a bit nauseated, from the subject matter she supposed. She got to a question about the consistency of his stool, which forced her to pause because she nearly threw up. She took a moment to sip some water from her water bottle and managed to compose herself and finish the interview. Gavin was nonplussed, but he did look relieved when it was time to rejoin his lady friends (minus the one who had snooped and therefore had been banned from the lab) and head home.

After lunch, Morgan approached Gena with a strange question.

"Gena, I have the weirdest taste in my mouth. Like I bit my lip and I'm tasting blood. But I didn't. What could it be? Am I sick?"

"I don't know. What'd you eat for lunch?" asked Gena. Morgan had eaten lunch at her desk while catching up on some work. Gena had gone for a bike ride.

"Yogurt. I've been craving plain yogurt," said Morgan.

"Maybe the yogurt was bad."

"Yeah, maybe. I'll check the date on the container when I get home. I'm probably still grossed out from my session with Gavin. I had to ask him about his stool."

"Gross! Poor you," said Gena.

The next day, she still felt out of balance. "Gena, my boobs hurt," Morgan whispered from her spot at her desk.

"Hormones, probably," said Gena. She was focused on her work and didn't seem to be fully paying attention.

Charlotte paused as she walked by them. "My boobs hurt so much when I was pregnant!" said Charlotte, who had conceived a daughter via donor sperm a few years prior.

She lived in a house with several other women, who were raising their daughters together. Charlotte left the room. Morgan and Gena stared at each other. Strong smells, weird tastes, nausea, and sore boobs! Oh, dear! Could she be pregnant?

"Morgan, did you take the birth control pills like I told you?" demanded Gena.

"Yes, I did. I took them the next day after we spoke."

"You should've done it right away when it's most effective!" said Gena.

"I couldn't pick them up because I was dealing with a monkey emergency!"

"Well, it doesn't matter now. What're you going to do?"

"I don't know. I need to think about it. Oh, my God. I can't believe I'm pregnant." Morgan's mind went entirely blank.

"Well, you better make sure," said Gena. She found a pregnancy test in a supply closet and handed it to Morgan, who took it to the bathroom to pee on it.

In the moments before the result came up, Morgan's two possible futures flashed before her eyes. In one version, her life stayed the same—she worked, took care of Jonas, and longed for something more emotionally fulfilling. In the other version, she held a baby, and nothing else mattered but the powerful love she felt for her child.

She remembered a pregnancy test taken a million years ago at the apartment she shared with a friend right after she graduated from college. She and her friend had held hands as she waited for the results, hoping desperately that one mistake with her boyfriend hadn't led to a baby. She had felt so much relief when that test came up negative.

She had never had the chance to take a test with Jonas. The time hadn't ever been right to try. She would never be able to gleefully show him a positive result that foretold of their future child.

Back in the bathroom at the lab, sure enough, after a few minutes, the plus sign came up. Morgan came out of the bathroom, crying tears of joy. No matter what happened, she had a baby inside her. No one was going to take that away. She was going to be a mother.

Several coworkers walked by Gena and Morgan on their way to a meeting in another part of the building. They were unfazed by Morgan's crying. At least once a week, someone had a tearful meltdown at work about a deceased family member, the stress of caregiving, or simply missing the touch of a man.

Gena stared at Morgan, unsure what to say.

"I'm going to have to tell Jonas. He did want a child. But what if he found out how it was conceived?" Morgan pondered.

"Morgan, what if it's a boy?" Gena's eyes were as big and round as dinner plates.

"Oh, no! You're right. Everyone would know that it wasn't planned, and that it was with someone who is not Jonas. Please let it be a girl!"

"And what about the risk of manflu?" asked Gena.

"Right, surely that would be terrifying to think about for a baby," said Morgan, "but I could protect a child. He would only be at risk for a little while, until the vaccine is ready." Morgan needed to believe the vaccine she was working on would be ready in time for this baby.

"It sounds like you want to keep it," said Gena practically.

"I very much do. I've always wanted a child, and this could be my last chance to carry one. But it's so complicated. And with my luck, it will be a boy, and I will probably die of embarrassment and worry. Meanwhile, my parents will be rolling over in their graves," Morgan said in a jumble of words and tears.

"There's a blood test you can take to find out if it's a girl. I'll help you do it. You'll need to wait a few weeks, though. It's going to be okay, Morgan. We'll figure it out." Gena held her while she cried a fresh set of tears.

Morgan couldn't believe that one careless night had thrown her life into such disarray. More than ever, she needed this vaccine to work. Now, it was personal.

CHAPTER 16

. . .

Morgan resolved not to say anything to anyone until she found out the gender of the baby. That meant acting like everything was totally normal, both at home and at work, while also fending off nausea, exhaustion, strange smells, sore boobs, and the urge to use the bathroom every three and a half minutes.

Jonas, used to watching Morgan for signs of a virus, even if just the common cold, that could prove deadly for him because of his reduced immune system, noticed something was wrong. Morgan told him she had been thinking about her family members a lot recently and was experiencing some depressive symptoms. He seemed to accept her explanation, at least for the time being.

At work, she had a harder time being discreet. Her work was full of women, many of whom had been pregnant and were intimately familiar with the first trimester's constellation of horrific symptoms. When Charlotte heated up some leftover salmon in the communal microwave, launching fish smells throughout the lunchroom, Morgan turned a shade of green that surely clashed with her outfit and ran to the bathroom. From then on, she got a lot of vague, sympathetic comments from her coworkers and offers of help with lab work. She knew they must assume she had been inseminated by donor sperm with a planned baby girl that she and her husband wanted to raise, but no one asked her outright. Only Gena knew the truth, and Morgan trusted her not to say anything yet.

Morgan thought often of Nate, and she wondered how he would react if he knew. Would he have any interest in a child? It was not a topic they had ever discussed. She would eventually tell him, but she didn't feel ready yet. A couple of weeks ago, he had called, and she had let it go to voicemail. He had tried a few more times, but she hadn't picked up.

Morgan was home during the day on a weekend, letting her mind wander to Nate and the baby as she watched a pre-pandemic movie on the 24/7 Romantic Comedy Channel with Jonas, when the doorbell rang. Old movies were very popular because the newer ones lacked male actors.

Morgan answered to find one of her neighbors, Bree, clipboard in hand, button on her shirt, canvassing in support of Ximena Álvarez, who was running for her second term. Bree was such a big fan, she wore her tightly curled brown hair cut extra-short on one side with the initials "X.A." shaved into it. Eyebrows festooned with piercings completed the look.

"Bree, you can't come in unless you want to take a shower, but if you don't mind, I'll sit with you on the front porch and chat for a while," said Morgan. She needed a distraction from the constant nausea and other pregnancy symptoms she had to deal with without revealing to Jonas what was happening in her body.

"That'd be wonderful, Morgan," said Bree.

Morgan went to get some iced tea for them both. She had never been interested in politics, preferring to keep her head down and focus on her lab work, but she knew that there were issues in the upcoming presidential election that affected her vaccine research.

As Morgan returned with the pitcher of iced tea, she spotted Sarah across the street taking her garbage bin to the curb. Morgan waved and motioned for Sarah to come over. Morgan knew that Sarah was the type to keep up with the news and was curious about her opinion.

"Come join us," Morgan said.

Sarah walked across the street, wiping her hands on her black stretched-out yoga pants. "I've got a chicken in the oven, so I can't stay long, but I won't pass up the chance to be a friendly neighbor. Hi, I'm Sarah. I'd shake hands, but, you know, garbage."

"Sarah, this is Bree from my book club. She lives a few blocks over. She wants to talk politics."

Sarah and Bree nodded at each other.

"Would you like some iced tea?" Morgan offered.

Sarah declined, and the three women settled into the slightly rusty wrought-iron chairs warm from the sun.

Bree launched into her elevator pitch. "Let me talk to you about Ximena Álvarez. She has done so many great things for this country in her first term. She's an inspiration for immigrant families like her own and for the rest of us. She fought for prison closures, saving a ton of money that she got Congress to spend on infrastructure. This country has never had such strong roads, bridges, and Internet connectivity. The job training programs have been super successful, and the stock market is up. Her new platform is about taking care of the caregivers.

"So many politicians these days are single and don't understand the realities of caregiving. Or they want to cater to the newer generation having babies on their own or with female partners. What about those of us caring for ill fathers, husbands, and sons who are struggling to get by? Where is our assistance? Ximena wants to pass a law providing a trained caregiver to any family who needs one. And she will ramp up R&D spending on more household robots. If you believe in less drudgery for all, Ximena is the candidate for you."

"Amen!" said Sarah. "I'd kill for some caregiving relief. My husband's not the easiest patient, and I'm on my own here. I'd love to spend more time working on my interior design business, but Robert's so demanding. They should spread some of that financial assistance around—if they can give it to women having babies, they can send some my way, too."

Morgan said, "Bree, I agree that caregiving assistance sounds great, but I'm concerned about vaccine funding. Where does Ximena stand on that? Funding levels have been very low since she's been president. We're so close to finding the vaccine. There's a German lab working on it, too, but this should be an American achievement. I've been working on this for ten years, and we're so close—with a little more funding we can make this happen." Morgan was slightly out of breath after her speech.

"I see how important this is to you, Morgan. But cuts have to be made in other places to pay for caregivers. I don't think there's enough to go around for vaccine research, too. Isn't there any private funding?" Bree asked. She tapped her pen against her clipboard.

"Private funding? Who's going to pay for that? Healthy men don't want any competition. Vulnies don't have much money. Men who are already sick aren't interested. And most women are happy with the status quo. I would have to identify Vulnies from wealthy backgrounds. I don't have time for that kind of fundraising. I want to focus on my lab work." Morgan crossed her arms and blew out air.

"Morgan, you know I love you, sweetheart, but I'm not sure how much public money we should be spending on vaccines. There're a lot of other pressing needs in society. And I'm not keen on a resurgence of men. The one I live with is enough for me to deal with," said Sarah, shaking her head to get her blonde bangs out of her face without touching them with her dirty hands.

Morgan was surprised. She hadn't ever discussed her work with Sarah and didn't know she felt that way. She assumed that the people in her life wanted science to progress and for things to go back at least somewhat to how they had been, with men healthy and thriving, but she guessed she had been wrong. With a baby on the way who could be a boy, she felt hurt by this attitude. What kind of future would her child inherit?

"Well, none of the major candidates are supporting vaccine research in this election," said Bree. "You're going to have to choose the best one from the lot, and I think that's Ximena."

Morgan was silent for a while, considering. Politics was not something she enjoyed discussing. She hated conflict of any kind. Choosing to spend her time with monkeys was no accident—they didn't talk back. She drank her iced tea and searched for a safer topic while she seethed inside. "Have either of you read any good books lately?"

"I wish I had time to read," said Sarah.

"I read that new book, *Before: A Time of Violence, Greed and Hypocrisy*. You have to read it. I will bring my copy next time I see you," said Bree.

"That sounds fascinating. Thanks for the recommendation. I'd love to borrow your copy," said Morgan. "Look, I've got to go back inside and take care of Jonas now. Thank you for stopping by. I appreciate hearing your point of view."

"Nice to meet you, Bree," said Sarah, standing up.

Bree also stood. "Nice to meet you, too. Thanks for listening. See you at book club next week, Morgan."

CHAPTER 17

...

Morgan and Jonas were eating dinner a few days later in the bedroom when Morgan brought up Bree's visit and support for Ximena Álvarez.

"Jonas, you follow politics much more than I do, what do you think about Ximena Álvarez? Are you planning to vote for her?" Morgan asked. "Bree says she wants to increase funding for caregivers."

"Remember that scandal she was involved in before she was elected president? It's funny how no one talks about that anymore," said Jonas. He waved his soup spoon in the air as if to emphasize his point.

"Well, it's not very relevant, is it?" Morgan could barely even remember the scandal to which Jonas referred. She stared into her bowl of food as if searching for the memory.

"I think it is. Remember how when her husband died during the pandemic, his *other family* showed up at the funeral? She was governor of Colorado at the time, and it was all over the news." The memory hit Morgan. It was a bit of a blur because it had happened when she was in the midst of dealing with her father's and brother's deaths and Jonas's illness.

"Oh my gosh. I remember now. The look on her face when the other woman approached her in the church! That photographer got some great pictures, and I remember seeing them on the covers of the tabloids at the supermarket. You could see her glance over to the pew where the kids were sitting and back at the woman, and the lightbulb went on. That woman's kids looked exactly like her husband. They had the same angular cheekbones and jutting chins. He must have had strong genes. I would have died of embarrassment if that had been me. Imagine the whole world knowing your husband cheated on you and you never caught on." Gosh, she hoped Jonas didn't feel this way when he found out about the baby.

"It must have been devastating," said Jonas, shaking his head. "I guess that's what drove her to push forward in politics and run for president—she wanted to help women in difficult situations like the one she'd been in."

He finished his dinner. Morgan placed their bowls on the nightstand.

"I guess this isn't relevant to her campaign now. If we're going to dig into her past, we should talk about how she overcame the hardship of her parents being refugees from El Salvador to become governor and then president—that's pretty impressive. I'm trying to decide whether to vote for her or not. It seems like she's done a good job in her first term. And I wouldn't want to judge her based on her personal life from years ago."

"Don't you think you should judge her at least somewhat based on the situation with her husband? I mean, she must have had a huge blind spot not to realize her husband was cheating for so long. He had two children with this other woman. How smart can she be if she was unaware of something as big and important as this?" Jonas asked. He was too weak to talk with his hands as much as he used to, but he gestured a bit for emphasis.

"I don't know. I feel like there's a double standard at play here," said Morgan, taking a sip of her water. "Remember back in the time *before* when male politicians cheated all the time and no one even blinked? Now we have a female candidate for president, and she did nothing wrong. It was her husband who cheated, and it happened ten years ago, and we're still blaming her? This feels unfair."

"All right, I do see your point," said Jonas, "But I was never a fan of all those cheating male politicians either. I think how you behave in your personal life says a lot about who you are professionally. There are no clean lines, especially not when you're running for president. I think she should've known. I don't want to vote for someone who is oblivious to basic facts, or worse, someone who lives in willful denial." He crossed his arms over his frail chest.

"But Jonas, Ximena has done some great things for this country. The improvements that you're always talking about in government spending priorities and infrastructure projects—those are her accomplishments. And I can see why Bree and Sarah support Ximena for those reasons, but I'm upset that vaccine research isn't more of a priority to them."

"People have different opinions, and that's okay, Morgan."

"I know. But I wish that society as a whole cared more about the vaccine development. We could put an end to this disease if everyone made it a priority. And my lab could be the one to make it happen."

"Do you know who you're going to vote for?" Jonas asked.

"I'm not sure. I'm going to do some research on the other candidates. If no one's supporting vaccines, I might as well vote for Ximena—it sounds like she's the best of the bunch."

"I'm going to do some more research, too," said Jonas. "Let's make it a date—we can read up together."

"That sounds nice, Jonas. I love that I can talk about anything with you," said Morgan, standing to clear the dishes. She remembered that she wasn't, in fact, comfortable talking about everything with Jonas these days. She still hadn't told him she was pregnant with another man's child. Soon, the pregnancy would start to show on her thin frame. She needed to tell him. Once she knew the baby's sex, she would, no matter how hard it was.

CHAPTER 18

• • •

Near the end of Morgan's first trimester, when Morgan and Gena had a free moment in the midst of their busy work schedules, Gena helped her with the blood test that would tell her with near certainty if her baby was a boy or a girl and how much of a disaster she was facing. Morgan's small but growing belly was hidden under stretchy pants and a loose top, which was not much different from what she normally wore.

It was late at night, and they were the only ones left in the lab. Morgan had finished checking on the monkeys. While Gena settled herself in front of the computer, nearly ready to pull up the results, Morgan paced behind her. Suddenly, she heard a "squeak," and Morgan nearly hit the roof. It was harmless, just one of the rodents used for vaccine testing chattering to his or her buddies. However, with the lab nearly empty and silent, the normal noises the critters made sounded much louder.

Morgan took a breath and calmed down a bit although her head pounded as she waited for the results of the blood test. "Please hurry, Gena. I can't stand it," she said. Her palms felt cold and sweaty. Gena looked at the computer and then at Morgan. There was no trace of a smile on her mouth.

Morgan knew instantly—a boy. Her stomach lurched. She sank into the nearest chair. Her face was wet with tears she was unaware of having shed. Her whole body felt heavy. She rested her head on her arms and sobbed while Gena patted her shoulder in a fruitless attempt to comfort her.

After Morgan had pulled herself together, the two women headed to Foot Bar to talk about it. They were silent on the way over. Morgan ordered a virgin piña colada and hoped the fumes from the nail polish wouldn't kill all the baby's brain cells. Gena offered to lay off the alcohol in solidarity, but Morgan said she didn't mind, so Gena had her usual Manhattan. They settled in the comfy chairs, soaking their feet in the warm bubbly water and sipping their drinks. In contrast with Morgan's busy brain, their surroundings were peaceful and calming.

Morgan's mouth soon started going a mile a minute to match her brain. "Gena, I have an idea. What if I pretend the baby's a girl? No one will know. It's not like anyone is going to look in her diaper. Everyone will assume that I used donor sperm. Although, I would still need to think of something to tell Jonas."

"Morgan, that's a terrible idea. What are you going to do when the baby hits puberty? Pretend he is transgendered? Or even before that, when he realizes he doesn't look like the other little girls? Plus, you're not going to be able to take him out of the house. He'll be susceptible to manflu."

"You're right. I haven't thought this through. I keep assuming the vaccine will be ready soon, I'll be able to give it to him, and he'll have a normal life. But he won't, will he? There isn't even any such thing as a normal life anymore. Remember how it used to be? Mom, dad, 2.1 kids, a dog, and a house in the suburbs. That's never coming back, not with all the vaccines in the world. Now it's mom, maybe two moms or even three, four, or five, one daughter or several, maybe a sick dad, brother or grandpa in the attic, and a sperm donor in a mansion on a hill. What is this baby's place going to be in the world?"

"How it used to be was a world without a place for me. I was never going to form a mom, dad, 2.1 kids kind of family. You know my own parents disowned me when I came out. I'm happy that the world has changed. No one questions my relationship anymore. People are accepted for who they are. Don't forget how different things used to be *before*. There's no use romanticizing it," Gena said. Deep lines appeared on her forehead which had, until a moment before, been smooth.

They paused their conversation as the woman came over to place the machines on their feet to paint their toenails. When she finished and the machines were busy whirring quietly, Morgan picked up the discussion where they had left off.

"I understand what you're saying, and I agree, everything is much better for women now and for anyone who doesn't fit the old mold, but what about boys and men? Don't they deserve a life, too?" asked Morgan. "And maybe there's something special about this child who was created naturally, without science. Maybe he was meant to be because he's destined to serve a special purpose. I have to protect him." Morgan hadn't meant to offend her friend. She was just deeply worried about the future of men and even more so now that she was having a son.

"He's going to be okay, Morgan. He'll find his place like we all have. We don't know what the future will bring, but he has you looking out for him. I'm more worried about you. The way people talk, everyone in each other's business, they're going to be out for blood."

"You're going to have to help me come up with a plan, Gena. You're so much more level-headed than I am," said Morgan, resigning herself to a difficult future.

"I hate to say this Morgan, but I have to ask—are you sure you don't want an abortion? They're not so common, but I'm sure you could find a doctor from *before* who would still know how to do it. You could always try again the proper way—you know, getting X-chromosome sperm at the sperm bank."

"I can't do it. I want this baby so much. An abortion is out of the question. I have to believe we will get the vaccine to work and he will be able to have a normal life. We're working harder than ever, and I feel like we're so close. What do you think, Gena?"

The woman came back to remove the machines, causing them to again pause their conversation.

"I think it's crazy to have a boy right now," said Gena when they were alone. "But if you want to keep this baby, I'll support you. Yes, I do think we're close to having a vaccine. But it's hard to know how long it will take, and meanwhile, you'll have to keep your baby bubble-wrapped!" Gena closed her eyes, looking deep in thought. "What're you going to do now, Morgan?"

Morgan looked down at her freshly painted pink toes. "I can't know the future, but I do know that the first step is to tell Jonas before he figures it out for himself. I'm going to march my pink toes home right now and do it. Wish me luck."

"Good luck, Morgan," said Gena. They both got up to leave the salon, giving each other a big hug before parting ways.

Morgan drove home and showered, mulling over what she would say to Jonas. She was going to have to come straight out with it. She wondered what his response would be. Would he ask her to leave the house? Could he accept her and the baby? Even after all these years together, she had no idea how he would react to this news because it was so far out of the range of possibilities she had imagined for their lives.

CHAPTER 19

...

Morgan finished her shower and walked to the bedroom to find Jonas watching the news. The German lab had recently made a major breakthrough with their research. Morgan tried not to get distracted, since she had already heard their news. No matter what the Germans were doing, she intended to focus on her own work. She sat on the bed as Jonas muted the TV.

"Jonas, I've got to tell you something." She swallowed nervously. Her heart pounded, and her stomach twisted into a knot.

"What is it, dear?" He looked deep into her eyes and raised his eyebrows. "Is it about the progress the Germans made?"

"No, it's not. Jonas, I'm pregnant," She looked down, frightened to return his gaze.

"Beth's nephew?" he asked, his tone mild and matter-of-fact.

Morgan met his gaze. "How did you know?"

"Our neighbor Robert has been watching your comings and goings, and he tries to report them to me. I finally blocked him on social media. Poor man has nothing better to do cooped up at home with his eyeballs glued to the window."

"I'm sorry you found out that way. I should've talked to you about it. It happened one time, and I haven't seen him since." She sighed, wondering how to tell him the rest of what she needed to say.

"It's okay. I understand. We've talked about it before. I told you that I want you to live your life. Just because I'm stuck in this bedroom all the time doesn't mean you should be. But now there's going to be a baby?" Jonas asked. He smiled.

Morgan thought he must be picturing a sweet girl child. A toddler playing with her toys on the floor of the bedroom he was confined to. When she got older, she would go to school in the mornings and spend her afternoons telling him all about the other kids in her class and what they had learned that day. His smile would soon disappear when he learned this child would not be able to attend school. At least, not for the foreseeable future.

"Jonas, you are the sweetest man. I'm so glad you said that. Yes, there's a baby. The neighbor doesn't know about it yet. I'm not sure how involved he will want to be. Regardless, I want you to know that I consider you to be the father-figure to this child."

"Thank you, Morgan. I'm so happy. I think this'll be a wonderful opportunity for us to finally have a family."

"Jonas, there's something else you should know." Morgan drew in a steadying breath as she paused, looking anywhere but at Jonas. Her heart raced again, and she felt so light-headed, she feared she might pass out.

Jonas frowned, although his eyes still glowed with what Morgan assumed was the vision of a beautiful daughter.

"Jonas." Morgan briefly closed her eyes. "It's a boy."

She opened her eyes and saw Jonas processing the information silently. She imagined he was replacing images of a daughter happily returning from school with one of a son trapped in the house, pale and depressed. Her hands shook as she waited for him to react.

"Jonas, please say something." Morgan dropped to her knees on the floor by the bed and pressed her face against the blankets.

"Are you sure? How do you know it's a boy?"

"I'm sure. Gena ran a blood test for me."

"So Gena knows."

Morgan nodded as she lifted her face from the blanket.

"You're bringing a person into this world who'll be at risk for manflu. How could you?"

Morgan felt a lump in her throat and began to cry. "Jonas, it wasn't intentional. I feel terrible about it, but I don't know what to do. I'm not going to have an abortion. This is my chance to be a mother. *Our* chance to be parents. Remember how much we wanted this? And we're so close to finding a vaccine. I know the baby's going to be okay. You have to believe me."

"Morgan, I need some time alone." Jonas turned away, hiding his face in his pillows. This was his version of storming off. Morgan quietly left the room and went to the guest room where she cried until her eyes burned and her stomach ached.

CHAPTER 20

...

Morgan and Gena arrived at work at the same time the next morning, both running a little late after the exhausting events of the previous evening. Morgan had been on the phone with Gena until 2:00 a.m., sharing her distress about her conversation with Jonas.

Unusually, the reception desk was empty. Morgan thought Andrea must have been getting herself a cup of coffee or gossiping with Charlotte. However, Morgan paused when she discovered Charlotte and Andrea deep in conversation with two policewomen. They stood just past the reception desk in an open area of the office.

When she looked back to Gena, entering the open area behind her, she saw that the expression on Gena's face matched the shock Morgan felt. Why would there be police officers in the building? Had a crime been committed? Morgan motioned to Gena with a finger to her lips and a hand cupped around her ear. They slowly walked toward the four women speaking so intensely and waited off to the side, listening.

"But that's where the vaccine samples are kept!" Charlotte exclaimed. "Why would anyone want to take them? We have expensive lab equipment they could have stolen but didn't, so this must be sabotage." Charlotte looked devastated.

Andrea placed an arm around Charlotte and murmured something in her ear. Andrea's cat earrings jangled softly as she shook her head in disbelief.

"The vaccine samples were taken?" asked Morgan, forgetting her plan to listen quietly but charging forward and butting in instead. It was unlike her to interrupt, but a risk to the vaccine triggered her fight or flight response. And today, she was spoiling for a fight.

"Are you talking about the samples meant for the next round of testing with the primates?" Her heart pounded, tears of anger and frustration stinging her eyes. A wave of pregnancy nausea hit her, too. "Why would anyone take those?" she squeaked out. It would take weeks to make those samples again. Time that she didn't have to lose in the race to finish the vaccine before her baby boy was born.

The police officers looked at Charlotte. "Can we speak to you somewhere more private, ma'am?"

"Certainly." Charlotte led the officers into a conference room along with Andrea. "I'll check in with you later, Morgan," she said before closing the door.

"Morgan, let's go take a look and see what happened," said Gena.

"Isn't it a crime scene, though? We probably shouldn't disturb anything." The adrenaline propelling Morgan forward with the police had subsided. She now felt nervous and cautious.

"Don't you want to see what was taken? What if they've stolen more than the vaccine samples? Let's make sure everything else is still there."

Morgan reluctantly followed Gena to the area where the vaccine samples were kept. Strangely, there was no broken glass or any other signs of a break-in. They finally reached the refrigerator that contained the samples.

Gena glanced at Morgan. Before she could say anything, she quickly yanked open the door. The refrigerator was completely empty.

CHAPTER 21

...

Morgan was horrified. All that hard work, gone. Gena's face instantly turned bright red and her eyes looked ready to pop. Morgan had never seen Gena this enraged before. Gena paced around the office, muttering to herself. Morgan felt the blood drain out of her head, and dizziness suddenly came over her. She turned around to look for a chair and was surprised to find Gavin right behind her. He must have arrived for his appointment and walked right in when he didn't find Andrea at her post.

"What's going on?" he asked.

Gena looked first at Gavin and then at Morgan's pale face, and she frowned. "Let's all go find somewhere to sit down," she said.

They walked into the staff kitchen where Gena got Morgan a cup of water while Morgan and Gavin sat. Morgan took a small sip and then rested her head on her arms folded on top of the table. Gena remained standing with her fists balled. She bounced from one foot to the other. "Gavin, that friend of yours who was snooping around here, have you seen her lately?"

"Do you mean Stacey? No, I haven't seen her. And snooping is a strong word, don't you think? My understanding is that she got lost on her way to the bathroom."

"Well, there was a break-in here today. Do you think she might know anything about it?" Gena asked, crossing her arms in front of her chest. She managed to keep her voice calm, but doing so required noticeable effort.

"Stacey? I doubt it. She's as dumb as a box of rocks."

"Ever consider that playing dumb was an act?" asked Morgan, lifting her head briefly, feeling dizzy again, and lowering it back onto her arms.

"She must be a great actress. And she really *got into* the part, if you know what I mean!"

"Seriously, Gavin! Now is not the time." Morgan was so frustrated, she lifted her head to speak again, ignoring the nausea rising in her chest. "Maybe she's been spying on us."

"She might be working for the Germans," said Gena.

"What're you even talking about? What do the Germans have to do with anything?" Gavin stood and paced around the small kitchen. Gena and Gavin would soon crash into each other if they couldn't keep still, thought Morgan.

"The Germans are working on a vaccine, too. They may be trying to learn about our progress so they can finish their vaccine faster," said Morgan.

"That makes no sense! From what I understand, scientists have been cooperating to get this done. Isn't there an international consortium or something?" Gavin looked from Morgan to Gena. His hands were in the air, asking the question, too.

Morgan's phone rang loudly, startling everyone. She pulled it out of her pocket and glanced at it to make sure there was no emergency with Jonas. It was Nate. She sent the call to voicemail as she had done with most of his previous calls over the last few months. A few times, they had managed a quick, surface-level conversation before she had said she had to go because she was busy with work or Jonas. She was surprised he hadn't given up yet. Morgan put her phone back in her pocket. She would think about Nate later.

"Maybe they've been acting like they're cooperating while secretly sabotaging us," theorized Gena.

"Look, the police are here, and I'm sure they're going to solve this," said Morgan. "Why don't we get back to work and let them do their job? Gavin, I'm sorry, but we'll have to reschedule today's session. I don't have time to do the interview now. I must tend to the monkeys." She mentally re-arranged her schedule to account for the time it would take to re-do the samples.

"That's fine, Morgan, but you're wrong about Stacey. I really don't think she's involved," said Gavin.

"Please let us know if you hear from her, Gavin," said Gena.

"I will," he said before he showed himself out.

"Do you think he had anything to do with this, Morgan?" asked Gena when he was gone.

"Gavin? No way. He wants to help. He may be crude, but he's a good guy. He's on our side." Morgan thought back to their conversations and how open Gavin had been with her.

"Okay, but I think you should keep an eye on him, too," said Gena.

"Gena, I don't have the energy to keep an eye on anyone, and now I'll have to re-make the vaccine samples!" said Morgan, putting her head down again. "You remember the situation I'm in, right?" She put a hand on her small baby bump, still hidden under baggy clothes.

"I'm sorry, Morgan, I didn't mean to pressure you," said Gena. "I'm not sure we can trust the authorities to resolve this. We have to do some of the sleuthing ourselves."

"Sure, Gena." Morgan stood and left the kitchen, Gena close on her heels. "I'm going to get some of my actual work done first, though."

Morgan went over to her desk to prepare for the day. She saw Charlotte and Andrea still in the conference room with the police officers. Gena sat at her own computer, typing furiously. Morgan got irritated at the loud banging of the keys. Between the exhaustion and the nausea, everything and everyone annoyed her these days, even her best friend. She opened a folder containing some paperwork and started going through it. She signed several check requests relating to monkey supplies. Among the finance papers, she noticed something that didn't belong. This was very strange. It was an invoice made out to Andrea for work supposedly occurring today. The description simply said, "Research." Instead of a company name, there was the name of a woman, Mikayla Bascomb. Morgan didn't know who she was, but that last name felt familiar. What work could Andrea have requested on the same date as the break-in? Was this a coincidence?

Morgan turned to look at Gena, who seemed to be deep in thought. Morgan decided not disturbing her made the most sense. This was probably nothing, just a payment for a research intern or something, although they didn't usually subcontract out research projects. Maybe they were short-staffed because some employees were out caring for sick family members and needed external help. That would make sense.

There must be a logical explanation. Morgan's imagination was in overdrive after the stress of the morning. What she needed to do was focus on her work so she could maintain momentum on the vaccine despite this break-in. She would let the police do their job, and she would do hers. The future of her son depended on it.

CHAPTER 22

...

The next day, Morgan finally got a moment alone with Charlotte, who had been walking through Morgan's work area when Morgan stopped her. She felt nervous about confronting her boss, but she was deeply worried about the previous day's events and needed more information. She had never thought of herself as an anxious person before, but the pregnancy amped her up and made her feel like a guitar with all the strings pulled tight.

"Charlotte, what's going on? What did you find out about the break-in?" Morgan asked, placing her hands on her hips.

"We don't know much yet, Morgan. I'm sorry I don't have any information to share. I'm working very closely with the police to help them solve this."

"Why don't we know more? There can't be that many people interested in stealing vaccine samples!" Morgan fumed.

"You would be surprised. There're a lot of people who don't want to see men re-gain any power in society." Charlotte shook her head, sending her trademark red glasses swinging on their chain and bouncing on her chest.

Morgan thought about mentioning the invoice she had seen made out to Andrea. It could be an important clue. But what if it was nothing? She would look petty and foolish, and it would seem she had something personal against Andrea. That was definitely not the impression she was trying to give Charlotte, who was very close to Andrea, for reasons Morgan could not begin to puzzle out. No, she wouldn't mention it for now.

"I understand that, but stealing vaccine samples is pretty extreme. We have to find out who did this and prevent it from happening again. Are you increasing security? What's being done? What if these people come back?"

"Morgan, I don't want you to worry, especially in your condition," said Charlotte soothingly. "The police are handling it. We have to trust them to take care of it." Morgan was temporarily rendered speechless by the phrase "in your condition." First of all, it sounded straight out of the 1950s. Secondly, did Charlotte know about her pregnancy? Was this how she was going to bring it up?

By the look on Charlotte's face, Morgan could tell that she regretted mentioning it. She started to backpedal, "I mean . . . I thought . . . some of the women were talking . . ." That only made it worse. Morgan didn't know what to do. Should she tell? She could reveal the pregnancy without mentioning the gender. She might as well spill it. Everyone would know soon enough. And apparently, people were already talking about it.

"Yes, Charlotte, I'm pregnant. But that has nothing to do with my desire to be informed about a situation at work that threatens my safety and the progress I'm making on this vaccine. I expect you to keep staff up-to-date on any information you hear from the police."

Before Charlotte could respond, Morgan ran off to the breakroom and started crying. She had never stood up to an authority figure like that before. Her whole body shook. She was terrified—

would she be fired? She was so used to doing what she was told without question. She wasn't sure if it was the threat to her vaccine or her unborn child, but something had unleashed a new side of her, and she was not sure she liked it.

At that moment, Morgan received a page over the intercom announcing Gavin had arrived for his rescheduled session. She couldn't believe that she had to deal with this right now. Luckily, his entourage was not with him. As she escorted him to the exam room, Morgan noticed whispered conversations among some of her colleagues. A few of the women looked from her to Gavin and stared pointedly at her stomach. Looks like her pregnancy was common knowledge after all. The women continued whispering rapid-fire to each other. Morgan rolled her eyes and showed Gavin into a room. Why were they pointing at Gavin? It took a moment to sink in—oh no, they must have thought he was the father! Could this day get any worse?

Gavin coughed to get her attention. "What's the topic of the day, Dr. Digby?" he asked.

Morgan refocused her attention on the ever-present HERO. "It's all about your prostate today," Morgan said fake-cheerfully. Oh dear, evidently it could get worse.

"Is that why everyone out there was whispering?" Gavin asked. "Is my prostate the hot topic of conversation around here?"

"No, actually. The world doesn't revolve around you. They're whispering about me," Morgan said in a less than professional manner.

"Really? Who would've thought?!" Gavin said, taken aback. "What'd you do, forget to rinse a test tube?"

"No, actually I got myself knocked up," said Morgan, relieved at the opportunity to confess, "and they think you did it."

Morgan couldn't believe she'd just said that to Gavin. Something about being in this small room with him so frequently had created a feeling of intimacy in their relationship. It had been frustrating being unable to talk to anyone at work besides Gena about what was happening in her life.

"Me?" Gavin was startled. "Why would they think that?"

"Well, there are not a lot of candidates who fit the bill. Certainly not my husband. And we've been spending a lot of time alone together."

"Didn't you go to the sperm bank? Why wouldn't they assume you did that?"

Morgan had a thought: yes, that's what she should tell people. She had gone to the sperm bank, and they had made a mistake and given her Y-chromosome sperm. That's what made the most sense. People would believe that. So what if it had never happened before. There's a first time for everything. Then no one would ever have to know she'd cheated on Jonas and been so irresponsible about birth control, allowing for the possibility of a child who was at risk of contracting manflu.

"You know how people are. They love to gossip. And I haven't officially announced my pregnancy yet, so they're suspicious. The women here normally tell people when they're getting inseminated."

"I see. Well, congratulations to you! Babies are ... delightful!" From his tone and hesitation, it seemed that he thought they were perhaps delightful for other people. "Want to have a little fun and pretend that we've been messing around in here, Dr. Digby?" Gavin asked with his customary wink.

"No, I prefer not to get fired," Morgan said. "Let's talk about your prostate now."

"I thought we *were* talking about my prostate," said Gavin with a chuckle. "All right, all right. Let's go, I'm ready for it."

The rest of the session unfolded professionally, apart from

another anti-government diatribe delivered by Gavin, who worried Ximena Álvarez's scheme to fund more caregivers would hit him where it really hurt—his pocketbook. Morgan had been so preoccupied with the affair and pregnancy, she had barely given a thought to the election, other than a brief update she had gotten from her neighbor Bree a few weeks prior at their book club meeting.

"I hope lab funding isn't cut further," said Morgan. She usually tried to avoid talking politics with research subjects but felt comfortable with Gavin after so many conversations about intimate topics.

Gavin stood and focused intently on Morgan. "I know you think I'm not a serious person, but I do care about science, and I want men to be able to thrive again. It's lonely in a world full of women. If you need anything for your lab, please let me know. I'll see what I can do to help."

"Thanks, Gavin. I appreciate it. I'll let you know," said Morgan, shaking his hand. "And you can call me Morgan."

"Congratulations on the baby, Morgan," he said with a smile before heading out of the exam room.

She felt her phone vibrate in her lab coat pocket. She pulled it out. It was Nate calling her again. This was the day that would not quit. She was fiddling with her phone, trying to send the call to voicemail, when she nearly crashed into Gena.

"Sorry, Gena!"

"That's okay. Hey, is that Nate calling you again?" Gena whispered.

Morgan glanced around to make sure they were alone. "Yes, he keeps calling. I don't know what to say to him."

"Are you planning to tell him about the baby?" she asked.

"I think I should. But I have to talk to Jonas first. He was so upset when I told him the news. If it'd been a girl, he would've been thrilled.

But bringing a boy into the world we live in where he won't even be able to go outside—he thinks it's cruel, and part of me agrees with him. But what can I do now? What's done is done." Morgan fell quiet, overwhelmed by all the what-ifs going through her brain. Gena grabbed her hand and gave it a squeeze.

Morgan remembered the brilliant idea that had come to her while she interviewed Gavin. She perked up and decided to run it by Gena. "Gena, listen, I had a thought. What if I tell people at work that I went to a sperm bank and they messed up and gave me Y-chromosome sperm? That way, no one would have to know about Nate."

Gena pursed her lips. "It's not the worst idea you've had," she said. "I mean, I've never heard of that happening to anyone, but there's a first time for everything. It is pretty far-fetched that a sperm bank would make a mistake like that, but it's not impossible. It could work." She tilted her head from side to side, as if examining the notion from a variety of angles in her brain.

"Well, I don't have any better ideas, so I'm going with that for now," said Morgan. "Now that I've figured that out, I feel like I can talk to Jonas again and then tell Nate. Worrying about what everyone might think has been holding me back."

"I can see why you wouldn't want people to know about Nate. The women here would definitely gossip about a juicy nugget like that. I'm glad you found a way to keep this quiet. It's no one's business but yours."

Gena always knew exactly what to say. Morgan gave her a quick hug. She felt so lucky to have her as a friend and co-worker.

She needed to steel herself for these upcoming conversations— they would not be easy. She hoped Jonas had come around since they had last talked. Knowing him, he probably would. He was tender-hearted and loved children. But she had no idea how Nate would react to the news. She barely even knew him. What if he didn't like children? She wasn't even sure why she felt the need to tell him except it seemed like the right thing to do.

CHAPTER 23

...

For several weeks, Morgan and Jonas avoided conversations about anything more involved than the flavor of Jell-O on the menu. She knew they needed to talk, but he hadn't brought up her pregnancy, and she hadn't felt the time was right to talk further about it. Since telling Nate was on hold, pending the conversation, she had to move forward no matter how uncomfortable she felt.

That night, Morgan sat on Jonas's bed for what felt like ages until he finally turned off the TV and looked at her. She felt a sense of calm settle over her, because she knew she would achieve resolution, and she trusted Jonas to be reasonable. However, she noted a hint of disdain in his eyes where there had never before been anything but love and respect. She almost broke down but blinked back her tears and cleared her throat.

"Jonas, it's time to talk. I want to keep the baby and raise him with you. Will you do this with me? I know it'll be hard. It's not what we planned. He won't be able to go out for now or live a normal life. Even so, can we find a way to be parents to this boy?" Morgan stared straight into his eyes and waited, not daring to move.

Jonas struggled to sit up but shrugged off Morgan's offer of help. He finally situated himself amongst the pillows and met Morgan's gaze. "Where else could I go? I hope I can find it in myself to love him when he's born. It'll be a struggle every single day. I'll look at him and be reminded of what we couldn't have and what you did have with someone else. And that the child will be born into the same prison I inhabit. I hope that with time and with the joy children bring, I'll be able to overcome these feelings. I don't see another path forward."

Tears pricked Morgan's eyes. She couldn't speak, so she sat quietly as a mix of relief and sadness washed over her.

"Yes, we can raise the baby together. You don't give me much choice, Morgan."

Although his words were hard to hear, Morgan was glad Jonas was able to put his thoughts into words. His training as a therapist made him very aware of what was going on in his own mind, and he always communicated clearly.

Morgan nodded. "Thank you, Jonas. I think you'll find that the baby will breathe new energy into our lives and into this house. Our marriage is still a partnership. You have to know that I'll always take care of you and consider your feelings in making decisions. If the situation were reversed, I know you'd do the same for me." Morgan felt the comfort that comes with being a part of a team. She trusted that Jonas would grow to love the child as much as she already did.

Morgan did something she had not done for a long time. She picked up a book of poetry from a shelf to read aloud to Jonas, who closed his eyes to listen, his faint smile giving his face a serene expression. For the first time in a while, Morgan felt content, and her chest swelled with love for her husband and for the baby growing inside her.

She found the poem she sought, which matched the mood that

day, "Ode to Melancholy" by John Keats: "But when the melancholy fit shall fall/Sudden from heaven like a weeping cloud . . ." The poem exhorted them to "dwell with Beauty—Beauty that must die; And Joy, whose hand is ever at his lips . . ."

CHAPTER 24

...

The next weekend, Morgan resolved to tell Nate. She felt he had the right to know about his son. Morgan wondered if he would react with indifference or perhaps take some interest in the baby. He was so young himself.

She took several walks past Beth's house until she found her neighbor's car gone. She imagined Robert watching her from his window across the street. He was probably trying to text Jonas at this very moment. She pushed those thoughts aside and rang the bell, speaking to Nate through the intercom.

In the disinfecting shower, the strong water flow hurt her newly sensitive breasts. She briefly flashed to an image of Nate's long fingers stroking her there, and she experienced a rush of desire for his strong, pale body. Exiting the shower and slipping into the short robe, she remembered how she had let it fall to the floor and kissed Nate deeply, their naked bodies pressed together. She blinked until the image in her mind faded.

Nate met her as she entered the house. He took her hands in his. "I missed you, Morgan. I didn't have anyone to help with my piano playing." He smiled sadly at her.

Her inner tension eased somewhat. "Oh, Nate," sighed Morgan.

Their attraction was powerful, especially with only fabric separating them. Morgan stood on her toes and kissed him full on the mouth. He responded, his lips soft and his tongue tentative. They walked to Nate's bedroom, managing to sit on the bed without separating their lips. Nate was pulling down his sweatpants when Morgan remembered herself.

"Nate, we need to talk," she said, voicing those most-dreaded words in the English language.

Nate calmly looked at her, his curly hair already disheveled and his clothing in disarray.

Then she spoke the second most-dreaded phrase in the English language, "I'm pregnant." She felt like a rock had been removed from her chest, and she could finally breathe. She hated keeping secrets from people she cared about.

Nate stared, mouth agape. At least he had the sense not to ask, "Is it mine?"

"It's a boy," Morgan added softly.

"Morgan, I don't know what to say." He resembled a small, scared child. He shrank into himself like a tortoise retreating into its shell and looked at Morgan searchingly from under his curls.

She moved next to him on the bed and clasped his hand in both of hers. "I'm keeping the baby. I've already told Jonas. We're going to raise him together."

"What do you mean, you're keeping the baby? What else would you do with him?" Nate asked, sounding confused.

"Oh, well, I might have had an abortion." Why *would* he immediately assume abortion? He probably didn't know anything about abortions.

"Oh, right. I think I've heard about them. I'm glad you won't do that. It'll be so nice to have a baby. You said you'll raise him with your husband? What about me? I'm the father. I should be involved in raising him, right?" He looked at her like a puppy trying to track a stuffed toy.

Morgan stared back at him. She hadn't thought about him wanting a relationship with the baby. He would be a good father. She pictured a little boy sitting on the piano bench next to Nate, tiny hands sporting long fingers poised over the keys, a small head topped with curly black hair. But Jonas wanted to be the father. Could the baby have two fathers? Could Jonas and Nate share the baby? When Morgan was a small girl dreaming about her future, she never in a million years would have anticipated this situation. All she'd ever wanted was a normal life.

"Nate, Jonas has accepted the baby, and he wants to raise it. He is my husband, and I'm committed to him. I'd love for you to be involved with your son. I'm just not sure how it could work. Things would be so awkward. And can you imagine explaining it all to the child?" Morgan paced around the room.

"Morgan, from everything you've told me, Jonas is a good man. I know we'd be able to do this," said Nate. "I really want to be a father to this baby. And you may need my help."

That was a good point. Morgan had not thought about the hands-on assistance Nate could provide that Jonas could not. She would have to think about the role she wanted him to play. She also needed to be honest with him.

"Nate, there's something else. I don't want people at work to know what happened. I'm telling them that the sperm bank messed up and gave me Y-chromosome sperm. No one will know you're the father," said Morgan.

"Do you think anyone will believe you? From what I've learned in my online biology classes, separating sperm by gender is pretty hard to mess up these days," he said.

In truth, she was counting on people believing her. "I don't have any other options. I'm not going to tell people about us," insisted Morgan.

"I'm used to being hidden away. I don't care about that. But I want to be a dad to my son," said Nate.

"We'll have to see how things go, Nate," said Morgan. She couldn't imagine how any of this would go.

Nate looked like he wanted to say more, but he stopped himself. He put an arm around Morgan, and she returned his embrace. They held each other silently for a while until she got up to leave. When Nate opened the bedroom door, Morgan saw Beth in the living room fluffing the sofa cushions. Had she heard their conversation?

CHAPTER 25

• • •

"Hi, Beth," said Nate, "I didn't realize you'd come in."

"I popped out to pick up some brown sugar for the cookies I'm baking," she responded, looking first at Nate and then at Morgan. She seemed to take in their emotional state. Morgan wondered what she'd heard and what she might be thinking. Was she judging them for their irresponsible behavior?

Morgan hadn't thought about discussing her pregnancy with Beth yet, but knew she would eventually tell her. Now seemed like as good a time as any. She glanced at Nate to try to read his expression, but he simply looked overwhelmed.

"Does anyone want some tea? The cookies should be ready soon. I'll go make us some tea to go with them." Beth briskly walked to the kitchen to escape the awkwardness.

With Beth gone for the moment, Morgan turned to Nate and motioned for him to sit with her on the couch. Nate settled in next to her.

Morgan whispered, "I'm going to tell her. She's going to find out soon enough, anyway. And she probably overhead us talking just now."

Nate sighed deeply, but he didn't protest.

Beth returned, carrying a tray with a plate of brown sugar cookies, a teapot, three mugs, and a sugar bowl. She served everyone tea and offered around the cookies, which Morgan took out of politeness. Nate, with the appetite of a young man, grabbed a handful.

Morgan felt ridiculous clad in a short robe as she perched on Beth's couch. "Beth, there's something we need to tell you. I'm pregnant."

"Congratulations, Morgan!" Beth stood, wiping tears from her eyes.

Beth didn't even look surprised. It probably took a lot more than an unexpected pregnancy to shock a nurse. She went to Morgan and reached out to hug her. Morgan gently stopped her embrace.

"Wait, Beth. There's more." Morgan wiped tears from her own eyes. She started to cry and laugh at the same time, her emotions in a tumult. "It's a boy."

"Oh, darling," Beth said. And she embraced Morgan and held her in her arms for a long time, letting her cry as long as she needed. Morgan missed her own mother so much at that moment but was grateful for her dear neighbor, who had stepped in to fill the role. Morgan wondered what she'd gotten herself into.

CHAPTER 26

...

Weeks passed, and Morgan's belly grew. In order to avoid shocked coworkers once she had the baby, Morgan had asked Gena to leak the news that she would deliver a boy. When her coworkers started to fish for information about how the baby came to be a boy, Morgan always demurred. Many a time, she ran off to check on her monkeys. Progress on the vaccine continued. The Germans still hadn't finalized their own vaccine, but Morgan felt certain they were getting closer by the day.

The party planning committee at the lab threw her a surprise baby shower, complete with those silly games that Morgan actually hated, but she pretended to enjoy herself. Charlotte won the "guess the flavor of baby food" contest (squash), and Gena won the "guess the number of M&Ms in the bottle" competition (973), though it was unclear who counted them.

The party planners always held these types of celebrations potluck-style due to the low budgets that were part of life at a government-funded lab. Most of the women brought in food representative of their cultural backgrounds, mixed in with some modern touches. Gena made her famous vegan enchiladas, a nod to her Mexican heritage. Charlotte shared a healthier version of a family potato salad recipe. Aparna, head of the party planning committee, lugged in a big pot of dal with freshly baked naan. Andrea contributed a box of store-bought alfajores (Argentine cookies) representing her parents' homeland. Morgan checked the package and saw that their best-by date was a month past.

Everyone sat around eating lunch companionably, enjoying the break from work, commenting on how delicious all the food was. During a pause in conversation, Andrea loudly asked Morgan, "What's your plan for passing off your work during your maternity leave?"

Morgan swallowed the big mouthful of naan she was chewing before she answered. "My goal is to finish the primate testing so that the vaccine is totally ready for Phase I human trials when I leave. That would be a natural point to pass it off." Morgan hoped that she was being realistic with this plan.

"Andrea, have we started recruiting the human volunteers yet?" asked Gena.

"No, not yet," replied Andrea. "Was that supposed to be happening?"

Morgan looked shocked. Recruitment was supposed to have been happening for quite some time, and she felt sure that Andrea knew it.

"Yes, Andrea. I asked you to pass the contract along to the recruiting company we normally work with weeks ago," said Gena, frowning deeply.

"Ladies, let's have this discussion later, shall we? We don't want to ruin the baby shower," said Charlotte. "Isn't it time for cake?" Aparna went off to get the cake out of the breakroom fridge.

Morgan could not believe that no one had begun recruiting the human volunteers. This threatened to completely upend her timeline. She so wanted to yell at Andrea, but on the flip side, she didn't want to make a scene at the party.

Andrea swiftly changed the subject. "So the baby's a boy?" she asked, with a smug expression. Everyone else had been polite enough not to bring it up. Morgan suddenly felt all of her coworkers' eyes boring into her. She felt a scarlet flush creep up her chest and neck.

"Um, the sperm bank must have mixed up the sperm they gave me," said Morgan, suddenly finding her plain black shoes to be very interesting.

"Oh, my goodness! Are you suing them? I can't believe they did that," said Charlotte, always ready to go to bat for the women. She could be a tough boss, but she was protective of her employees.

A woman from HR said, "My aunt received defective sperm from the sperm bank. She threatened to sue, and they settled for like a million dollars. And it wasn't even Y-chromosome sperm—her baby had straight hair, but she wanted curly! I'm going to text her and get her lawyer's info for you." The woman immediately pulled out her phone and started typing furiously.

Aparna said, "Forget lawyers. You should go straight to the press! The public ought to be informed that this is happening. What if this happens to someone else, and you didn't warn anyone?" She crossed her arms over her chest.

Morgan instantly felt damp under her arms and breasts. Her face grew hot and prickly. The room started to spin around her. Luckily, Gena noticed her deteriorating condition, and she was ready with a chair for her to fall into.

"Folks, this is very upsetting for Morgan. Please stop telling her what to do. The situation is delicate, and she's handling it to the best of her abilities. The most helpful thing you can do right now is to go back to work and make a vaccine for her baby! This party is over. Thank you."

Morgan thanked Gena for her intervention, then made her way to the bathroom for the millionth time that day. She washed her face. She was standing at the sink, letting the cold tap water run over her wrists, when Gena walked in.

"Do you want to take a break and get some tea?" Gena asked.

"Sure, that would be great," said Morgan, recalling a ginger tea that always calmed her stomach on the menu at a café down the block. "Fresh air would be good right now."

CHAPTER 27

...

Morgan breathed in the air outdoors as she and Gena walked over to the café. They ordered drinks and sat at a small table. On a muted TV mounted up on the opposite wall, Ximena Álvarez gave a short speech displayed in subtitles about her plans for her second term, if she were to be elected. Morgan watched for a moment as Gena collected their drinks from the counter.

Ximena looked confident and strong in her signature red, loose dress, which picked up the russet tones in her bronze skin. Red for power, loose for comfort. She must have a closet full of similar dresses. Morgan always found the style jarring because, even after so many years, she still expected a politician to don a suit.

The TV program switched to an old clip of one of Ximena's famous moments from when she was running for governor of Colorado many years prior. Her opponent, the state treasurer at the time, had run an attack ad implying that a woman wasn't fit to be governor because women were bad at math, whereas he had successfully managed state funds. Ximena gave a speech tearing him to shreds. She played up her humble origins and described adding up the grocery costs in her head at the supermarket as a child to make sure her mom had enough money to pay for their food. She reminded voters of her advanced degree in economics, which she had paid for by waiting tables between classes. And the finale was her plan to invest the state pension funds in a way that would guarantee higher returns than her opponent had earned in his years as treasurer. The tagline that made her famous was "Women Know Money."

That election was so long ago! Morgan wondered if anyone still thought about it or remembered what things had been like when men dominated politics. Switching her thoughts to the current election, from the research Morgan had done with Jonas, she knew both Ximena and her opponent opposed new vaccine funding. The opposing candidate was a bit more fiscally conservative than Ximena, who was in favor of significantly more spending for caregiver services. Morgan supposed that since both candidates were equally negative on vaccines, she would probably vote for Ximena. Her need for caregiving services was about to increase dramatically. Morgan turned away from the TV as Gena returned to the table with their hot beverages. She had enough going on without worrying about the election too.

"Well, that went about as well as could be expected," said Gena, sipping her hot tea.

"I almost fainted at work," said Morgan incredulously.

"Yes, but people seemed to believe what you said about the sperm mix-up," replied Gena.

"I guess so." Morgan stirred sugar into her tea.

"Hopefully no one will bring it up again, and you'll be all set."

"Let's hope!"

"Morgan, don't you think it's weird that Andrea never contacted the recruiting company?" asked Gena.

Morgan nodded. "Yes, I feel like she's trying to slow us down.

Certain supplies are always missing, too, like cell culture."

"I know! There was one whole week when I couldn't get a test tube. A damn test tube!" Gena said.

"It's amazing she hasn't been fired," mused Morgan.

"And don't forget she didn't let you into that antibody workshop even though she knew you were interested. I've never liked her, but now it seems like something else might be going on. Like she's working against us." Gena rested her chin on her hand in a pose reminiscent of the famous Rodin sculpture.

"And she completely messed up the paperwork for the lab to keep its license to conduct research on primates. It took me forever to sort that out, and we're still working under a temporary license that can be revoked at any time. I have nightmares about it."

"I had no idea we're still under a temporary license. Gosh," Gena sighed.

Morgan took a long, slow sip of her ginger tea. "Gena, I didn't say anything before because I didn't think it was important, but now I'm starting to think it might be related."

She took a steadying breath. Gena eagerly leaned forward, almost knocking over her tea.

Morgan ignored the commotion and continued. "I found an invoice for 'research' (she made air quotes) to be conducted on the date of the break-in. It was made out to Andrea from someone named Mikayla Bascomb. Does that name mean anything to you? Do you think Andrea could be connected to the break-in?"

Gena's eyes widened. "No, I don't recognize that name. But I'm definitely going to look into it. Can you imagine if Andrea is actually trying to sabotage the lab?"

Morgan couldn't believe it. She wondered what other explanation there could be, though. "It doesn't seem possible. She's so close with Charlotte, whom I trust 100%. But her behavior has crossed the line recently from cranky and incompetent to actively harmful. Anyway, I'm glad you're looking into it, Detective Gena."

"Yup, that's me. Detective Gena." She laughed throatily. "Hey, Morgan, switching gears here. What's going on with the whole Jonas-Nate-baby situation?"

Morgan had kept Gena posted over the past few weeks. She knew Jonas was warming up to the idea of the baby and that Nate was also excited to be a father figure. They had spent many late nights on the phone talking about how it all would work.

"Gena, I have a crazy idea. Tell me what you think. What if Nate moves in with me and Jonas? He could help take care of the house as I progress in the pregnancy and help with the baby after he's born." Morgan sipped her tea.

"Um, I can see why that makes sense from a practical point of view, but wouldn't it be incredibly awkward?" Gena's left eyebrow was arched up so high, it looked ready to take flight.

"Yes, it would be awkward, especially at first, but I think we could overcome it. We're all adults. Nate wants to be involved with the baby. There's no way I can take care of Jonas, a baby, and the house all on my own. I won't be able to bring in outside help, because the baby will be at risk of contracting manflu, at least until he's vaccinated, and Jonas is immunocompromised. It's a win-win." She sat back in her chair, satisfied her argument was persuasive.

"Hoo boy, Morgan. I don't know what to say except good luck." She slurped the dregs of her tea.

"Thanks, Gena. I'll need it. I'm going to talk to them both about it ASAP."

"Your husband and your lover in the same house—wow!"

"I know, I know. You don't have to remind me. Thank goodness my parents are not around to see this. I never expected my life to look like this, yet here we are. I'm just being practical now. Maybe they would be proud of that. And nothing else's going to happen with Nate anyway."

"Don't you think you'll be tempted with him living in your house? And won't he be tempted, too? That's if he even agrees to it."

"I think we can be mature about it."

"Maybe *you* can be mature. Isn't he like a teenager or something?"

"He's not a teenager. He's in his early twenties. It will be fine, Gena. It has to be." Morgan stood and looked around to make sure she wasn't forgetting anything. She had been distracted and forgetful recently—another side effect of pregnancy, she supposed. "Let's get back to work on this vaccine, shall we?" They headed back to the office.

CHAPTER 28

...

Morgan raised the idea of Nate moving into their home with Jonas one evening, and to her great surprise, he had no real objections. As usual, they spoke while they slurped their evening soup, Jonas tucked into bed and Morgan sitting beside him. She had a pillow behind her to support her tired back.

Jonas's brow furrowed as he considered Morgan's idea. "Morgan, it would be a huge burden for you to care for the baby and me all on your own. Moving Nate in is actually a good idea."

"Are you sure, Jonas? Won't it be awkward having Nate here with everything that has happened?" Would Jonas feel hurt every time he saw Nate? She wondered how she would feel if the situation were reversed and Jonas planned to move a woman he'd cheated with into their house. She couldn't even fathom it. Jonas was far more accepting than she would be.

"Having him down the block or down the hall is all the same to me. You're free to get your needs met in whatever way you can and wish to."

Jonas spoke practically and logically, his voice free of emotion.

Morgan stared at him as he sipped his chicken broth, wondering what he was really feeling. He must have been jealous of all the things Nate could do that he could not, and having Nate in his house would only rub it in his face. Or was Jonas so accepting that he didn't mind having his wife's former lover in the next bedroom?

She was loath to question Jonas much further because it was such a relief that he was willing to have Nate move in. She didn't know how she would manage without help.

With that settled, the next evening, Morgan went over to talk to Nate. She went through the disinfecting shower, gently cleaning her growing baby bump. When she was clean and dry, she put on the ever-ready white robe, which grew tighter by the day. Nate welcomed her into the living room and fetched her a glass of milk and a stool upon which to rest her feet, now somewhat of a ritual for them. Over the last several visits, as her stomach grew, Morgan had felt the heat dissipating from their relationship, more so on his side than hers. She found him as attractive as ever, if not more so now that he was being so attentive to her needs. However, the way he looked at her had changed. Desire was replaced by reverence. He treated her like a beautiful, glass sculpture that could shatter at any moment.

"Nate, I have a crazy idea," said Morgan, putting her glass of milk down on a side table. Nate sat sprawled on the sofa opposite her. "What if you moved in with me? It's going to get harder for me to take care of everything around the house as I get bigger, and once the baby is born, I will need even more help. That would give you a chance to bond with the baby and be a father figure to him. What do you think?" Morgan tried to keep her face neutral, but there was a pleading look in her eyes.

"It's a great idea! I would like to be there for you more and to have the chance to develop a relationship with my son. But what does Jonas think? Have you asked him?"

"Yes, I checked with him first. He says he's fine with it. He knows I'll need the help." Morgan cradled her stomach, her hands making a heart shape around it. "It'll be awkward, but I think it's the best solution."

Nate nodded.

"What about Beth? How do you think she'll feel?"

"I'll talk to her, but I think she'll be fine with it. She wants what's best for me, you, and the baby."

"Looks like it's settled. I guess it's time for you and Jonas to meet. Do you want to come over for dinner? Are you comfortable doing that?" Morgan wondered how Nate felt about leaving the house, even for a short walk down the block and into her house, which was always carefully sanitized.

"Yes, totally. I really want to meet Jonas. From everything you've told me, he sounds like an amazing guy." Morgan was surprised to hear that. She barely recalled mentioning Jonas to Nate, but she must have talked about him more than she realized.

"Wonderful! It seems that I'm now responsible for planning a dinner party to introduce my husband to my..." Morgan paused, struggling for the right words, "baby's father," she finished. She was thinking "lover," but there was no way she could say that word aloud.

CHAPTER 29

...

The evening of the dinner party arrived. Morgan walked from room to room, absent-mindedly tidying as her mind occupied itself with worst-case scenarios. A half hour before Nate was expected, she went into the bedroom and sat by Jonas.

"Jonas," she said, "please be open-minded when you meet Nate. He has the best of intentions."

"I already told you he can move in. I don't know what else you want me to say," said Jonas a little testily.

"Please do try to be friendly," said Morgan, attempting to take Jonas's hand. He quickly pulled it away.

After a few minutes waiting for Jonas to say something, anything, Morgan gave up and went to the kitchen to check on dinner.

Wearing a face mask, Nate took the small risk of leaving his aunt's house and walking over to Morgan's. Like everyone else who entered the house, he passed through the lemony disinfecting shower. Morgan had some of Jonas's old clothes waiting for him to change into. They were more formal than Nate's usual style and a little too big and made him look like a child playing dress-up.

Morgan welcomed Nate politely and led him into the master bedroom where Jonas was sitting up in bed. The two men needed no introduction.

"Welcome, Nate," said Jonas in a neutral tone.

"Nice to meet you, Jonas," Nate responded.

Morgan realized that she would have to leave them alone together when she went to get the food. She ran off to do so before the awkwardness of the situation paralyzed her. As she stepped out, Jonas asked Nate about the remote work he did. Nate seemed grateful for a topic to speak about. Morgan returned quickly with a tray that held a serving dish of chicken soup, three bowls and spoons, and a plate of rolls. Morgan and Nate sat precariously on the bed, twisted around to look at Jonas. Morgan's childhood charm school classes had failed to prepare her for a dinner party in bed where the guest of honor was her affair partner. The room was quiet for a while, except for the sounds of slurped soup.

When they all finished eating and the dishes had been cleared away, the real conversation began. Nate, with the bold confidence of youth, spoke up first, "Jonas, first let me say thank you for welcoming me into your home this evening and being open to this conversation."

Jonas nodded in acknowledgement.

"Morgan's getting farther along in her pregnancy, and it's going to get harder for her to take care of everything around the house. Plus, you will need help when the baby comes. I want to be there as a father-figure for the child. Not the only father, but one of two, maybe? What do you think of me moving in here to help?"

Jonas paused to consider his words. "Obviously this situation is neither traditional nor ideal. Times have changed, and we must adapt. Families look different than they used to. Children can have several parents. In my personal and professional opinion as a therapist, the more people who love a child, the better. To be clear, this situation does not come without challenges. I ask you to keep any personal relationship between the two of you, how shall I say this, discreet." He looked from Nate to Morgan and back again as he made this statement.

Morgan, curvy with pregnancy, flushed, starting at her face and ending at her newly full breasts. She was committed to remaining respectful toward Jonas. However, she had to admit that now that she had passed the nausea phase, the pregnancy hormones and increased blood supply had led to more racy thoughts than at any time in her life since she had stared at posters of teen heartthrobs on the walls of her childhood bedroom while suffering through puberty.

Morgan looked at Nate from under her ink-black eyelashes, hoping he would respond. He took the hint. "Absolutely, Jonas. This is your house and your marriage. I'll respect that completely, and I know Morgan does, too."

Morgan closed her eyes and imagined a late-night rendezvous at Beth's house. She and Nate would sneak out of her house together and run over to Beth's, hop in the disinfecting shower where they could lather each other up, and run straight to his bedroom. In this fantasy, she moved lightly and gracefully despite the extra weight her body carried. He would marvel at her lovely, large breasts, hopefully not get distracted by her growing belly, and satisfy her considerable needs.

"Morgan, dear!" said Jonas. "Are you alright?"

Morgan started as her name was called. "Sorry, yes? What were you saying? I was feeling the baby move around." Luckily, she could pretend it was the pregnancy that distracted her rather than lust. She fanned her face with her hand.

"I was asking when Nate might want to move in and what his aunt thinks about our situation," said Jonas.

"Oh. Beth is fine with it, right, Nate? And you can move in

whenever you want. If you do it on a weekend, I can help you," said Morgan.

Now the men's faces featured identical scowls. "You're not lifting anything!" they said more or less simultaneously.

Morgan could not believe this crap. Women were doing everything these days and they were going to give her a hard time about carrying a few boxes while pregnant? And it's not like Jonas could help, either!

"Calm down, guys. I'll figure it out with Beth. We'll get the stuff moved over. I won't lift anything too heavy." And with that said, Morgan went into the kitchen to get some chocolate chip cookies for everyone to nibble for dessert. At this stage of pregnancy, if she went more than a few hours without chocolate, violent tendencies at odds with her normally sweet nature emerged. She gave thanks to the researchers who had created the new low-calorie chocolate.

CHAPTER 30

...

Later that night, Morgan's phone rang as she brushed her teeth. She saw the call was from Nate and answered immediately.

He launched in without saying hello. "Morgan, Beth said that while I was over at your place, she saw a woman prowling around outside her house!"

Morgan spit out a mouthful of toothpaste and wiped her face on a towel.

"Oh, my goodness! Did she call the police?" Morgan whispered as she walked out of the bathroom and past a sleeping Jonas. She stepped into the guest room, closing the door behind her and sitting down on the bed. She felt pressure in her chest, closed her eyes, and immediately flashed back to how she had felt after the break-in at work. A wave of nausea hit her, and she put her head down on her knees until it passed.

"Yes, but they arrived too late. The woman was gone. Beth had turned on the floodlights, so she must have gotten scared and run off."

"Who was it? What did the woman look like?"

"Well, Beth didn't get a good look because it was dark, but she said she was a Caucasian brunette, with nothing else identifiable that she could see."

Morgan thought about women she knew who might fit the description. Gavin's friend Stacey was a Caucasian brunette. What were the chances, though? Probably not her.

"That's so strange. I'm glad you're back there with her now. Is she going to take any additional precautions?" Morgan tried to control her breathing.

This was probably nothing. Maybe some grief-stricken woman who didn't know where she was. It happened sometimes that a woman would get lost in her memories of a departed husband, father, brother, or son, start wandering around, and become disoriented.

"She's having security cameras installed tomorrow."

Morgan felt better. If anyone showed up again, the cameras would capture them. "That's good. Thanks for letting me know. I'll keep watch around here, too." Morgan fell quiet for a moment. "I thought this evening went pretty well," she said, changing the subject.

"Yeah, me, too. Jonas is pretty cool." Morgan was not in the mood to discuss Jonas. She was busy imagining Nate standing between her and some unknown source of danger, and she felt warm all over. When she closed her eyes, she could almost feel his flexed biceps with the tips of her fingers. Nate coughed. He was probably waiting for Morgan to say something.

"Thanks for being so open to this, Nate," she finally responded.

"Sure."

"I'm exhausted. I'm going to bed now. Please keep me updated, okay?"

"I will. Talk to you later. Goodnight, Morgan." She immediately imagined Nate giving her a goodnight kiss, which would lead to other types of kisses and other types of things. Respecting Jonas's wishes would be challenging. She reached into the bedside drawer.

CHAPTER 31

...

The next day was Saturday, and Morgan planned to go shopping with Gena for maternity clothes. Patty would run her own errands, and then they would all meet up for lunch. As they browsed through the racks of clothes, Gena asked how the dinner party had gone.

"Surprisingly well! Nate is going to move in."

"I can't believe Nate is moving in with you guys!" said Gena. "Jonas is totally fine with all this?" She picked up a jewel-toned, professional-looking maternity blouse and held it out to Morgan, who added it to her pile.

"Jonas is a rock. It's hard to believe, but it's truly the best solution," said Morgan. "These pants look comfortable, don't they?" she asked, holding up black pants with a stretchy panel in the center.

"Yes! Would it be weird if I got a pair?" asked Gena with a smile. "Won't it be hard with all the sexual tension between you?"

"Gena, you have no idea," said Morgan. "I can't stop thinking about sleeping with him again. But we can't do it in the house with Jonas right there. We're going to have to use Beth's place. But now

MANFLU

she's putting cameras up everywhere, so it's not like we can sneak around."

"Why is Beth putting up cameras?" Gena frowned as she studied a hideous floral dress the size of a tent. Morgan vehemently shook her head, and Gena moved down the rack. With women designing all the clothes, garish maternity dresses should really be a thing of the past, thought Morgan.

"I'm getting to that part of the story! So last night, some lady was prowling around outside Beth's house. The police came too late, and they missed her. Maybe it was someone with mental health issues. You know how some of the women get when they're missing their relatives. They start wandering around and lose touch with reality," said Morgan.

"What did she look like?" asked Gena.

"She was a Caucasian brunette." Morgan paused, watching Gena's reaction. "Are you thinking what I'm thinking?"

"You think it could be connected to the break-in at work?"

"It seems far-fetched, but possible."

"I don't think it's far-fetched. Remember how you ran that antibody test on Nate? Maybe the person who broke into the lab found his address on some paperwork and went to check it out."

"I didn't think about that, Gena. That is terrifying. But really, what are the chances? It can't possibly be connected. Maybe I should talk to Gavin about it to be sure." She went back to looking at clothes, but she didn't pick out anything else.

"You have to be careful. This could get dangerous," said Gena.

Morgan's stomach churned. She looked down and hugged her belly.

"We're going to figure this out, Morgan. Don't worry." Gena patted Morgan's arm reassuringly.

After they were done at the clothes shop, Morgan and Gena went to meet Patty at a fancy sandwich place on the other side of the mall. By the time they arrived, Patty was already seated and surrounded by bags from the knitting store and a worn-out giant purse. She perused the menu from behind tortoise shell reading glasses that matched her dirty-blonde stick-straight hair. Morgan was starving. She would normally wait to make sure everyone was ready to order, but she flagged down a server as soon as she could and ordered a very large chicken panini. After Gena and Patty ordered, Patty made conversation about Morgan's pregnancy. When she wasn't teaching poetry and philosophy classes at the local university, Patty occasionally worked as a doula.

"How have you been feeling, Morgan?" she asked, hands folded on the table and leaning forward as she looked at Morgan over her glasses.

"I'm feeling mostly fine. The nausea is getting better now."

"You've been feeling sick? That's wonderful!" Patty's honey brown eyes crinkled with delight.

Morgan's eyes widened. "Why do you say that?"

"Nausea is one sign of a healthy pregnancy. It means your body is producing a lot of hormones." Morgan could not argue with that. It felt like an alien had taken over her body.

Gena yawned, probably tired of hearing about Morgan's pregnancy symptoms.

"Do you have a plan for giving birth yet? You're getting pretty far along," continued Patty, ignoring Gena.

"Yes, I've talked to Beth about it. I think you've met her before. She's my neighbor who is a nurse. She's going to help me deliver at home and is training Nate so he can help out, too, in case she's not around. She's been stocking up on medical supplies for me and the baby from the hospital where she works."

"What about the pain, though? You won't be able to have an epidural at home," asked Gena.

"Not to worry! I did some research, and it turns out they've made huge advances in pain control over the last decade. They had one of those contests for best new technology for pain management during labor and delivery, and a team at MIT developed a machine that uses acupressure to completely relieve labor pain. Well, acupressure plus laughing gas mixed with a new anesthetic they discovered. It's supposed to feel amazing. Beth is going to bring all this stuff over next week so we can get set up and she'll return it after the baby is born," said Morgan.

"Sounds like you have it all figured out," said Gena, taking a big bite of her high-protein veggie sub.

"I would gently recommend that you take some time to prepare for the emotional component of birth, as well," said Patty.

"Between work and taking care of Jonas, I don't have much time to prepare for anything!" Morgan sighed. "I really want to finish the primate testing before I go on leave." She took a sip of water.

"We'll get there, Morgan," Gena said encouragingly.

"Patty, I feel uncomfortable saying this, but I have a weird pregnancy symptom I want to ask you about."

"Really? Weirder than nausea, sore boobs, a funny taste in your mouth, and a large belly?" asked Gena with a laugh.

"Yes, listen. I know this is normal, but it still feels very weird. This pregnancy is making me super extra horny," Morgan whispered, shrinking into the depths of her chair.

"Oh yeah, I read about that. Extra blood flow and all that," said Gena.

"It is normal, Morgan. You should take advantage of these feelings now because post-birth, it is common for your sex drive to decline precipitously," said Patty.

"Are you going to make things happen with Nate?" asked Gena.

"I don't know! We haven't done anything since I told him I was pregnant. He looks at me differently now. I mean, I may be about to become a mother, but I'm not *his* mother. I've got to work on my flirting skills. I'm not sure how sexy I am with this giant belly, but I've got to do something! It's all I can think about."

"You mean, all you can think about is sex and vaccine research, right?" joked Gena.

All three women laughed, and the conversation moved to other topics. In the back of her mind, Morgan tried to puzzle out whether she should try to seduce Nate, and if so, how in the world she could draw his interest.

CHAPTER 32

...

As Morgan drank her decaf coffee the next morning at the kitchen table, she thought about calling Gavin to ask for help on the prowler situation, but she wasn't sure if it was a good idea. She didn't want to talk about it with Jonas, because there was no point in frightening him. Still, she felt the need to process her thoughts with someone. She kept coming back to Gavin. Strangely, no matter what nonsense came out of Gavin's mouth, Morgan's gut always told her that he was trustworthy. She had to know if his friend Stacey could be involved in the break-in and was now prowling around her neighborhood. She decided to call him.

Morgan thought about where to meet Gavin where no one would notice them but couldn't think of anywhere where a pregnant woman and a relatively attractive healthy man out together wouldn't attract attention, so when she reached him, she invited him over to her place. Nate was at Beth's that day, packing up a few boxes. Jonas stayed in the bedroom while Gavin and Morgan had coffee in the living room (regular for him, more decaf for her). Gavin looked ridiculous in Jonas's old clothes, which were several sizes too big. Prior to manflu, Jonas had been a substantially built man. Gavin had the slim body of a computer nerd who had never seen the inside of a gym, although he was blessed with a good metabolism.

"It feels strange to see you outside of the lab, but thank you for coming," said Morgan.

She had never encountered Gavin in a social setting. He had an ease to him that was very attractive as he settled effortlessly into his surroundings. She looked around at her faded furniture, purchased as a wedding gift by her parents, and felt slightly embarrassed by how old and worn everything looked. At least her dad had insisted on good quality items that would last.

"Sure, happy to be here. Why didn't you want to talk at the lab or over the phone?" said Gavin, his curiosity apparent as he studied Morgan.

"I have some sensitive matters to discuss with you." She felt confident she had made the right choice to invite him over.

"Oh, really?" Gavin asked, eyebrow arched.

Oh, great, she thought. This is not a joke. "Gavin, this is important. We need your help. This vaccine must work. The baby I'm carrying is a boy." She prayed she could trust him.

"A boy? Shit, how'd that happen?" Gavin asked, eyes wide beneath his dark-framed glasses.

"Please lower your voice," Morgan angry-whispered. "My husband is in the other room. Listen, I'm involved with another man. He's a Vulny. So obviously, he needs the vaccine, too. Will you help us?"

"Ho ho, I'm not the only busy one, I see!" He smirked. "I knew there was more than meets the eye with you. Still waters run deep. Mm mm mm."

While she expected his reaction, it still stung a bit. "Gavin, I know this is all very exciting, but we need to focus on the matter at hand here. Will you help?" she repeated.

"I already told you I would help you! Now let me enjoy the process," said Gavin. "What do you want me to do?"

"First, I need to ask you about those women who've come with you to the lab. How well do you know them?"

"We hang out—nothing serious. They're party girls. You know how it is."

Morgan was amused that Gavin thought she knew anything about being a party girl. She pushed again. "After the break-in, I asked you about Stacey. Have you heard from her? Do you know anything else about her?"

"When you asked me about her, I called a friend of mine who is on the police force and asked her to do a background check on Stacey as a courtesy. She was happy to oblige in return for certain favors." Morgan felt like she might throw up, and not from pregnancy nausea. "We don't have to get into it," Gavin continued after noticing the look on Morgan's face, "but she couldn't find anything about Stacey."

"Couldn't find anything bad, or couldn't find anything at all?" Morgan asked.

"Nothing at all. Like she doesn't exist."

"That's strange," said Morgan.

"She must've given me a fake name."

"That's both frustrating and suspicious."

"It is what it is," said Gavin, spreading out his hands.

"What about the other women? Do they know anything about her?"

"No, I met them separately. What can I say? Lots of fish in the sea."

Morgan rolled her eyes. "Well, did you ask them if they know her real name?"

"Of course I did! They said no."

"And did you have them checked out, too?"

"Jeez, am I supposed to do background checks on all the women I sleep with?"

Morgan stared at him. What could she even say?

"Okay, okay, I'll have my police friend do some more digging. This is going to be exhausting," said Gavin.

Morgan tried not to picture Gavin exhausting himself with his police officer friend but found the images entering her brain unbidden. She blinked a few times to clear her mind. "Thanks, Gavin. I appreciate it."

"Anytime." Gavin got up to leave. "Take care of yourself and the little guy." He nodded toward Morgan's belly.

She intended to do exactly that.

CHAPTER 33

. . .

A few days later, Morgan received a call from Beth while she was at work.

"I hate to ask you this, Morgan. You know I don't like to interfere in your private business, but was Nate with you last night?"

Morgan found this question strange. Nate had not yet moved in with her and Jonas, so he should have been at Beth's house.

"No," Morgan answered cautiously.

"I went to his room in the evening to ask him if he wanted a piece of the German chocolate cake I had baked, and he wasn't there. I checked the video camera, and he was out of the house for a few hours. He's sleeping now, and I didn't want to wake him, but I'm worried. Where could he have gone?"

Morgan, too busy to deal with Nate, was in the middle of writing up her findings investigating the primate's immunity levels as they varied with different doses of the vaccine. The trial had been very successful so far. The sick monkey from the night she couldn't pick up the morning after pills had been a fluke. None of the other primates had shown negative reactions to the vaccine at reasonable doses, and all displayed impressive levels of antibody production.

"I don't know, Beth. He's pretty careful about the virus. Maybe he just went for a long walk at night when there are fewer people around. It must be hard to be cooped up in the house all the time."

"You're probably right, Morgan. I'll ask him when he wakes up. Sorry to bother you."

"No problem, Beth. Talk to you soon."

Morgan finished up her project. She invited Gena to accompany her to the mall to check out baby furniture during their lunch break. It would also give them a chance to catch up.

The store was empty when they walked in, and the saleslady approached them right away. She was an older woman with straight gray hair fashionably flipped out at the bottom, wearing dark purple glasses matching her outfit, which, while still loose and comfortable, passed for trendy these days. Her eyes softened when she saw Morgan's considerable baby bump.

"I'm so glad you came in today," she said rather excitedly. "I love to help young couples shopping for their babies!"

Morgan and Gena exchanged glances but said nothing.

The saleslady pressed on. "And what will you name her?" she asked.

Morgan started to stammer, gratitude flooding her when Gena took over. "We haven't decided on a name yet," she said politely. She pulled Morgan along with her toward a display of stuffed animals and away from the overly solicitous shop assistant. Morgan was relieved when the woman took the hint and moved to straighten items on another table.

"Has Nate finished moving in yet?" asked Gena, picking up a fluffy stuffed bunny and flopping its ears.

"Not quite. He's almost settled in the guest room." Morgan examined a pack of tiny baby onesies.

"How has the move been going?"

"It's a little weird having him in and out of the house, getting everything ready. It's taking him a while to set up the equipment he needs for his job. He's doing his best to stay out of the way, but it's still distracting."

"I can imagine! Do you think something will happen between the two of you?"

"I don't know, I'm not sure if he's interested in me at the moment," said Morgan, making a gesture that encompassed her growing body. She had never felt less attractive in her life. Whenever she caught a glimpse of herself in the mirror (which she tried to avoid), she couldn't believe that the image reflected back belonged to her.

"Even with the giant belly, you're gorgeous. I'm sure you'll figure it out. Here," Gena, said, handing Morgan a tube. "Do you want to buy some nipple cream?"

They both laughed until tears streamed down their faces. The sales lady gave them a curious look. They moved toward the back of the store where the larger items were kept.

"Did you speak to Gavin about his friend? Was he able to find anything out?" Gena asked as she experimentally rocked a display bassinet.

"I did ask Gavin again for any info on his companion. Apparently, he tried to have a friend run a background check, but the name she gave him was fake." She peered through the slats of a wooden crib.

"That's too bad."

"He said he would keep looking, but I'm not hopeful."

"I have something to share, too," said Gena.

"Have you been digging? What did you find out?" Morgan asked as she ran her hand over a changing table.

"Obviously Andrea has been acting weird, right?" Morgan nodded. How could she forget?

Gena continued. "This might be why. And I didn't even have to dig for this nugget. It came to me. I got a voicemail from a debt collector looking for her. She must be dodging them. I'm not sure how the message ended up in my voicemail, but it seems she owes a significant amount of money."

"Wow, she must really be avoiding them if they're calling her employer." Andrea had always seemed like a goody-two-shoes type to Morgan. It was weird that she had unpaid debts. Morgan wondered what it could be. Shopping addiction? Gambling? She didn't appear to be on hard drugs.

"Probably. Imagine what she might be willing to do if she's in dire straits financially. Maybe someone's paying her to spy for them. She could be funneling all kinds of information to the competition or helping them in other ways. That could explain why she's been going out of her way to slow us down."

"Do you think we should talk to Charlotte?" She couldn't imagine Charlotte's reaction to troubling financial information about the teacher's pet.

"Not yet, I think we need more. For some unknown reason, Charlotte seems to worship the ground Andrea walks on. Maybe it's some kind of weird single mom bond or something. Who knows? Bottom line—we need more dirt. And I'm going to keep looking."

The sales lady approached again. "Finding everything all right, ladies? You make such a beautiful couple. I want to be certain you have what you need for your precious little one," she said, looking a little teary.

Morgan pointed out the items she wanted to order, struggling not to correct the woman's assumptions. What difference did it make if she thought Morgan was a lesbian? It's not like Morgan was about to tell her that, in fact, the baby had two fathers living in the same house with her. And she certainly wasn't going to tell the woman that the baby she carried was actually a boy. She could imagine the look of shock on her face upon hearing that piece of news. Her well-groomed eyebrows would hit her hairline.

As the sales lady rang up her order, Morgan flashed back to when she and Jonas were about to marry and went shopping for items to add to their registry. A similar shop assistant had gone around the home furnishing store with them as they zapped barcodes on kitchen items and décor together with a special device. She remembered how Jonas deftly maneuvered the conversation, knowing that she could be shy when she spoke to people she didn't know. Now, she was accustomed to doing those types of errands without him. His illness had forced her to become more independent. But somehow, she had always thought when she bought furniture for a nursery, she would be doing it with him. She wiped a stray tear from her eye. Gena stood next to her at the register, patting her arm silently and reassuringly.

After they finished at the furniture store, she and Gena returned to the office. They stopped by the bathroom first, because of course. Then Gena went off to a meeting. Morgan sat at her desk and opened her email. The first one looked ominous. She clicked it open, and the first line read, "Permission to Conduct Research on Primates Suspended."

Devastating news.

CHAPTER 34

...

What could she do? She was weeks away from finishing her vaccine research and meeting her goal of having the vaccine ready for human trials, assuming all went well.

She wondered what, practically speaking, this email meant. What would happen now? Would enforcers from some branch of government come to the lab and remove the monkeys? How long would the bureaucratic process take? Weeks? Months?

What if—crazy idea—she simply ignored the email and continued her research. She could pretend that the email went to spam and she never received it. Happened all the time, right?

This thought process was totally unprecedented for Morgan. Always a huge rule-follower, she'd been the type of kid who did homework she was sure the teacher would never collect. She wouldn't consider jaywalking at midnight on a deserted street. She made certain her taxes were accurate to the penny, year after year. Pretending she didn't see an email from a government agency was such a foreign idea, she was not even sure how it had slipped into her brain. Although, getting pregnant by a man other than her husband was not exactly following the rules, so Morgan supposed she had changed at least a little somewhere along the way. That one transgression was, perhaps, opening the door for more.

She resolved to say nothing to anyone about the email, not even Gena, for a few days to see how she felt. Delaying for a few days would surely cause no harm. She could have been on vacation or wrapped up in a primate emergency. Not everyone checked their email every day, surely.

Charlotte walked behind Morgan on her way to another part of the building. When Charlotte said hello in passing, Morgan nearly jumped out of her chair. She would have, in fact, jumped, if she had not been carrying an extra thirty pounds on her slim frame, slowing her down considerably. She didn't know how long she could keep up this charade. It had been hard enough to hide her pregnancy and the baby's gender for so long, and that only affected her own life and the people close to her. How could she hide information that impacted not only her entire lab, but also the health and safety of all the men and boys who awaited this vaccine? Keeping the email a secret, even briefly, would be harder than she thought.

She was totally distracted when she got home that evening and was unprepared to find that Nate mostly had finished moving in while she was at work. She found him in the living room with his eyes closed, listening to a piano concerto on her speakers.

She cleared her throat.

His eyes flew open. "Hi, Morgan. I got myself moved in, and then I made dinner," he said.

Well, that was a pleasant surprise. "Great," she said, "I'll take some into Jonas."

"I already did."

She was pleased he felt comfortable interacting with Jonas without her there.

"I have to talk to you about something," he said. She could not handle any more surprises today. "Beth mentioned she'd called you the other day because she didn't know where I was." He paused, looking at his feet.

She nodded, encouraging him.

"I went to a classical music concert."

Morgan gasped. She couldn't imagine him taking such a risk.

"Wait, I'm not done. It was outside, and I stayed away from the other people. I know it's still not totally safe, but I was careful. I felt like I was losing my mind, and I had to do something, go somewhere. I just wanted you to hear it from me instead of Beth. Can you understand?"

Morgan felt her heartbeat return to normal. The risk of an outing like that was nonzero, but minimal. "Yes, Nate. I know you feel trapped staying at home all the time. But now your actions affect Jonas, too. And soon, the baby. We really need to minimize all risks. Please don't do that again."

"I won't, Morgan." He sighed. "It was amazing, though." He stared off into the distance, and his fingers moved as if playing a piano.

CHAPTER 35

...

One evening a few days later, Morgan slipped into the bath, the only place in the house she felt she could be alone and relaxed, and called Gena.

"How are you feeling, Morgan?" Gena asked.

"Huge," was the only response that felt appropriate.

"How's it going with both the men living in the house?"

"Ugggggggggggggg," Morgan groaned in frustration.

"What's that about?"

"I can't stop thinking about having sex with Nate."

"That's not good."

"I know! I feel so awkward around Jonas. It's like I'm living parallel lives. Jonas and I talk about the baby and how we're going to be a family, and then I see Nate, and I want to grab him and do things to him. And he's right on the other side of my bedroom wall—I can hear him breathing!" Morgan regretted the layout of her small house with the master bedroom and guest bedroom sharing a wall.

"Morgan! Wow! I've never heard you talk that way. You are like a different woman."

"It's the pregnancy hormones! They've taken over my brain."

"Is there something deeper going on with Nate, or is it just lust?"

"I don't know, Gena. He's really sweet, and he tries to take care of me. But he's so young."

"I can see that it might be hard to relate to him. And you already have that strong connection with Jonas."

"Yes, Jonas and I have an amazing bond. But he's not going to be around forever . . ."

"Don't tell me you're lining up Jonas's replacement already?"

"I know it sounds horrible, but the baby's going to need a father! I've always wanted to have a family that includes a partner and a baby. Maybe that person can be Nate someday." Was it so terrible to consider forming a family with the father of her child?

The women discussed other topics and soon hung up. Morgan tilted her head back and dipped her hair into the warm bathwater, closing her eyes and imagining herself and Nate walking through a park with a toddler between them, reaching up to hold both their hands. Jonas was not in the image. For one moment, she let herself savor the thought without allowing in any guilt. The dream felt cozier wrapped around her than the warm bathwater.

CHAPTER 36

...

Finally! Morgan knew Beth was at work and Nate had just gone over to the other house to get a final box. Morgan's desire for Nate seemed to increase at the same pace as her stress at work. She wasn't sure if it was the hormones or if she was craving a distraction, but she could not stop thinking about him.

"I'm going for a walk, Jonas," Morgan called out. She speed-walked her pregnant self down the block toward Beth's house. It could have been pouring rain, and she wouldn't have noticed. She didn't even bother to enter through the shower, figuring that she hadn't picked up any germs on the short walk, and she refused to let anything slow her down. She burst clumsily through the front door of Beth's house, belly first, right into the living room. A startled Nate spun around from a box he was taping and met her gaze. He wiped sweat from his forehead with the back of his hand.

"Nate, let's go in the bedroom really quick," Morgan said.

"What for?" asked Nate.

She couldn't do cute right now. "Nate, please fuck me—right now." She spoke calmly and politely, as though ordering dinner from a menu. Nate started at her word choice. She now understood the phrase "tunnel vision." She was able to ignore the heightening crisis at work, her growing midsection, oh, and the fact that the person in front of her was living with her and her husband, all for the promise of some relief.

"Uhhhh, I thought we had to lay off because of Jonas, and you know, our whole new living situation," said Nate.

Logic would not sway her. This was a desperate situation.

"Yeah, yeah, that would make sense, but these pregnancy hormones are making me crazy! I need you to do this for me. Please, don't make me beg." Morgan parked her fist on one larger-than-normal hip, eyes darting around like a caged animal.

"I, uh, I'm not sure . . ." stammered Nate.

She didn't need this. "I realize that I'm not at my sexiest right now. Please just do your best," said Morgan, beginning to seethe with frustration.

"Okay, fine, let's go to the bedroom." Nate placed his hand on her back and guided her in that direction.

Was this actually going to happen, or was he trying to get her out of the living room? Morgan couldn't tell.

After he closed the bedroom door behind them, Morgan looked at Nate. His blue eyes stared into the distance rather than taking her in. She did not want him thinking about anything beyond the bedroom walls for fear that he would get cold feet. She took his face in her hands and pulled him close, feeling the prick of the stubble on his chin. She placed her lips on his mouth and thrust her tongue toward his. He responded automatically, rewarding her with the minty flavor of his mouth, but not much else.

She drew back from him to undress. She struggled to pull her simple maternity dress over her stomach and off while he easily slipped off his sweats and t-shirt. Nate stood there ogling Morgan's belly. She tried to perch enticingly on the edge of the bed, but by the state of him, she guessed that sexy was not the word that came to mind. Her senses heightened by her pregnancy, she felt hyper-aroused by his sweaty scent punctuated with notes of caramel and salt.

He lay down beside her and she leaned over and kissed him again, more gently this time. She could feel her belly between them, forcing them to meet at an awkward angle. She kissed him deeply, using her tongue the way she remembered him liking it. He finally responded with some enthusiasm, gently prodding her tongue in return. He reached for her swollen breasts, but she batted his hands away because they were so sensitive to the slightest touch. This confused him, and he retreated until she reached down and grabbed him where he had finally grown hard. She wanted to slide him into her, but they did not fit together as they had before. After a few awkward moments, she got on all fours and he entered her from behind, caressing her back with his chin as he stroked in and out. Her belly hung down, nearly hitting the bed. Morgan climaxed almost immediately, on the verge of crying from the desperately needed release. Nate continued for a few minutes after but soon pulled out and lay next to her, looking uncomfortable.

"Are you okay?" Morgan asked.

"Yes, fine. I'm sorry. The pregnancy is making things hard for me," said Nate.

"Or not so hard." She smiled to let him know she was teasing him. For a quick moment, she thought she had hurt his feelings, but then he laughed.

"I appreciate the effort. It paid off for me, at least," said Morgan.

"That must have been record timing," said Nate.

They lay next to each other, barely touching. Morgan felt less desperate and distracted and more able to focus on their looming life changes. Somewhere in the quiet recesses of her brain rang a soft alarm bell. Obviously, he wasn't attracted to her right now. That would change when she was no longer pregnant, wouldn't it? She pulled her thoughts to the more important matter at hand, their unborn child.

"Nate, are you excited about the baby?" asked Morgan.

"Yes, I keep wondering what he's going to look like. Too bad we couldn't risk going for the 4D ultrasound."

"Right. We didn't want to let the entire world know there's a boy on board." Morgan rubbed her belly tenderly. "Ah, he just kicked. Do you want to feel?"

She never tired of feeling the baby's movements inside of her. She thought back to pregnant monkeys she had cared for and how they would sit with a hand on their bellies, feeling their own babies move. She felt so connected with mothers across species, all sharing the same experiences.

Nate placed his hand over the spot Morgan indicated and was rewarded with a baby jab. "Oh, Morgan, this is amazing," said Nate.

"I know. I feel him move all the time, and it never gets boring."

"My little guy. I can't believe he's really in there. I never allowed myself to imagine being a father, and now it's happening. This might sound weird, but I love him already," said Nate. "I can't wait to hold him in my arms."

Morgan laughed. She closed her eyes, trying to picture her baby first with Nate's curly hair and then with her straight hair. They both had black hair, so the color wouldn't be much of a mystery. "Oh my gosh, what if he's bald? He'll probably look like a little old man."

"I think he'll have beautiful hair," said Nate. "Hey, have you thought of any names?"

"I was thinking of naming him after my father or brother. Or maybe both," said Morgan.

"What were their names? Maybe a first and a middle?"

"My brother was Mark. My parents thought "M" names were strong and American-sounding. And my father was Jing. Mark Jing Digby sounds nice, doesn't it?" asked Morgan.

"Oh," said Nate quietly.

"What?" asked Morgan. "You don't like the name?"

"Mark Jing is a great name. But he won't have my last name. It's okay, I understand. I just hadn't thought about it," said Nate.

Morgan took Nate's hand and looked in his eyes. There wasn't anything she could say to change things. The baby would have her and Jonas's last name. She noticed that, rather than meeting her eyes, Nate's eyes had drifted downward and come to rest on her full breasts. He looked up and met her gaze with a question. Her answer was to kiss him deeply, pressing her chest against his and resting her hands on his muscular shoulders. They made love again, more slowly this time, creatively finding their way around Morgan's large belly. Nate's skills in the bedroom were improving rapidly.

When they finished, Nate and Morgan got up and located their clothing. They dressed quickly—or as quickly as possible with a beachball-sized stomach. Morgan walked back to her house, taking a moment to notice the sound of the birds chirping at the sunny day, and Nate followed a little while later with his last box.

As Morgan walked, she thought about how something shifted the moment Nate felt that kick. It was as if the baby were suddenly real to them both. And now that she had gotten her needs met, it was as if the cobwebs had been swept from her brain and she could focus again. Not a moment too soon—she had a lot of work to do to get the vaccine ready before little Mark Jing came. Mark Jing—she liked the sound of that. Her baby was a real person with a real name. She wouldn't stop working until she developed a real vaccine that would protect him.

CHAPTER 37

. . .

In the final weeks of her pregnancy, Morgan grew more anxious with each passing day. She received another email repeating the message that the lab's license was no longer valid for working with primates. Then, nothing. No phone calls, no visits from federal agents, nothing. She settled in to wait for the other shoe to drop.

On the other hand, she began to feel more confident that she could pull this off. It would be amazing to finish the primate stage of the manflu vaccine before anyone caught on about the expired license. She did regret leaving her colleagues at the lab to deal with the paperwork mess that would occur during her leave, but that was not her fault. Andrea should have taken care of it properly the first time.

Sex with Nate had cleared her mind. Morgan became laser-focused on her final tasks at the lab. She was at the point where the major work had already been completed, and she was just handling some final details. Before testing the vaccine on humans, all the "I"s had to be dotted and the "T"s crossed, which she needed to accomplish before the baby was born.

She was at the lab triple checking on the primate's bloodwork when she received a page to come to the front desk. Oh, dear. Could it be lab inspectors? Her heart started to pound, and she couldn't take in a full breath of air. Her lungs, already squeezed by the baby, now felt as if she were inhaling through a straw. She forced herself to breathe in through her nose and out through her mouth, counting out the seconds. When she had gotten herself somewhat under control, she made her way as quickly as she could on her swollen feet to the reception area.

There, she found two women who made a mismatched pair despite their matching outfits, one dark-skinned and very tall and the other a pale, very short redhead, both wearing khakis and polo shirts and with plastic badges hung around their necks identifying them as working for the federal agency tasked with lab inspections. Andrea ignored them as she typed on her computer. Morgan would be unfailingly polite.

"Hello, I'm Dr. Morgan Digby. Can I help you with something?"

"Yes, hello, Dr. Digby," they said, introducing themselves and greeting Morgan with small bows. Morgan still remembered a time when they would have offered their hands to shake.

"We're here to notify you that this lab has had its license for primate research suspended and must cease all such research immediately."

Now Morgan decided to play dumb. "Really? How can this be? We're doing critical research that is government-funded."

"Well, it says here that you failed to submit form W52-AX35 on time."

Here Morgan turned to Andrea. "I'm sure you submitted that form, didn't you, Andrea?" Morgan asked, knowing that she had not.

"Um, yes, I absolutely did," said Andrea.

"We don't have a record of it."

"What if we submit the form now, would that resolve this?" Morgan asked. "I'm sure Andrea has a copy handy, don't you?" she asked, turning to Andrea.

Morgan was counting on a hunch she had that Andrea had prepared the form so as to be able to show it to Charlotte but had not submitted it. Sure enough, Andrea easily pulled up a copy.

The agents accepted the document. "Yes, this looks in order," said the taller one.

"Great, so are we all set?" Morgan asked hopefully. It was never this easy with government agencies, but she could dream.

"Well, we need 60 days to process the form," said the shorter one.

Of course, they do.

"Can you grant an exemption? We are at a critical phase of the research," pleaded Morgan. She was fairly certain they would not.

"No, absolutely not. No exceptions."

"Well, what can we do now? What do we do with the primates already located in this facility?" She thought of the dozens of monkeys that relied on her and other staff members for their care. She had bonded with each and every one of them.

"The primates can stay here provided absolutely no research is conducted on them pending the outcome of the process."

Well, that was good news, Morgan thought. They weren't going to take away the primates at least. She could probably complete what was needed without technically conducting any research on the primates. Much of the data to be collected could be couched as part of basic care, such as taking their temperatures and the like.

"I give you my word on that," said Morgan, putting out her hand and quickly withdrawing it to instead bow. She glanced over at Andrea while she finished her conversation with the agents and noticed that she looked irritated. Her plan hadn't worked, had it? The primates could stay. Andrea must be fuming.

At that moment, Morgan felt her lower abdomen squeeze harder than it ever had before. So this is what a contraction felt like.

CHAPTER 38

...

"Oh!" Morgan doubled over from surprise and pain.

"Are you alright, ma'am?" asked the shorter agent.

When she stood up, Morgan noticed that Andrea had continued typing without even glancing over to check on her.

Morgan took a deep breath. "Yes, I'm fine. It's nothing," said Morgan. "Thanks again for your flexibility. Good day." She waited for the agents to leave and went back to her office so she could think. When she got there, she looked around for Gena, but she wasn't at her desk.

It seemed like she might be going into labor, although it was a few weeks early. The timing was out of the danger zone for the baby, but she was definitely not prepared. There was so much she had wanted to finish at work before taking her leave. She had wanted to give the human trials the highest possible chance of success.

She knew what she had to do. She would take all the information currently floating around in her brain and get it down on paper so that she could hand it off to Gena or another trustworthy person to finish the trial. Another contraction gripped her midsection. Ready for it this time, she breathed through it. She had to get these notes written quickly so she could go home and give birth. She also needed to call Beth and warn her the baby was on his way. First babies took a long time, right? She felt sure she would have time to complete her notes.

CHAPTER 39

...

Morgan completed a good number of notes before the contractions became too distracting. At that point, she got into her self-driving car, for which she was very thankful because she surely could not concentrate well enough to drive, and asked it to take her home. She sat in the front seat, weathering one contraction after another. She wasn't exactly able to time them, but they seemed very close together. The pain increased with each squeeze. In between contractions, she called Jonas.

"I'm on my way home, Jonas. The baby's coming," she said. She paused to let a contraction pass and catch her breath. "Beth already knows. She'll be over when she can."

"How are you feeling?" he asked. His voice sounded so weak, weaker than she remembered.

"The contractions are painful," she paused, gasping—this was a bad one. "I'm okay, though. I have to go. Be there soon," she managed before another contraction hit.

Morgan soon arrived home. Even though she was doubled over in pain, she still entered through the disinfecting shower so she wouldn't bring any germs from the lab home to Nate and Jonas, or worse, the new baby. She straightened up just enough to clean her body thoroughly with the lemon-scented cleanser. When she was about to get out of the shower, she felt a gush of liquid between her legs. She felt a sense of relief that her water breaking had not made a mess in the house. She turned on the faucet and cleaned herself again.

When she got out of the shower, she shrugged into a robe without bothering to fasten it closed and went to the couch to rest. She wanted to see Jonas, but she didn't have the energy to go into the master bedroom. Instead, Nate came out of the guest room to greet her.

"Morgan, how are you? Beth called and told me the baby was on his way," he said, sitting beside her on the couch and trying to take her hand.

She pulled her hand out of his, not wanting to be touched. Nate looked surprised. "I'm fine, Nate," she grunted.

"Can I get you anything? Water? A blanket? Should I rub your back?"

Morgan glared at him. Could he please leave her alone? Would that be rude to say? She said nothing. He continued to stare at her, so she shook her head and closed her eyes, focusing as much as possible on her breathing. Nate continued to sit there, staring at her awkwardly.

Morgan was relieved when, soon, Beth arrived and helped her to the guest bedroom where she conducted an exam. She felt an odd mix of embarrassment at having her friend and neighbor see her body so intimately and comfort that a woman was there to be with her and help. She wished she could have what other women had, a collection of female friends and family surrounding her and supporting her as she brought new female life into the world. But her mother was dead. She had no sister, sister-in-law, aunt, or grandmother. She couldn't have her best friend over, because every additional person increased the risk of germs that could infect her husband, her lover, or her new baby. Her male baby.

Morgan began to cry from a combination of emotional and physical pain. She felt so lonely. Her contractions were peaking in strength and duration. Finally, Beth set up the MIT-invented machine, which would provide relief at least for what her body was experiencing. As the pain reduced in intensity, Morgan settled down, relaxing on the bed. Nate came in quietly, unsure of whether he was welcome. Morgan looked up at him and smiled, less annoyed now that she was no longer in pain and remembering that they were going to have a beautiful son whom everyone would love. A son who would heal some of the emotional pain.

Nate and Beth sat on either side of Morgan, each holding a hand. Jonas was on the other side of the wall, aware, and yet excluded. Morgan could hear him breathing. She wished that he was there with her.

"Do you feel ready to push now, Morgan?" asked Beth.

She nodded. She had felt the baby's head bearing down for a little while now. Nate helped her prop herself up at the edge of the bed, and Beth settled below, waiting to catch the baby.

"He's crowning! He has a beautiful head of hair," said Beth excitedly.

Morgan pushed through a few contractions, resting in between. Finally, she bore down hard one last time and the baby slipped out and into Beth's waiting, gloved arms.

Baby Mark Jing did have a shocking amount of black curly hair for a newborn and a strong pair of lungs. Beth toweled him off gently and placed him on Morgan's chest, where he calmed down immediately. Morgan felt love like she had never felt before swell up, and she cried while cradling the baby in her arms.

"Morgan, he's beautiful," said Nate, standing over mother and child. "You're amazing." His face radiated joy, and the three of them formed the picture of a perfect family. "I love you, Morgan," he said for the first time ever in their relationship.

In the rush of emotions from the birth, Morgan felt love for Nate, too. She smiled at him, too tired to voice her feelings but hoping he understood. They heard a cough from the next room. Was Jonas struggling over how to be included in this moment?

"Nate, will you take the baby over to Jonas for a minute?" asked Morgan.

Morgan lifted the baby, but he fussed and cried. Nate frowned. "Maybe you should feed him first?" he said.

Morgan put the baby back on her bare chest, and he moved to her nipple and began to suck. Morgan stared at him in wonder. Everything he did was fascinating. Beth quietly and professionally took care of Morgan while she bonded with little Mark Jing, cutting the umbilical cord, helping Morgan pass the placenta, sewing a small tear, and cleaning her up with no fuss, as nurses have always done.

The baby soon finished nursing and fell asleep. "Nate, can you take him to the other room now?" asked Morgan. She so wanted Jonas to be included in this miracle. Nate carefully picked up his son, supporting his tiny, floppy head. He carried him into the next room where Morgan knew that Jonas was awake in bed, listening to the activity of birth. She heard Nate say, "This is our son, Mark Jing Digby," including Jonas as one of the parents with his tone of voice and by stating the baby's last name, which was Jonas's. The springs on the bed creaked as Nate sat at Morgan's side. She imagined the look on Jonas's face as he saw the baby for the first time—he wouldn't have the strength to hold him.

"He's beautiful," Jonas said softly, with a touch of sadness but also love.

CHAPTER 40

. . .

Beth stayed over on the couch for a few nights to help but soon had to return to work at the hospital. Morgan and Nate cared for their infant son and also for Jonas. Little Mark Jing wanted to nurse almost constantly. Morgan felt glued to the large armchair in the living room, which was the most comfortable nursing spot in the house. Staring at her son, fascinated by every little movement, she could forget for hours that other people existed in the world. That is, until she heard Jonas's faint voice calling her, requesting assistance to use the bathroom, or wanting food or drink. One day, she had finally gotten the baby to latch on to her painfully sore nipples when she heard Jonas calling her in an urgent tone. She knew he needed to use the bathroom.

"Nate!" she called out.

Nate came running from the guest bedroom where he had ensconced himself, having returned to his remote job because he couldn't sit around staring at a baby all day, no matter how lovely the baby. Nate had taken on many household tasks so that Morgan could tend to Mark Jing. He ordered groceries, cooked, cleaned, and more.

However, he still kept a distance from Jonas, taking the baby whenever Morgan had to assist with Jonas's more personal needs.

Nate jogged into the living room and stood by Morgan in the armchair, holding his long arms out for the baby.

"Nate, can you please go help Jonas?" asked Morgan. She peered at him out of puffy, red eyes. He stood back and looked at her. She followed his gaze and thought about what she must look like. Her hair was pulled into a ponytail with loose strands flying out in every direction. A large black maternity t-shirt hung on her like drapes and was covered with milky baby puke. Half of it was pulled up over a breast, leaving her loose belly bare where the baby did not obscure it. For some unknown reason, she wasn't wearing any pants, just a stretched-out pair of cotton panties holding a brick-sized pad. On one level, she felt embarrassed for him to see her looking like this, but on another, deeper level, she was simply too tired to care.

"Um, sure, Morgan. I can do that." She could tell from Nate's hesitation and tone that he felt awkward about helping Jonas in the bathroom. Well, hopefully he would get over that and quickly.

The doorbell rang, which was strange because she was not expecting anyone. She picked up the baby, still latched onto her breast, and walked to the door, peering out through the peephole. A delivery woman bearing a bouquet of flowers.

Morgan opened the door, not bothering to cover herself, and accepted the flowers, a colorful mix. She wondered who could have sent them. She carried them over to a table and pulled out the card. "Dear Morgan. Congratulations on your son. Take as LONG as you need to recover." They were from the lab. She had no doubt who had written that message—a certain someone who wanted her out of the lab for as long as possible.

CHAPTER 41

...

Morgan awoke with a start in her bed to the sound of a tiny baby mewl. Oh, no! She hadn't meant to sleep in the bed with Mark Jing. What if she rolled over him in her sleep? She must have fallen asleep while nursing him, and now he was ready to nurse again. What she wouldn't give for a hot cup of coffee right now. The baby cried louder—the coffee was not meant to be.

If her parents had been alive, her mom would be here with her, offering congee or a special tea made from herbs to help her recover from the delivery and regain her strength. Her mom would take the baby when she wanted to rest. She would have nourishing meals available to restore her to health rather than watery soup and Jell-O. It would be unheard of for her to do anything strenuous for a month after giving birth. She closed her eyes, allowing herself a moment to grieve over what might have been.

Morgan soon opened her eyes and looked down at herself as she pulled baby MJ to her breast. Her pajamas were crusted with unidentifiable guck. She tried to run a hand through her hair, but it got stuck in a rat's nest which was a natural consequence of having failed to wash her hair for at least a week. She wiped off a stream of drool that dripped from her mouth and had already soaked the pillow. It was upsetting how unlike her usual self she felt.

Jonas, sleeping beside them, slowly opened his eyes and focused his loving gaze on her. "Good morning, my darlings. I want you to know that you're a beautiful mother, Morgan. You're everything I knew you could be." His voice sounded raspy, and he coughed roughly after he spoke, but his eyes shone with warmth.

Her? A beautiful mother? She felt like a dead animal left out in the rain and run over by multiple cars. She appreciated Jonas, though. He was such a sweet man. "Thank you, Jonas," she managed, tears in her eyes. She wasn't yet sure if she was a good mother, but she knew that she loved her son more than anything.

Jonas reached for his phone and summoned Nate from the other room to help him in the bathroom. Nate entered the bedroom, rubbing the sleep out of his eyes, but did not complain. After those first exhausting weeks, the four "housemates" (including baby Mark Jing) had settled into a routine. Nate awkwardly cared for Jonas to free up Morgan to nurse and otherwise tend to the baby. Jonas grudgingly accepted assistance.

Morgan was getting used to life as a mother, but she missed her work and being in the lab driving forward critical research. She hadn't received any updates yet from coworkers—she wondered if the human trials had begun. If those were successful, the baby could be vaccinated—Nate, too—and they could live normal lives. If she were at the lab, she could help make everything happen faster. But she was stuck at home with a baby glued to her breast all day and night. She loved him so much, but she wanted more. She longed to return to the world of science, where her brain was engaged and her passion fed.

Nate and Jonas returned from the bathroom. Morgan noticed that Jonas looked thinner than ever. In all the chaos with the baby, had she not made sure he ate enough? She felt guilty that she hadn't taken as good care of him as she had before MJ's birth. It wasn't fair to cast Jonas aside because she was busy with the baby. Or maybe it wasn't anything to do with her, and it was the natural progression of manflu-related complications? It was true that those who survived manflu with lingering effects tended to weaken and worsen over time. Either way, she resolved to pay more attention to Jonas and to monitor his health more closely in the future. She looked over to see him settled back on his side of the bed, and she smiled reassuringly at him.

CHAPTER 42

. . .

Although Nate and Jonas were accustomed to being home all the time, Morgan was not, and she was going stir crazy. She called Gena and begged her to come over to sit on the front porch and chat. Morgan couldn't risk going out anywhere and exposing herself to germs that she might bring home to all the guys, especially little Mark Jing, who had such low levels of immunity to something as simple as the common cold, let alone manflu.

Gena arrived one cloudy afternoon, carrying a bottle of red wine, two plastic wine glasses, and a bottle of nail polish that was the same shade of red as their drink, Morgan's favorite color. She set her portable Foot Bar up on the small table on the porch while she waited for Morgan to hand off the baby and come outside.

When Morgan opened the door, Gena's pupils dilated with shock. Morgan saw the expression on her friend's face and thought about how she must look. She straightened up her stooped back and smoothed her messy hair away from her face. Gena leaned forward as if to embrace Morgan but held herself back, clearly remembering that they needed to stay several feet apart.

ust Oz

"Congratulations, Morgan! Thanks for all the pictures. Little Mark Jing is beautiful. I love his full head of hair."

"Thanks, Gena! At the rate I'm going, I'll be bald soon, though. How come no one ever told me that you lose your hair after giving birth?"

"Yikes, I didn't know that either," said Gena, patting her own curls as if afraid that someone was going to yank them out.

"Gosh, I'm so tired. I didn't know it was possible to be this tired. I'm in a fog all the time. I can barely remember my own name, and it's a struggle just to keep my eyes open."

"I'm sorry, honey," said Gena, pouring them each a glass of wine. "Isn't Nate helping?"

"Well, it's kind of awkward. The baby is stuck on me, nursing most of the time, so he's helping . . . but with Jonas. He's had to help Jonas use the bathroom. It's not great. And I'm up all night nursing because we want Mark Jing to get as many antibodies from me as possible, so I can't pass the baby off then."

"That sounds really hard."

"Also, Nate's home, but he has a remote job. I don't know what we're going to do when I go back to work. It's not like we can put the baby in daycare. But how are things going with you? And with the vaccine? Please talk to me about anything but baby stuff!"

"I'm fine. Patty's doing great. She's still knitting. Hasn't finished that Christmas sweater yet. Wouldn't it be a shame if she didn't." Gena winked, then leaned forward in her chair. "The vaccine development process is moving along. We took your notes and completed the work so that it's ready for human trials."

"Gena, that's so exciting!" Morgan half-jumped up, nearly knocking over her wine. Then she quickly sat back down, because jumping was not on the menu yet—any more sudden moves and she was likely to pop a stitch or pee herself or both.

"Here's the thing, Morgan. We really need you back. You have so much expertise on this vaccine. I know you're supposed to be on leave for a few months, but any chance you can come back sooner?"

A few moments of silence passed. Morgan saw Gena surreptitiously checking to make sure she had not fallen asleep. But no, she was just deep in thought watching the clouds drift by floating on a delicate breeze.

"Thank you for making me feel so critical to the team. It means a lot. I will try to come back as soon as possible, but I'm not going to be very helpful right now. I'm exhausted, and I'm in pain, and the baby needs me to nurse him what feels like nonstop."

"I totally understand. Listen, there's something else. I did some research on that invoice you found. Remember the name Mikayla Bascomb?"

"Oh, that's right. Thanks for doing more digging. What did you find out?"

"Mikayla Bascomb is the niece of Ximena Álvarez's deceased husband."

"What?" Morgan was shocked. A connection going all the way up to the president? She was awake now.

"I think the delays to the vaccine may go beyond Andrea."

Morgan was scared to think what all this could mean, although it made sense that someone was paying Andrea to do their dirty work. She thought back to the calls Gena had received from Andrea's debt-collector. With those large debts due, Andrea was vulnerable to unfortunate influences.

"Could this be a coincidence?" asked Morgan, hopefully.

"I don't think so. I'm going to keep looking for information. You should be careful. There are high-ranking people actively working against us."

"Thanks for letting me know, Gena. I wish I could do more to help."

"Just take care of yourself right now. And the baby."

"Morgan!" Nate called from just inside the house.

Morgan heard the baby crying. "I have to go. Thank you so much for coming."

"All right, hang in there, Morgan," said Gena as Morgan stepped back into the house, leaving her friend to grab the unused nail polish and clean up the wine bottle and glasses.

CHAPTER 43

. . .

When Morgan got inside, Nate was standing in the living room right by the door, furiously bouncing the crying baby up and down.

"I can't get him to calm down, Morgan," he said. "The only person he ever wants is you. I don't know how we're going to make this work." He immediately handed her the baby. Her instinct was to refuse to take him because she was so annoyed, but she couldn't let him fall to the floor, so she reached for her son, who stopped crying right away.

"Nate. It's still early days. It's going to get better. The more time you spend with Mark Jing, the more he'll love you. This is the hardest part." She couldn't believe that in addition to a bedridden husband and a needy infant, she now had a manchild who needed coddling. "I'll feed him now, but then you're going to have to take him so I can take a nap. I was up all night with him." She had been planning to plop herself in the armchair but instead took the baby into her bedroom and sat to nurse him next to Jonas, who was in his usual spot on the bed. She needed some space from Nate.

"He's beautiful, Morgan. He looks exactly like you," said Jonas, himself looking very pale and drawn.

"Thank you, Jonas, I appreciate it," said Morgan. She smiled and searched his eyes. The couple communicated a thousand words in a few minutes simply gazing into each other's faces while the baby slurped eagerly at her breast. Morgan gently rubbed Jonas's arm, and as she paused to switch the baby to the other breast, she gave him a gentle kiss on his colorless, thin lips.

"Jonas, Gena was just here. They finished all the prep work for the human trials. She wants me to come back as soon as possible to help."

"I'm glad to hear that things are moving along with the vaccine. Hopefully, it will be ready for little Mark Jing soon," said Jonas, reaching weakly to pat the nursing baby's bottom. "How do you feel about going back to work so soon?"

"Well, I love the little guy. I would miss snuggling with him all day, but it would be nice to be out in the world, working with other women on what I love." She couldn't say this to Jonas, but the prospect of being around people who could feed themselves and clean up their own poop was tantalizing. She admitted, "And it would be a dream come true to see this vaccine through to completion."

"It sounds like you know what you want to do," said Jonas.

"If only it were up to me alone. I'm not convinced Nate can handle the baby by himself. We haven't even tried to give him a bottle yet."

"People generally rise to the occasion," said Jonas. "Nate will figure it out if he has to."

CHAPTER 44

...

The next morning, Morgan was, as usual, in the armchair in the living room nursing MJ when her phone rang. If she hadn't had the phone in hand, searching for updates on the German lab's vaccine progress, she wouldn't have been able to answer because she was completely trapped under the baby, who was about to fall asleep. She really wanted to beat the Germans. She hadn't found anything about their lab, which she took to be a good sign. It was Gavin calling, which was a bit strange, especially so early in the morning.

"Good morning, Gavin," said Morgan.

"Morgan, I'm so glad you picked up," said Gavin, sounding out of breath.

"What's going on?"

"I was supposed to go into the lab for a session later today."

Morgan was taken aback. She hadn't imagined someone else conducting these sessions with Gavin while she was out. Feeling a little jealous, she wondered who it could be. Maybe Shoshanna was back from leave.

"And what happened?" Morgan asked.

"I got a call that the session was canceled because there was a fire in the lab."

"Oh, no! A small fire, or did the whole lab burn down?" Morgan held her breath while she waited for his answer.

"The call came from the lab, so I think it was only a part. But I don't really know anything else. I've been looking for news online, but I haven't seen anything."

How strange. A fire at the lab should generate news coverage. This was a major government building. Unless someone was blocking the media from reporting on it. Someone like Andrea, covering up for whomever it was that paid her off. She better get in touch with Gena to see what she thought. Oh dear, Gena! What if she had been in the building?

"Gavin, do you know if anyone was hurt?"

"I don't know. They didn't tell me anything."

"I have to call Gena. I'll let you know what I find out."

"Please do, Morgan. I really hope everyone's okay."

"Me, too, Gavin. Thanks for letting me know. Talk to you soon." Morgan hung up. She looked down at MJ, relieved that he had slept through the call. She immediately called Gena's cell phone. The call went directly to voicemail. Morgan felt her chest tighten, and she tried to control her breathing. If anything happened to Gena, she didn't know what she would do.

Oh my goodness, what about the animals? No, she prayed the animals were safe. Thinking about animals caught in a fire horrified her. *Breathe, Morgan. Breathe.* She called Charlotte. The call went straight to voicemail, too. *Oh, dear.*

CHAPTER 45

. . .

M organ next called Patty, Gena's partner. While the phone rang, Morgan chewed her bottom lip. Patty *had* to pick up. Finally, she answered.

"Patty, I heard about the fire. Is Gena okay?" Morgan asked without taking time for pleasantries.

"We're at the hospital, Morgan. I can't talk long. Gena is okay. She was at the lab late last night, preparing for the human trials when a fire started somewhere close to where she was in the building. Luckily, she got out in time, but she suffered from smoke inhalation along with a few cuts and bruises. They kept her overnight for observation. No one else was hurt, and the animals are all fine, too." She spoke quietly, presumably to avoid disturbing Gena, and she sounded tired.

Morgan felt a rush of different emotions hitting her all at the same time. Thank goodness Gena was not seriously hurt, and what a relief it was that the animals had not been injured! However, she was concerned because it seemed someone was targeting Gena. Surely whoever started the fire was still after her, and her life was in danger.

She was so worried for her friend. And what about the lab? Would the human trials still be able to continue? Her baby, who was sleeping on her body right at this instant, was waiting for the vaccine that would come out of these trials. They needed to continue.

"Patty," she said cautiously, not wanting to upset her, "do they know anything about who started the fire?"

"No, no one's told us anything."

"I don't mean to frighten you, but someone may have specifically targeted Gena."

"Who'd want to do that?" asked Patty.

"There are people who don't want the vaccine to succeed. I can't say more right now." Morgan didn't want to put Patty and Gena in any more danger by speculating over the phone.

"What should I do?"

"See if they'll keep Gena a little longer while I try to figure things out. She's probably safest in the hospital right now." Morgan tried to sound more confident than she felt, which was terrified.

"All right, Morgan, I'll try."

She shouldn't keep Patty on the phone any longer. Surely, she would want to focus on Gena. "I'm so glad we were able to talk, Patty. Please let me know if anything changes, and give my best to Gena when you speak to her."

She wished she could run over to the hospital to visit Gena and see that she really was safe, plus ask her more about what had happened. But she knew she couldn't risk it. A hospital was not a safe place with all the germs she might bring back to her family.

Now more than ever, she had to know who was working against them. Who was pulling the strings that Andrea was attached to like a marionette? Morgan resolved that no matter her exhaustion and difficulty in completing any tasks apart from nursing her son, she would get to the bottom of this. Her best friend was hurt, and the lives of her son and her son's father hung in the balance. Whoever was slowing them down every step of the way would be found out and stopped. Morgan knew how determined she was—when she set her mind to something, it happened. This time would be no different. The perpetrator would be found out, and the vaccine would be successful with human subjects. It had to be.

"Morgan, come quick," yelled Nate from the master bedroom.

What now?

CHAPTER 46

...

Morgan couldn't exactly go anywhere quickly with a sleeping infant attached to her. She stood gingerly, trying not to wake him. Holding MJ in front of her like a frosted cake, she speed-walked to the bedroom. When she entered, she saw Nate holding a plastic trash can up to Jonas, who was leaning over and vomiting into it, barely able to hold up his own head.

Morgan carefully settled the baby into the bassinet she kept on her side of the bed and approached the two men. She put a hand to Jonas's cheek—sweaty. His whole body sagged.

Nate's eyes were wide with fear. "I don't know what to do, Morgan," he said in a pleading voice that begged to be relieved of this responsibility.

"I'll take care of him, Nate. Can you please call his doctor? The number is in my phone. Dr. Veronica Santiago. Describe his symptoms and ask her what we should do." Nate looked around the bedroom confused. "My phone's in the living room."

Nate left the bedroom, and Morgan heard him in the living room on the phone. She turned to Jonas, who was still heaving but had nothing left in his stomach to bring up. She stroked his damp cheek with her cool, dry hand.

"You're going to be fine, Jonas. We'll get you some medicine. Don't worry, darling," she whispered. She rubbed his back. He breathed shallowly, struggling to get enough air with each attempt.

Soon, Nate returned and stood in the doorway of the bedroom. "Morgan, the doctor is on the phone. She wants to speak to you," he said. "I'll stay with Jonas."

Morgan took the phone from him. "Hello, Dr. Santiago," she said. "Are you calling in a prescription for Jonas?"

"Hello, Dr. Digby. Yes, I am calling in an anti-emetic. The pharmacy will deliver it in a few hours. I wanted to speak to you, because this kind of vomiting may indicate that Jonas has entered the late stages of manflu post-viral syndrome. He may not have much time left. We can treat the symptoms, but it's likely that his health will continue to decline very rapidly."

Morgan trembled with the shock of the woman's blunt words. She knew Jonas's health was poor and that he was not likely to live a long life, but she hadn't expected him to go so soon. She thought they still had years together. Years for him to watch the baby grow up. Years of family time.

She flashed back to their wedding day. Barrel-chested and standing tall in his black tuxedo, he waited for her to walk down the aisle to him. She remembered the vows they had made and when "till death do you part" had seemed like an absurd thing to say. Death was something that could never happen to either of them or would happen so far in the future it was unimaginable. She closed her eyes and remembered the kiss that had sealed their promise to each other. How could she live a life where she would never be able to kiss Jonas again?

"Isn't there anything you can do, Doctor?" Morgan asked, choking back a sob.

"There are some medications we can try, but the prognosis is not very good. I'm sorry."

"How, um, how much time does he have?" Morgan stammered.

"At this point, it's most likely a matter of weeks."

Morgan's eyes felt hot and liquid and a sob threatened to burst from her throat, but she looked toward the bedroom and restrained herself. She didn't want Jonas to hear her break down and worry. And she didn't want to wake the baby. She would cry later. She thanked the doctor, hung up, and walked back into the bedroom. Jonas barely turned his head to look at her from where he lay propped up on pillows, his chest still heaving, Nate sat beside him, holding his hand.

"Dr. Santiago is calling in a prescription. You'll feel better soon, Jonas." She nodded to Nate that he could leave and took over his position beside Jonas. She squeezed his hand. He didn't have the strength to say anything or squeeze back. Morgan blinked back tears she didn't want Jonas to see.

CHAPTER 47

...

The medication the doctor sent over via drone stabilized Jonas, but he remained extremely weak and barely accepted any food. Morgan ran herself ragged taking care of both him and the baby as the days unfolded. Her body dragged with every motion. As Jonas improved slightly, Morgan regained some energy, and her thoughts turned back to the fire in the lab. She woke up after an improved night's sleep (meaning two solid chunks of three hours each) and resolved to get to the bottom of what was happening at work. She owed it to her best friend.

Gena was still in the hospital, and Morgan had not yet spoken with her. She didn't know the extent of damage from the fire or why it had started in the first place. She feared the worst. What if the vaccine samples meant for the human trials had been destroyed in the fire? That would cause more painful delays.

Morgan placed a large coffee bean delivery order and made sure not to get decaf. She had a lot of work ahead of her, and she refused to allow sleep deprivation to stand in her way. Moving some furniture around, she created an office space in the living room with a playmat and bassinet nearby so she could work on her computer while she watched the baby. Nate came in while she was lifting a table and jumped in to assist, but it was too late.

"Morgan, I would've helped with that. Why didn't you come get me?" he asked.

She looked at him, puzzled. It hadn't even occurred to her to ask for help. She was accustomed to doing everything herself. She shrugged. "It's done now," she said.

He shook his head and went back into the guest room.

After she had put MJ down in the bassinet for a nap, she began to comb the Internet. She started with a general search, which didn't generate any interesting findings. Then, she remembered a political gossip website Sarah had once mentioned. Sarah followed the page as a distraction from life with Robert, the way some people obsessed about celebrity news. Clicking link after link, Morgan found an old article about Mikayla and Ximena becoming close after her husband's death. Mikayla had harbored political ambitions and was using her aunt as a stepping stone to her own career by acting as her personal gopher. A tiny photo accompanied the article. Morgan clicked to enlarge it and found herself staring at Stacey, Gavin's former companion who had been caught snooping. Bingo!

Gavin was pretty naïve to think that "Stacey" was dumb and innocent. Obviously, she had been using him as a way to gain access to the lab where he was a research subject without raising any red flags. She should have been a little more careful when she was snooping and maybe picked the name of a person who actually existed. Morgan felt vindicated in her suspicions of the woman. It was simply unnatural to spend one's day following a man around.

MJ woke up screaming. Morgan nursed him, and he calmed down a bit. She tried to put him down on the playmat so she could go back to her research, but when she let go of him, he wailed. Why had she even bothered to set up this area? She wasn't getting anything done. Nate came in and cooed at MJ on the mat. The infant stopped screaming. Soon, Nate had MJ smiling when he shook a stuffed owl around and made hooting noises. Morgan's heart swelled with gratitude and love.

She returned to her computer to hunt for clues about Andrea. Who could be paying her off? Morgan thought about everything she knew about Andrea. Annoying and meddling, yes, but that wasn't anything to go on for an Internet search. Wait, there was something—she always wore those weird cat earrings. Plenty of people wore cat earrings once in a while, but not every single day. Maybe that meant something beyond liking cats. Morgan clicked through a million pictures of cat earrings on the Internet. Nothing jumped out at her.

She took a break for a cup of coffee. While the coffee brewed, she thought more about those earrings. There were different pairs, but they all shared the same color scheme—orange and white. She brought her mug of coffee back to her computer and did some more searching.

Aha! There was a clue. She found a sorority with a cat mascot and the official colors orange and white. Chi Alpha Theta. What university had Andrea attended? Morgan racked her brain. She finally remembered. It was Stanford. Morgan recalled seeing tree posters mixed in with the cat gear in the reception area. What a couple of stupid mascots. Morgan hoped the cat from Chi Alpha Theta climbed up the Stanford tree and got stuck. She shook her head to clear her brain. *Must stay focused.*

Morgan ran some searches on Andrea's name and Stanford University and came up empty. She went back to the coffee pot for a refill. Hadn't Andrea been married *before*? Yes, Morgan vaguely remembered her referring to her daughter's deceased father. Maybe she had taken her husband's name upon marriage. Gosh, how was she going to find out what Andrea's maiden name had been?

Nate looked up from the floor where he was still playing with MJ. "What are you working on?"

"I'm trying to figure out the reason for the fire at work." Morgan had told Nate all about it when she got the call from Gavin.

"You should be careful, Morgan," he said. "It sounds like there are some powerful people working against you."

"I realize that, and I'm trying to figure out who they are and what they want," said Morgan. "Maybe you can help. Do you know how I can find out someone's maiden name?"

"Are you using me for my IT skills?" he joked.

She tapped her foot impatiently and said nothing. It was not the time to be funny.

"Sure, I can help you. Let me pull up a website." Morgan stood up from her desk, and Nate got up off the floor and sat at the computer. As soon as he was left alone, MJ started to cry again. Morgan scooped him up and bounced him up and down gently, patting his back to the same beat as her bounces.

"Here is the website. What's her name now?" Nate asked. Morgan told him, and he typed it in. After a minute, the website spat out the name "Domingo." "Looks like she used to be 'Andrea Domingo,'" said Nate, standing up and making his way to the kitchen to get some coffee.

"Thanks!" called Morgan to his back as she sat in the chair, still holding the baby and typing awkwardly around him. She immediately ran a search on "Domingo" and "Stanford University." Several results came up. Apparently, Andrea was quite a talented swimmer in college. Finally, Morgan hit the jackpot. It was a yearbook picture group shot of a sorority—Chi Alpha Theta. The pledge class was in the front row, and the upperclasswomen stood behind them. In the center of the front row was Andrea, looking young and fit, presumably from all that swimming. Next to her, their arms slung around each other's shoulders, was a youthful Ximena Álvarez. Neither woman was smiling.

CHAPTER 48

...

Morgan jumped up, gingerly holding baby MJ away from her computer as if it were a hissing snake. She had suspected this went all the way to the top, but now she felt even more certain. Andrea and Ximena looked too cozy in that photo. And now Ximena's niece, who had used a fake name with Gavin and was caught wandering around the building, submitted an invoice to Andrea for work done the day of the break-in? Much too coincidental. Morgan still didn't know the *why*, but she was confident about the *who*.

Nate walked back over to her with his mug of steaming coffee. "Did you figure it out?"

Should she tell him? She didn't want to scare him unnecessarily. But now, with this new information, she knew they were all in danger. They had to do something to protect themselves, and his help would be essential. How could it be that her very own government was working against her while she was trying to save lives? Not for the first time, she considered the world a cruel place.

"Nate, you may want to sit down for this," said Morgan. "And put down that coffee."

Nate sat on the living room sofa, sliding his mug onto the table. He looked at her attentively.

Morgan swallowed. She glanced at his clasped hands, and she remembered playing piano with him. She also recalled him touching her with those long fingers. Pushing those images out of her mind, she looked up at his face, which was kind and open and so incredibly handsome. She wished things could be different, that they could be enjoying their time together rather than discussing how to handle the dangerous situation in which they found themselves.

"Nate, I'm fairly certain that the President of the United States is paying the office manager at my lab to sabotage the manflu vaccine every step of the way while covering up what she's doing. I think they're responsible for the break-in and the fire, among other things. And they may come after me next. We should consider going into hiding to protect everyone's safety." She held on tight to the baby and stroked his curly hair as she spoke.

Nate whistled. "That's a lot, Morgan. Are you sure?"

"I don't have time to get into all the details, Nate, but look at that photo." She pointed to the computer screen. "It's Andrea and Ximena Álvarez, standing side by side in a Chi Alpha Theta photograph from Stanford."

Nate walked over to the computer and squinted at the photo caption. "Looks like they're the only Latinas in their pledge class," he said. "That explains a lot."

"Why do you say that?" asked Morgan, bristling at his racist-sounding comment, which was out of character.

"You haven't heard about the Chi Alpha Theta scandal?"

Morgan shook her head.

"I guess there's no reason why you'd be up on sorority gossip. The only reason I know is because one of my sisters went through sorority rush a few years ago at Colorado State University, and apparently Chi

Alpha Theta is still pulling this crap decades later."

"Pulling what crap? Nate, we don't have a lot of time. Please just tell me." Baby MJ made an adorable squeak, punctuating Morgan's statement.

"The national organization is disgusting. There was a scandal a couple of decades ago—probably around the time Ximena and Andrea were in college. The national president was caught on video at a private gathering describing the ideal Chi Alpha Theta woman— above all else, she had to be pretty, white, and blonde. But each chapter needed to be sure to recruit a couple of minority women every year to avoid discrimination lawsuits. The president recommended plenty of hazing so those minority women would *know their place*. My sister is blonde, and they were all over her to join. Luckily, she knew the history, and after talking to some people, figured out the sorority hasn't changed at all. She joined a different sorority."

"I had no idea. How horrible! And to think that type of racism still goes on to this day."

He nodded. "It's terrible. I think going through that type of experience must have closely bonded the people who were hazed. That's why I mentioned the fact that they appear to be the only Latinas from their year. Though I wonder why they put up with it instead of leaving the sorority."

"The connections they made there were their ticket to success. Isn't that why anyone joins a sorority? I guarantee Ximena wouldn't be president without the help of people she met there." She looked down at her son, wondering if and how he would be able to succeed in life. Not only was he male, but he was half-Asian. When he was an adult, would he face this type of racism and cronyism?

Morgan pointed to the computer screen. "Andrea's in a large amount of debt, making her open to bribery and manipulation. Ximena's niece has been implicated very clearly—I saw her name on an invoice, and I recognized her picture as someone caught snooping around the lab. This evidence of a connection between Andrea and Ximena seals it. They must be working together against this vaccine."

"It's hard to imagine anyone working against this vaccine," said Nate. "It would transform my life." Nate picked up his coffee mug. He stared into its contents, as if expecting an answer to appear in the liquid. "Morgan, Ximena Álvarez was governor of Colorado before she became president."

"So?"

"So, she was probably responsible for the government agent spreading manflu on the mall food court tables in the video I showed you. Similar videos were taken starting when she was governor."

"You're right! I'm sure she was behind that, too. I'm sorry I ever doubted you."

"It's okay, Morgan. The important thing is we're on the same team now."

"Nate, we need to think about leaving." Morgan sighed. She didn't want to leave her home, where she had spent so many happy years with Jonas before all the hard years. Also, this was where her son had been born, so it would remain a special place in her heart forever.

"What about Jonas? Moving could kill him with how sick he's been. And where would we go?"

Morgan thought through her options. Maybe she could leave Jonas with Beth? But Beth had to work. And Jonas was close to death whether or not they moved, so she couldn't let that affect her decision. Nate was right, though. Where would they go? It's not like she could book a hotel for this motley crew. She was the only one in the group with a functioning immune system. And even if she could, putting anything on a credit card would signal their location to the government.

She had spent the prime of her life working in government labs on solutions that would benefit all of society. She felt so betrayed. It was all so unfair. She hadn't done anything wrong, and her own government was probably after her.

MJ started to cry, startling Morgan out of her thoughts. She turned to Nate. "I'm going to nurse MJ. We'll talk about this later. I need some time to think." She brushed past him, carrying the baby to her favorite armchair.

"Morgan?" Nate called out quietly.

"Yes?"

"I trust you," he said.

CHAPTER 49

...

Morgan spent most of the night tossing and turning. With the amount of stress she was under and the volume of coffee she'd had to drink, sleep proved almost impossible. Whenever she managed to close her eyes for a moment, a nightmare began in which faceless government agents burned down her house. In her dream, the fire caused her to grab MJ and run out into the street where they were captured, Jonas left behind in the burning building. When she thought of Jonas, she startled awake.

In her lucid moments, she thought through all of the possibilities. They couldn't go to Gena's house because Gena would be on the government's radar. In fact, Gena probably needed a safe place, too, after she was released from the hospital. Beth's house was compromised—a prowler had already been spotted there. She wished she could stay with her parents. Her mom would make her tea and rub her feet. Her dad would explain to her why everything was not as bad as she thought it was. Her brother would tell stupid jokes and make her watch ancient TV comedies from decades long past while he recited every line in sync with the characters. She missed her family now more than ever.

In the wee hours of the morning, a thought occurred to her—maybe they could stay with Gavin. He had offered to help in any way possible, and his house was huge. In her desperation, she clung to this idea. It was her only hope. Had he meant what he said? Would he be willing to take in her family? What about her best friend?

CHAPTER 50

...

When the sky lit up pink with the start of dawn, an exhausted Morgan got out of bed. She left MJ asleep in his bassinet and Jonas resting peacefully in bed. She padded quietly into the kitchen where she brewed coffee. She needed to reach Gavin. She glanced at the clock. 6:00 a.m. Would he even answer?

"Call Gavin," Morgan said to her phone. She heard ringing. She also heard something else—Mark Jing's tiny hands smacking against the sides of his bassinet as he started to wake up for his early morning feed. She detected some adorable coos. In a moment, there would be full-blown wails.

"Morgan?" Gavin said sleepily when he picked up the phone after what felt like a million rings.

"Gavin—it's an emergency. Can I come stay with you for a little while and bring my family?"

"Uh, sure, okay. I have some visitors, though . . ."

"Get them out, Gavin. Make something up. Pretend your wife is coming home or something."

"Is everything okay? This sounds serious."

"It's very serious. Please have your visitors leave immediately. I'll explain everything later."

"Okay, no problem. I'll do that, Morgan."

"What about Gena and her partner? Do you think there's space for them, too?"

"Sure, there's definitely plenty of space. The more, the merrier," said Gavin, finally starting to sound awake and like himself.

"Your place needs to be disinfected before we arrive. The baby is susceptible to everything, and Nate and Jonas are at risk, too."

"Hmmm. I've never done that before. I don't have the right supplies. I mean, I think I have a bottle of bleach somewhere that one of my guests was using on her hair . . ."

"Go through the place with trash bags and get rid of anything that is not essential," she said. "Take all the trash outside. Pick a room that you don't need. Anything you want to keep that cannot easily be wiped down, put it in there and close the door. Put all dirty dishes in the dishwasher and start a cycle. Pick up all the dirty clothes and linens, including what you're wearing, and start a load of laundry on hot. Pick a bedroom near the entrance and make sure it's spotless— I'll put all the guys in there when we arrive and then help you clean the rest of the house."

Morgan heard the baby crying in the bedroom. She held the phone between her ear and her shoulder as she went in to get him.

"Did you get all that, Gavin? Look at the place as if you were hunting for germs and try to kill them all. You can do it!"

Great, add cheerleader to her list of duties. She hoped he could handle it. A stray germ could be deadly for any of the males she loved.

Morgan hung up the phone and put the baby to her breast, holding him with one arm as she walked around the house. She went into the guest room to wake Nate.

"Nate," she said gently. "Please get up, we have to get out of here. I found us a place to go."

Nate groaned and rolled over, covering his face with a hairy arm.

"Nate!" Morgan turned on the light and went over to him. She shook him by the arm. "You have to wake up. I need your help."

Nate finally opened his eyes and sat up a bit in bed, blinking at the bright light. "What's going on?" he asked.

Morgan had been planning to ask him to pack the baby's stuff, but that was looking like it would take too long to explain.

"Just take the baby!" she said. Mark Jing had finished nursing on one side and was looking forward to the second course of his meal when Morgan handed him off to Nate. The baby began to cry. Nate placed him belly side down over his forearm and firmly patted his back to elicit a burp. Nate got out of bed, pulling the baby to an upright position against his chest, facing out at the world. He followed Morgan to stand right outside the master bedroom where she quickly shoved diapers, wipes, and baby clothes into a suitcase.

Morgan quietly and calmly explained the situation to Jonas as she packed. He was too ill to say much. Morgan was afraid he wouldn't survive the move. She wondered if he was thinking the same thing.

As Morgan packed, she called Patty. She didn't want to disturb Gena, who was still recovering from smoke inhalation, but she needed them to understand the gravity of the situation they were dealing with. She needed to convince them to join her. Luckily, she reached Patty, who had gone home to get some rest, and convinced her to pack up and stay with Gavin. Gena was supposed to be released from the hospital later that morning. Patty said she feared that whoever had set the fire would be back to finish the job and that she was grateful Morgan had found them a safe spot to stay.

CHAPTER 51

. . .

I t took forever to get out of the house. In addition to all the packing, Morgan disinfected the car and then herself in the shower. They had been all ready to leave, but the baby soiled his diaper and his entire outfit, requiring another round of bathing and changing.

Finally, Morgan placed the suitcases in the trunk. Nate slowly, painstakingly lifted Jonas into the backseat and joined him there. Morgan placed Mark Jing on his lap. They hadn't bothered to purchase a car seat—they hadn't planned to take the baby anywhere. Morgan paused with one hand on the door of her car, looking at her house. She had thought this would be a starter house for her and Jonas. A place where they could have one baby and maybe get pregnant with another before looking for a bigger place that they could have easily afforded on two salaries. Of course, things hadn't turned out that way. She climbed into the car, instructing it to drive to Gavin's after buckling up and wiping a tear from the corner of her eye.

CHAPTER 52

. . .

Morgan soon arrived at Gavin's house with her ragtag group. They pulled up to a multi-level modern mansion situated on a hill overlooking the Bay, which was dotted with tiny white sailboats. The enormous garage would conceal her vehicle once she got everyone settled in the house. The place looked like a fortress.

Leaving the guys in the car, Morgan knocked on the door. Gena greeted her at the doorway, wet sponge in hand. Morgan spotted Patty in the distance, mopping the floor of a giant, gleaming white kitchen.

"This house is freaking enormous!" said Gena in greeting, mopping sweat from her forehead with her sleeve. "I lost count at bathroom number seven."

Morgan was speechless. How had Gena and Patty gotten to Gavin's so quickly? And why was Gena cleaning the house when she was supposed to be resting?

Gena must have noticed Morgan's startled expression. "Oh, don't worry about me, I'm fine now. They were only keeping me at the hospital because of the danger from whoever started the fire, as you recommended to Patty. We've been trying to figure out where to hide out, so your call this morning came at the perfect time."

"I'm so glad you're all right!" exclaimed Morgan.

Gena was amped up. "You have to see this place. The basement is a sex dungeon. We couldn't sanitize it, so we just taped it off. Sex swing, whips, chains, pillows, the whole nine yards."

"Tell her about the bedrooms, Gena!" Patty shouted.

"You are not going to believe the bedrooms. They each have a theme, and the closets have costumes to match, which we dumped in the basement. Patty and I took the superhero room. It's painted dark blue and covered with decals of male and female superheroes. The closet had a bunch of superhero costumes along with foam swords, shields, toy guns, and all manner of superhero weapons and paraphernalia. It was less creepy than the other option, if you can believe it."

"What was the other option?" Morgan asked, gritting her teeth.

"The other choice looked like a classroom in a school to be attended by the children of Dorothy from Wizard of Oz and Mary Ann from Gilligan's Island. There were actually desks like you would find in an elementary school, a blackboard from the 1980s, an ancient pencil sharpener bolted to the wall, and all kinds of wigs and innocent young girl outfits. The bedspread was blue gingham like Dorothy's dress. We sealed it up right away."

Morgan could not imagine the purpose of a room decorated in that manner in Gavin's home. Nor did she want to.

"Where's my group staying?" she asked, almost afraid to hear the answer.

"Let me show you," said Gena. She led Morgan to a bordello-style room painted taupe and styled with rich burgundy fabrics and dark wood furniture. A mirror was installed on the ceiling above the bed.

"This is for you, Jonas, and the baby. The draperies, chaise longue, and lacy costumes that complete the look are in the basement."

Morgan looked up at the ceiling, taking in the room. "And Nate?"

"He's next door in the surfer room," Gena led Morgan over to another bedroom. The walls were painted blue with white foam caps to simulate the ocean. Surf boards were nailed to the walls. The bedding was a tan color that looked like sand. "You should have seen the room before. A six-foot shark replica from the movie Jaws is currently swimming in the basement along with enough sexy bathing suits to outfit the entire cast for the next season of *Baywatch*."

"Wow," said Morgan.

"We put Nate next to you guys so he could be near the baby."

Morgan nodded. Patty joined them, taking a break from mopping.

"Anything else I should know about the house, or should I not ask?" said Morgan.

"That's basically it. Gavin's bedroom, which looks like a man cave, and his office space are upstairs," said Patty.

Walking back toward the entrance on her way to the car to get the men, Morgan noticed the contrast between the common spaces of the house and the themed bedrooms. The main floor was open-plan style, and the upstairs landing opened up to it as well, so the house was filled with light during the day. The kitchen was all white from the tiles to the cabinets to the stools around the island. The living room had dark wood floors covered by a white fluffy rug that looked freshly cleaned. White leather couches also sparkled in the airy space. Off the living room, in what would have been the dining room in any other type of house, sat a pool table.

As Morgan looked around at all that was visible from her vantage point, Gavin appeared at the top of the stairs. Completely naked.

"Hi, Morgan!" he called out.

She sucked in her breath at the unexpected sight. "What's going on?" she asked Gena.

"I told him he needed to put his clothes in the washing machine and take a shower, and he's been walking around the house naked ever since. You should have seen the collection of women who skedaddled when Patty and I showed up! We had to pretend I was his wife, and she was my sister, and we intended to kick some butt. We've been cleaning up wine glasses and lingerie all morning. When this is all over, I might trade lives with this guy."

"I can't wait to hear more, but right now I need to get the guys inside the house. Are the bedrooms you showed me sanitized?"

"The bordello room and adjoining bathroom are ready. We haven't done surfer chic yet. You guys will all need to crowd in at the moment and we'll let you know when we're done," said Gena.

"Thanks, Gena. I'll bring in the guys. Once they're settled, I'll help you clean."

Morgan managed to get all the people and suitcases into the disinfected portion of the house. Jonas and the baby were soon tucked into the bed and asleep. Every step of the way had been slow and painful for Jonas. Moving his limbs proved exhausting. The journey seemed to have weakened him even further.

Nate paced the room. He watched the baby to make sure he didn't roll over and fall off the bed. Somehow Gavin's gigantic and well-equipped house did not feature a bassinet or crib for the little guy. Morgan went off to help clean.

CHAPTER 53

...

Hours of cleaning later, Morgan's back ached, and her stomach grumbled. Before she could take a break, she went into the bedroom to check on the guys. When she opened the door, she was startled at the sight of all three of them sleeping together in the same luxurious bed, the baby in between the men amidst the crisp white sheets. Jonas opened his eyes when she entered the room. His wispy gray hair contrasted with the rich brown wooden headboard.

"How's everything, Morgan?" he rasped. "Are we safe here?" His face appeared to be growing thinner and older by the minute.

"Safer than we were at home, Jonas," said Morgan, sitting at the foot of the bed. "I'm sorry we had to move you here. I know it was difficult for you to leave the house. We're going to have to take things one day at a time, but I think we're going to be fine." She and the baby would be fine. Jonas would not, but she didn't want to scare him unnecessarily. Jonas nodded and closed his eyes, drifting back to sleep.

Morgan smelled something delicious frying and remembered her empty stomach. She followed the rich and slightly greasy aroma into the kitchen. Gena and Gavin (now fully clothed) sat on stools around an island while Patty scrambled eggs and fried potatoes on a stovetop facing them. Morgan collapsed onto a stool, and Patty passed her a plate of food. Morgan gratefully smiled at her and ate quickly. When she was done, she looked at Gavin and Gena.

"Thanks so much for letting us stay here, Gavin," said Morgan, "You have no idea how much I appreciate it. It's such a relief to be in a safe place."

"Absolutely! I'm happy to have you all here."

"Gena, now that we have a minute to breathe, can you please catch me up on the fire at the lab?"

"I don't remember much. One minute, I was organizing vaccine samples, and the next minute I was on the floor, and there was smoke everywhere. There was an explosion that knocked me over, and I passed out briefly when I hit my head. Luckily, I came to quickly, saw the smoke, and got out of the building, crawling on my stomach the whole way. By the time I made it out, the fire department was already there and putting out the fire. I didn't see who set it or what caused it. It seems clear that it was set deliberately."

Patty stepped away from the stove and made her way to Gena, putting an arm around her shoulders. Morgan marveled at Gena's ability to stay calm in a crisis.

"Oh, my goodness, Gena," gasped Morgan. "I'm so glad you're okay! And thank goodness none of the animals were hurt." She reached for Gena's hand and squeezed it. Patty rubbed Morgan's back, and the three women briefly formed a triangle where love and care flowed freely.

Morgan broke the spell. "Gena, I hate to ask, but what happened to the vaccine samples you were preparing for the human trials? Have they all been destroyed?"

Gena's naturally pink lips curved into a sneaky smile. "I'm sure all the samples in the lab were destroyed, but luckily, I had some stored offsite. I had Patty grab them from the house, and we brought them with us."

"That's fantastic, Gena," she said, grabbing her friend and squeezing her shoulders.

"Wait, you have vaccine samples in my house?" asked Gavin. "That sounds dangerous." He folded his arms across his chest.

"It's fine," said Morgan. "Just don't accidentally drink them. I'm assuming they're in the fridge?"

"Yes, of course. You didn't use them to cook the eggs, did you, Patty?" Gena laughingly asked.

Patty stared at Gena, seeming not to find the joke particularly funny.

"We'll have to figure out what to do with those samples," said Morgan.

At that moment, Nate walked into the kitchen, carrying the baby. Morgan froze—the baby had never been around other people. She couldn't breathe for a moment because all she saw everywhere were germs. She fought the urge to yell at everyone to stand back. She took a deep breath and felt her pulse slow down. It was going to be okay. She could approach this calmly.

"Ladies and gentleman," announced Morgan to the small group, "this is Nate. And this," she gestured to the baby, "is Mark Jing." Everyone said how pleased they were to meet each other. "I know it'll be hard, but please don't touch the baby or get too close," Morgan reminded them. "We can't expose him to outside germs. Nate, either, for that matter."

There was a moment of silence—Morgan imagined that Gavin, Gena, and Patty were taking in the idea of being face-to-face with not one, but two Vulnies for the first time. Morgan hoped they would be understanding and respectful. Little Mark Jing yawned adorably, and everyone laughed, breaking the tension.

"Would you like some eggs and potatoes, Nate?" asked Patty, grabbing a plate.

"Sure, that would be great, thanks." Nate accepted the full plate and sat at the kitchen island. Seemingly unfazed by the others in the room watching him, he quickly cleaned his plate, shoveling food into his mouth and looking up only when he was done. Patty gestured for the plate and refilled it wordlessly.

"So, Nate, tell us about yourself, man," said Gavin when Nate had finished his food and had some water. Morgan felt the shock of her professional and personal worlds colliding as Gavin attempted to make conversation with Nate. Of course, she had destroyed all such boundaries when she showed up at Gavin's place with her entire household, but somehow, watching her research subject speak to her Vulny lover made her aware of how upside down everything was.

"Oh, sure. I'm from Colorado. My mom and my sisters still live out there. There was a big outbreak last year, so I came out here to live with my aunt Beth, who's a nurse at the hospital. I'm able to work remotely, so I can live anywhere, but I can't leave the house. Beth lives down the street from Morgan, and we met when she was visiting. Right before she had the baby, I moved in with her and Jonas to help."

"That must've been something, moving in with them after everything," said Gavin, shaking his head. Morgan flinched. An awkward pause ensued.

"So, what kind of remote work do you do?" asked Gavin eventually.

"Computer networking," said Nate.

"No way! I used to work in IT, too," said Gavin, smiling broadly.

"What kind of work do you do now?" asked Nate.

Morgan had not told Nate much about Gavin because she had to protect research subject confidentiality. She managed to suppress a chuckle, but Gena snickered.

"I guarantee the continuing of our delicate species," said Gavin smugly.

Nate's brow furrowed, and he tilted his curly head.

"He sells his sperm to sperm banks so women can have daughters," said Gena. "Most people can't do it the old-fashioned way these days, unlike you."

"Or they don't want to," said Patty quietly. Everyone turned to look at her since she had barely spoken up to this point.

"What? Everyone knows we're lesbians, right?" said Patty, face scrunched in confusion.

"Never done it with a man?" asked Gavin. "No interest at all?"

"I knew from the time I was in elementary school that I was gay," said Patty, placing the dirty pots and pans in the sink and running the water to soak them. "When the other girls would talk about boys they wanted to kiss, the thought would gross me out. Why kiss an awkward, smelly boy when you can kiss a soft, pretty girl?"

"Can't argue with you there," said Gavin. "What about you, Gena?"

"Gosh, this is a personal conversation," she said. "Some of us just met!"

"That's the way Gavin is, Gena," said Morgan. "He has a one-track mind. S-E-X. No need to answer."

"No, that's fine. As long as we're going to be holed up here, we might as well skip the small talk." She brushed a stray curl off her face. "My parents were very religious—I come from a large, Mexican-American Catholic family. I was taught that gay people go straight to hell. I didn't even consider that I might be gay until my senior year of high school. Prior to that, I had a few boyfriends, but it never felt right. And then Suzette joined the tennis team, and I knew as soon as I saw her. She had long legs that were beautifully tanned, and her brown hair flowed straight down her back with blonde highlights from the sun. The way she moved across the tennis court was so graceful. And she was smart, too. She knew exactly where to aim the ball to catch her opponent off guard.

"Anyway, we were friends for a few months, and then we became more. My mom caught us kissing one day in my bedroom. We fought, my parents prayed about it, things were tense for a while, and eventually they kicked me out of the house. This was a few years before manflu hit, and I haven't spoken to them since. I don't even know if they're still alive. I assume my dad passed away, but I don't know for sure. I have a younger sister who seemed to be heading down the same religious path they were on. I tried to reach out a couple of times, and she never responded."

Patty walked over to Gena and put her arm around her. Gena sighed.

The mood in the room shifted. The early start to the day, the move, and the intense cleaning suddenly caught up with Morgan. She could see Patty and Gena fading, too. Nate alone seemed well-rested and refreshed after his nap and meal. Passing MJ to Morgan, he took his plate to the sink and washed the dishes. Gavin, Gena, and Patty drifted off to other parts of the house.

Morgan thought to bring some food into the bedroom for Jonas and check on him. When she got there, he was sleeping. The move to Gavin's house seemed to have consumed every last drop of his energy. Morgan tried to wake him up to eat, but he shook his head and kept his eyes closed. She felt his cheek, and it was damp with sweat again—he must have been struggling to breathe. Worry overcame her. What if bringing him here worsened his illness and even hastened his death? Would she be responsible for ending his life?

CHAPTER 54

. . .

Despite her worry about Jonas's health, Morgan slept deeply that night with MJ tucked beside her and Jonas on the other side of the bed. She still worried about rolling over on top of the infant, but she was too tired to come up with a better spot for him to sleep in. She must have woken up briefly to breastfeed, but she had no memory of it, and MJ must have fallen back to sleep right away, too. Nate had slept in his own room next door.

Morgan woke up with the morning light, immediately turning to Jonas to check on him. She found him cold and still in the bed. *Oh no, it couldn't be true!* Had he died sometime during the night? She had known Jonas was gravely ill, but she had thought he still had time remaining. She hadn't said goodbye nor told him how much she loved him and how grateful she was to have had him in her life.

It couldn't be possible that never again would she be able to kiss him, tell him about her day, watch him smile at the baby, read a book of poetry together, or any other of a million ordinary things. Was their life as a family really over? She felt herself crumble deep inside. She made herself stand and walk over to Jonas's side of the bed to check his vital signs. If there were any to check.

Holding her breath, she squatted down and watched his chest closely to see if she could detect any movement, but there was none. Desperately, she placed a hand above his still-open mouth, but she felt no breath. She looked up and caught sight of the three of them in the garish overhead mirror, forming a tragic tableau.

Her mind refused to grasp the shocking reality of his death. Understanding creeping in, she collapsed to the floor. Her crying awakened Nate in the adjoining bedroom. He hurried into Morgan's room. The baby soon joined in with his own gasping wails. Nate picked up MJ and went over to where Morgan knelt next to Jonas, holding his face in her hands.

"No, Jonas, no. Don't go. Come back to me," she moaned. "I love you, Jonas. Don't leave me. Please. Please, Jonas." Tears streamed down her face, her devastation apparent.

Nate bent down to check on Jonas. Morgan followed his gaze to Jonas's face, which was white. His eyes looked vacant. Nate shifted the baby to one arm and reached down with the other. He brushed his fingers against Jonas's cheek. He caught Morgan's eye. "Morgan, he's gone."

She looked at him as if she didn't even know who he was, causing Nate to visibly shiver. In that moment, all she cared about was Jonas.

Gena, Patty, and Gavin entered the room, Gena confidently striding toward Morgan and the other two tiptoeing cautiously behind her.

"Oh, Morgan!" said Gena, wrapping her in her arms, her brown curls covering Morgan's face and creating a private space for them.

Morgan remained only peripherally aware of the other people in the room.

"Is he dead?" Gavin asked awkwardly.

"No, he's about to tap dance. Jeez!" said Patty in an angry whisper.

Nate said, "Jonas passed away during the night. Let's give Morgan some space."

He walked toward the door, holding the baby as he shooed Gavin and Patty out of the room, exiting behind them. Morgan felt vaguely grateful that he was taking charge and preventing the baby from seeing her so upset. She allowed herself to collapse into Gena's body and sob until there were no tears left.

"He was such a good man, Gena," Morgan said once she calmed down a little, her voice still shaking with emotion.

"I know, sweetie. He was," Gena soothed.

"He helped so many people with his support group. He never complained about being sick. He was always there for me." Morgan struggled to get the words out, another round of tears starting when she finished speaking.

"It's going to be okay, Morgan." Gena patted her on the back.

"I don't think anything will ever be okay," Morgan whispered as she sobbed.

"I'll be right back, Morgan." Gena promised. "Let me get you something."

CHAPTER 55

...

Morgan woke up totally disoriented in a blue and tan colored room. Suddenly, reality came rushing in, and she recalled waking up next to Jonas and finding him dead. The baby! Where was the baby? She remembered Nate holding him. And Gena comforting her, giving her medication, and putting her to bed in another room so she wouldn't have to lie down next to Jonas's body.

Her mouth felt dry. The room was flooded with light. And her breasts were full of milk and beginning to leak. She must have slept for hours. She stumbled out of the room, intending to return to her bedroom to change clothes, but she didn't know if Jonas's corpse remained in there.

Gena appeared out of nowhere. "How are you feeling now, Morgan?"

"I've been better, but sleeping helped. Thank you, Gena." Morgan finger-combed her wild hair into a ponytail. "Where's Mark Jing? I have to feed him."

"He's with Nate in the living room. We gave him a bottle, but he'll probably want to nurse again soon."

"Oh, you gave him a bottle ..." Morgan put her hand to her mouth. He had never had a bottle. Had he taken it easily? Had he missed her? Did he have any awareness that Jonas was gone?

"It's okay, Morgan. It's just one bottle. He'll be fine."

Morgan sighed. "You're right, but I thought I'd be there the first time he had a bottle." Tears ran down her pale cheeks.

Gena led Morgan back to the bed and held her while she cried.

"What are we going to do about Jonas?" Morgan asked after she regained her composure.

"We're going to bury him tonight in the backyard. We talked about it while you were sleeping. As soon as it gets dark, we'll start digging a grave for him. We can't do it now, because the neighbors might get suspicious."

"That's so soon. I can't believe everything's happening so fast."

"I know, Morgan. I wish things could be different. We can't risk any other type of funeral right now."

"Gena, this reminds me of when my father and brother died and my mother and I had to arrange their funerals in a hurry. She was so upset because we couldn't pick the date when the ceremonies would be held. It was at the peak of the pandemic, and we were lucky to have funerals at all. Yet again, this feels so rushed."

"That's a Chinese tradition, right? Finding auspicious dates for events?"

Morgan nodded.

"Maybe there are some other traditions we can follow for Jonas."

"Jonas wasn't Chinese. I don't know much about his family's funeral traditions, because they weren't close. All I can do is what I know. For example, there is a Chinese tradition in which we burn items our loved one might need in the afterworld. Usually, we burn fake paper money and sometimes miniature items like houses and cars or anything associated with the person's interests."

"Let's do that! What can we burn that would be special for him?" Gena asked.

"Jonas loved poetry. I would like to do a reading and then burn a copy of the poem to send it off with him. I think he would've liked that."

"That's a lovely idea. Why don't you ask Patty to suggest some appropriate poems?"

"Yes, I'll do that now. Thank you, Gena."

CHAPTER 56

...

Morgan watched through the window. She held MJ as Nate, Gavin, Gena, and Patty spent the evening digging with shovels Gavin had in a shed in his backyard. After a while, MJ became fussy. Morgan put him to bed in a blanket-lined dresser drawer Nate had repurposed into a bassinet while she had slept earlier.

Around midnight, Patty wrapped Jonas's body in a sheet from the bed. Gavin and Nate carried his remains to the makeshift grave. Gena stayed at Morgan's side as the body was lowered into the ground. Everyone stood outside together in a small circle for the impromptu service.

A chilling wind blew off the Bay and cut right through the mourners. The dark sky was studded with just a few distant stars. Despite no neighbors close enough to see them, they knew they had to make it quick. Morgan wanted to read the piece Patty had suggested. It was beautiful and true to Jonas. She cleared her throat as she opened the book of poetry Patty had lent her. Gena switched on a small flashlight and pointed it at the page. Morgan read the entire poem in a clear voice.

DEATH IS NOTHING, NOTHING AT ALL
by
Canon Henry Scott-Holland

Death is nothing at all.
It does not count.
I have only slipped away into the next room.
Nothing has happened.

Everything remains exactly as it was.
I am I, and you are you,
and the old life that we lived so fondly together is
      untouched, unchanged.
Whatever we were to each other, that we are still.

Call me by the old familiar name.
Speak of me in the easy way which you always used.
Put no difference into your tone.
Wear no forced air of solemnity or sorrow.

Laugh as we always laughed at the little jokes that we
      enjoyed together.
Play, smile, think of me, pray for me.
Let my name be ever the household word that it always
      was.
Let it be spoken without an effort, without the ghost of
      a shadow upon it.

Life means all that it ever meant.
It is the same as it ever was.
There is absolute and unbroken continuity.
What is this death but a negligible accident?

Why should I be out of mind because I am out of sight?

I am but waiting for you, for an interval,
somewhere very near,
just round the corner.

All is well.
Nothing is hurt; nothing is lost.
One brief moment and all will be as it was before.
How we shall laugh at the trouble of parting when we
        meet again!

Morgan finished reading and fought a sob. Gena put an arm around her and led her back into the house. Nate, Gavin, and Patty waited until they were out of sight to begin shoveling dirt over Jonas's body.

Gena guided Morgan to a stool in the kitchen and put on water to boil for tea. "This will warm us up," she said.

Soon everyone drifted into the kitchen. Gena poured the mugs of aromatic tea and handed them around.

"I'm sorry for your loss, Morgan," said Gavin.

"He was a special person," said Nate. "I could see that in the brief time I knew him."

"The poem you selected was beautiful, Morgan. So apt," said Patty.

"You had something amazing with him," said Gena. "But that bond doesn't disappear because Jonas is gone. It lives on in you."

Morgan cried a little. "Thank you, everyone. You're all so kind." She looked around at their faces, which were concerned, caring, and full of love for her. Maybe this was what a family was really about, not a man, a woman, and a child.

She took a copy of the poem to the stove and put a flame to it. Everyone bowed their heads as the piece of paper burned to ash and then disappeared.

CHAPTER 57

...

The next day around lunchtime the new housemates convened once again. Gavin and Nate had finished up a game of pool. From the way Gavin strutted into the kitchen, Morgan could tell he had handily beaten Nate. Poor Nate had probably never played pool in his life. Morgan was glad the two men seemed to be getting along. She supposed Gavin was thrilled to have another man around to talk to about his exploits, and she felt certain Nate was excited to catch a glimpse into his potential future—once a vaccine was ready.

Morgan and Gena sat on the kitchen stools, drinking tea and talking. Morgan's eyes and body suffered the ravages of her grief. Her loss had not been unexpected, and she felt that she could continue to function by putting one foot in front of the other until the blanket of sadness engulfing her finally lifted. The baby lay on his mat on the floor, staring at his hands as if they were the most fascinating television program.

People seemed to be getting hungry, because one after another, everyone wandered into the kitchen and poked around. Nate rummaged in a cabinet. Gavin examined the pantry. Patty opened the fridge and stared in. Morgan and Gena immediately shouted, "Close the fridge!"

"What? I'm trying to figure out what we can eat!"

"The vaccine samples are in there. They have to be as temperature-controlled as possible," Morgan explained.

Patty plopped onto a kitchen stool, chastened.

"Why don't you have a kitchenbot, Gavin?" asked Gena.

"I have one, but it's in the shop. Bad timing, huh? And the only thing I know how to cook is breakfast cereal."

"I can make spaghetti for everyone," said Nate, pulling pasta and sauce out of some hidden spot.

"Much appreciated, my friend," said Gavin. "So, no rush or anything, and I love having you all here, but can anyone fill me in on what's going on and what the timeline looks like?"

"And what are those vaccine samples?" asked Nate.

"Gena had some manflu vaccine samples hidden when the lab burned," said Morgan.

"For monkeys or people?" asked Nate, sounding cautiously hopeful.

"Human vaccine samples," said Gena.

Nate's eyes widened.

"Gena, do you think we have the ability to continue the research we were working on to test for human safety?" asked Morgan.

"We don't have enough samples saved for that. Nor the time. We need to test for efficacy right away. The government's going to track us down soon, and it'll all be for naught unless we can prove we have a vaccine that works." Gena set aside her tea, pacing the kitchen while she spoke.

"How do you prove the vaccine works?" asked Gavin.

Morgan and Gena looked at Nate.

Nate stood frozen at the stove, where he had begun setting up pots and pans, and sported a deer-in-headlights look on his young face.

"We could give Nate a dose, wait a week, and test to see if there are any negative reactions and if antibodies develop. It would be a sample size of one, but it's better than nothing," said Morgan.

"You want to test the vaccine on me?" Nate said, his voice rising in shock. He walked over to the sink with the large pot and turned on the water to fill it.

"We talked about this before, Nate, and you seemed to be fine with it at the time," said Morgan, surprised by his reaction.

"I didn't mean I wanted to be the first human to ever test this vaccine! I was willing to help out but after safety was already established."

"We have conclusively established safety in monkeys," said Morgan in a reassuring tone.

"I'm not a monkey, and I don't want to be your guinea pig, either!" Nate dropped the pot he was filling with water with a loud clang. Water splashed all over the kitchen. Patty went in search of a towel. Nate stomped off into a bedroom and slammed the door behind him.

MJ started to cry at the noise. Morgan picked him up off of his mat and soothed him.

"What was that about?" asked Gavin.

"I shouldn't have done that," said Morgan, looking down, tears in her eyes, at the baby in her arms. "I meant to talk to him about it privately, but I didn't get a chance. I really put my foot in my mouth."

"Are you going to go talk to him?" asked Gavin.

"I'll let him cool off a bit," said Morgan, shifting the baby from one arm to the other.

"Well, what about lunch?" asked Gavin as Patty mopped up the spilled water.

"Can't you do it yourself? No? Well, I'm happy to cook—it's not like I have anything else to do," said Morgan, making to toss the baby to Gavin.

"Calm down, Morgan. Patty and I will make lunch," said Gena. "I hope Nate comes around soon. It would be good to know if this vaccine works or not."

CHAPTER 58

...

Later that day, Morgan was playing with the baby on the floor of the living room when Nate asked if they could talk privately. She scooped up MJ from his spot on his playmat and followed Nate to the surf room. She hoped he had changed his mind about the vaccine. If not, she didn't know what they would do.

Morgan sat on the bed with the baby on her lap. Nate settled in beside her, his body tilted in her direction. "I'm sorry I stormed off like that, I was surprised. Can you tell me more about the vaccine?" he asked.

"It's okay, Nate. I understand," said Morgan. "I should've talked to you about it privately, instead of springing it on you in front of everyone. We've done extensive testing with primates, both for safety and for efficacy, and we're fairly confident it will be safe and effective for humans, too. We would inject you with the vaccine, wait a week, and check your immunity level like when I did antibody testing with you earlier. If it works, you'd be able to live a normal life."

"What if the vaccine doesn't work? Could I get sick?"

"With the way the vaccine is formulated, it's very unlikely that you'd get sick. It's an inactivated vaccine. If it doesn't work, nothing will happen. It'll be a very difficult week for you emotionally, but we'll all be here for you." She looked into Nate's worried eyes.

"What about Mark Jing? Would it be safe to give him the vaccine?"

Morgan glanced away. "It's a difficult situation. We have no way to know how safe the vaccine is for babies. He would be more at risk for an adverse reaction of some sort. But every day without the vaccine, he's at heightened risk for manflu. We also might be discovered by the authorities, and I don't know what we would do."

"Does it help the baby if I get the vaccine first?"

"Well, yes, that would be some indicator of whether the vaccine is safe for humans." Morgan twisted the wedding ring that she still wore on her left hand as she looked at Nate.

"All right, in that case, I'll do it. I owe it to him." He sat up straighter, squaring his shoulders.

"Are you sure, Nate?" She could barely get the words out, her respiration quickening.

"Yes, I want to do it."

"That's wonderful. I'm so excited. I'm going to go talk to Gena, and we'll get everything set up. We can do it this evening if you're ready." She couldn't believe this was happening. She held on tight to the baby, reminding herself to stay calm for his sake.

"Let's do it," he said firmly.

She leaned close and pressed a chaste kiss to Nate's cheek. He blushed and hid behind his mop of curls. Standing, she returned to the living room to let the others know, Nate following close behind.

CHAPTER 59

...

The unlikely housemates gathered in the living room that evening, minus the baby, who had been put to bed. Gavin had ordered pizza, which awaited them on the coffee table.

When they were ready, Nate took a seat on one of the stools. Gena and Morgan stood nearby, gloved and masked. Morgan soaked a sterile cotton ball in rubbing alcohol and sanitized the injection site on Nate's arm. Gena held the syringe. Morgan couldn't believe that the moment she had been waiting so long for was finally here. They were about to test this vaccine she had helped to develop on a human. If it worked, it would change the world for her son and for humankind.

"Do you want to do the honors, Morgan?"

"No. Please go ahead. My hands are shaking."

Before anyone could contemplate further, Gena jabbed Nate in the arm with the prepared needle. Nate let out a puff of air—he had been holding his breath. A drop of blood appeared. Gena wiped it away and covered the spot with a small, round flesh-colored Band-Aid. Nate rubbed his arm for a second, slid off the stool and headed to the coffee table in the living room. He grabbed a slice of pepperoni pizza and shoved the tip in his mouth, not bothering with a plate. After he inhaled one piece, he grabbed another to eat more slowly and dropped down onto the couch next to Gavin.

Morgan and Gena exchanged a long, complicated look before they started to clean up the makeshift vaccine station. Morgan already felt her stomach churning. She would not be adding pizza to the mix.

When everything was put away, Morgan and Gena made their way to the living room. Pizza slices were passed around on paper plates. Gena sat on the couch next to Patty to eat. Morgan remained standing and paced around the enormous living room. Everyone else followed her with their eyes.

"Are you going to do this for a whole week, Morgan?" asked Gena around a mouthful of pizza.

Nate sneezed, and all eyes whipped in his direction. He wiped his nose on his sleeve, causing Morgan to grimace.

"If anyone should be nervous, it's Nate," said Gavin unhelpfully, patting his friend on the back.

"At this moment, he is both immune and not immune," said Patty, "like Schrödinger's Cat is both alive and not alive." Morgan was not in the mood for one of Patty's philosophy lessons right now. Apparently, neither was Gena.

Patty started to explain further when Gena groaned, cutting her off. "Look, there's nothing we can do right now. Let's try to forget about it for the next week. Let's talk about something else, anything else!"

"All right, look at the lovely blanket I'm knitting for the baby," said Patty, "I can explain the type of stitching I used here . . ." She gestured to the knitting project that was next to her on the couch.

Everyone politely listened to Patty for a few minutes until Gavin said, "Please, let's talk about something else." Morgan was relieved he had said something, because she couldn't take it much longer and hadn't wanted to be rude.

"So, Nate," said Gena, "if the vaccine works, what are your plans?"

Gavin leaned forward. Everyone grew still, waiting for the response.

Nate took a deep breath. "I've thought about this a lot—what I'd do if I were free. I want to see the world! There are so many places I want to travel to. Seeing things on a computer screen isn't the same. I want to feel the sun on my skin, sand on my feet. Crane my neck up to look at tall buildings. And I want to go to concerts so I can hear live music while I watch the musicians' faces. I want to have real experiences."

Morgan sighed, recalling trips she had taken and concerts she had attended in her twenties, before the world had gone so horribly wrong. She thought back to her honeymoon in Paris with Jonas and how they tilted back their heads to see the top of the Eiffel Tower from the ground, squeezing each other's hands with delight. And a few years before that, the time they had attended an Ed Sheeran concert together. When "Shape of You" started, the crowd went wild, and Jonas turned to her and kissed her. They pulled apart, and he looked straight into her eyes and said, "I love you," for the first time. She would never forget that moment. Of course, Nate wanted his own moments, too.

Gavin broke the silence. "I know what you mean by *experiences*, my friend!" He winked. "No need to travel the world to get some of that. Finest women right here in the Bay Area."

Nate's pale cheeks turned pink. He opened and closed his mouth several times but didn't find the words he sought.

Patty stepped in. "You're a young man, Nate. It's important for your development to understand other cultures and societies. Absolutely, you should go see the world. Soak up all you can."

Morgan was about to speak but stopped when she heard the baby crying—the baby Nate would be leaving behind if he decided to explore the world like a teenager doing a study abroad program. Nate was not a teenager—he was an adult and a father. She went into the bordello-like bedroom and picked up her baby from his drawer/bassinet. She brought MJ to the bed and caught sight of their reflection in the ridiculous overhead mirror. Maybe, just maybe, this vaccine would work on Nate. Then she could give MJ a dose to protect him. Maybe he would be able to live a normal life.

CHAPTER 60

...

Morgan woke up ready to face day one of waiting for the test results. When she went to the kitchen to get her morning coffee, she saw Gena running up and down the main flight of stairs. Morgan figured Gena was trying to get a workout in—she knew Gena got anxious and worried about becoming deconditioned if she didn't exercise every day.

She also spotted Patty sitting in a corner of the couch, immobile save for her fingers furiously scribbling in a small notebook embossed with her initials. She looked so serious; Morgan didn't dare ask what she was working on.

As she poured her coffee, she thought about Nate. She was concerned about his emotional state. The waiting must be agonizing for him. He soon appeared and prepared a bowl of cereal. When she greeted him, he barely grunted a reply before taking his breakfast back to his room.

Morgan went through her morning routine with baby MJ, nursing him, burping him, changing his diaper and tiny outfit, and playing with him on the playmat. He seemed to grow tired of the hanging stuffed animals and miniature crinkly mirrors and began to fuss, so Morgan picked him up and bounced him around the house. She guessed he was picking up on her sadness and on everyone's anxiety as they awaited the results of the vaccine. Morgan still worried about anyone, apart from Nate, getting too close to the baby due to the possibility of infecting him. She was starting to feel desperate for a break, and she didn't feel she could barge in on Nate and ask him.

As the sun rose and the light grew brighter in the house and MJ continued to cry, Gavin emerged from his private office, where he had been ensconced for the whole morning. Morgan didn't want to think about the type of work in which he was engaged. She supposed *someone* had to keep the lights on. Gavin entered the kitchen, poured himself some coffee, took a look at the upset baby, and walked very quickly back upstairs.

Morgan was trying to make herself some lunch while soothing MJ as Gena approached. "Morgan, you must be exhausted. Please let me do something to help. We've been here for almost a week, and I'm not sick. Why don't you let me take the baby? I'd love to hold him." Morgan felt her body sag with relief. Had it been that long? She had lost all concept of time. She supposed it was safe to let Gena help.

Gena gently pulled Mark Jing out of Morgan's arms and sang him a Madonna song very out of key. "Like a virgin. Touched for the very first time. Like a viiiirgin. When your heart beats next to mine." Gosh, Gena was a terrible singer.

"Okay, Gena, you can take him, but you have to promise me you'll stop singing. I don't want you to torture the poor child!" said Morgan, laughing for the first time in days. "Also, couldn't you think of anything more appropriate for a baby? 'Wheels on the bus'? 'Twinkle Twinkle'? Literally anything not by Madonna?"

"All right, all right, I got the message. No more Madonna. Little MJ and I are going to sing some Michael Jackson instead. Look—

same initials! 'You Know I'm Bad, I'm Bad, You Know It.'" Gena danced around the kitchen with the tiny baby, who stared at her without showing any reaction. He was still too little to even laugh. At least Gena enjoyed herself. Morgan felt a sense of happiness and peace. Her best friend was finally able to bond with her son. This was what family felt like.

CHAPTER 61

...

On day two of waiting for test results, Gavin organized an all-day pool tournament to pass the time. The baby hung out with them as they played, getting passed around to whomever had free hands. Morgan had given up worrying about germs and welcomed the help. Between her grief over Jonas's death and her anxiety about the vaccine, on top of caring for a baby who nursed around the clock, she felt like a car on the verge of running out of electricity.

Unsurprisingly since she excelled at every sport she ever tried, Gena was an amazing pool player and kicked Gavin and everyone else's butts. Pool must have worn everyone out, because people drifted off to bed early.

Morgan was sound asleep when Nate entered her room.

"Nate, what's going on?" Morgan asked.

"Sorry to wake you, Morgan. I was getting a glass of water from the kitchen, and I saw a woman follow Gavin up to his room. We should make sure it's not the one who got caught spying or anyone else up to no good."

Morgan rubbed the sleep from her eyes and got out of bed, checking to make sure the baby was asleep in his drawer. She followed Nate into the hallway, and he led the way upstairs to Gavin's master suite. The door was open a crack, and Morgan did not hesitate before she peeked inside the room.

A red dress and a pair of matching stilettos lay on the floor where they had apparently been flung haphazardly. The bed was occupied by a dead ringer for Marilyn Monroe, who was giggling and moaning with Gavin's face between her legs. Her hands mussed his mud-colored hair.

Nate, standing right behind Morgan, pushed the door a bit farther open. Morgan was torn. She was shocked and fascinated and even a bit turned on by the scene in front of her, but she also felt guilty about invading Gavin's privacy. However, she felt indignant that he would put everyone at risk by bringing a stranger into the house. She didn't know what to do. She looked back at Nate and saw that his mouth was hanging open and his eyes were about to pop out of his head.

Morgan turned back to the bedroom. The couple, in a world of their own pleasure, didn't notice Nate and Morgan at all. After a few moments, Gavin sat up and plunged his (Morgan couldn't help but notice) *substantial* sex into the woman, who gasped and gripped his shoulders with her hands and wrapped her legs around his waist. He moved in and out for a few minutes, grunting audibly all the while, suddenly disengaged from her, plucked a plastic cup from the nightstand, and filled it with his seed.

Gavin picked up his phone from the nightstand table and pushed a few buttons. Morgan heard the rumbling of a garage door in the distance. Gavin popped a plastic cover on the cup and took it over to the balcony at the back of his bedroom. Morgan could no longer see what was happening but surmised that Gavin's self-driving Maserati was stopping near the balcony so he could drop his DNA through the sunroof and send it off to the sperm bank for a fat check. The woman, still nude, one leg crossed over the other, scrolled through her phone. Adorned with fire-engine-red toenails, her shapely foot tapped against the bed in time to her rapid thumb-typing.

Morgan and Nate backed out of Gavin's doorway and speed-walked silently to Nate's room before anyone noticed them. Morgan closed the door behind them.

"Oh, my goodness, Nate! I can't believe Gavin would do that. He exposed us all to her germs."

"Did you recognize her, Morgan?" asked Nate, slightly out of breath.

"No, she wasn't one of the women who's been in the lab."

"Should we say something to him?"

"You better believe I'm going to say something to him! As soon as that woman leaves, he's going to get a piece of my mind." She paced around the room, fuming like a bull about to charge a matador. After a little while, she heard footsteps coming down the hall and the front door opening and closing. Morgan slipped out of Nate's room and stood in the hallway, ready to pounce.

"Gavin," she said as he walked by, whistling obliviously.

"Ack! Holy shit, Morgan, you scared the hell out of me." Gavin grabbed at his chest as if afraid of an impending heart attack.

"What the hell are you doing, Gavin?" asked Morgan, whisper-yelling. Nate came out of his room and stood in the doorway with his arms folded across his chest.

Gavin looked from Morgan to Nate and back again. He seemed to be trying to determine what they knew.

"We saw her, Gavin," said Morgan. "How dare you expose us all to someone else's germs? We don't know what she's carrying. Outside germs could kill baby MJ." Morgan had stopped yelling and sounded sad. "And we have to think about Nate, too."

Nate nodded but didn't say anything. Morgan imagined it would be hard for him to confront Gavin, someone he admired.

Gavin looked downcast and apologetic. "I'm sorry, Morgan, Nate," he said, looking at each of them. "I'm not used to worrying about anyone but myself. I wanted to invite a friend over, and I didn't think through the consequences. I let the wrong brain guide my choices. It was wrong. I'm really sorry."

Morgan looked slightly mollified, but she wasn't ready to forgive him. "Gavin, you really don't show the best judgment when it comes to these matters," said Morgan. "Remember your friend Stacey? Her real name is Mikayla Bascomb, and I'm fairly certain she was involved in the break-in at the lab. I found an invoice made out to her for work done on that date."

"Really? Oh, wow. I guess you were right about Stacey. I'm so sorry, I was sure she was innocent."

"She's also the niece of Ximena Álvarez. She's why we believe the president is involved in stopping the development of the vaccine."

"Why didn't you tell me this before?"

"With Jonas dying, taking care of the baby, and giving Nate the vaccine, I didn't get the chance yet."

"What can I do to make it up to you?" asked Gavin.

"Well, you can start by sanitizing everything," said Morgan.

Gavin's eyes opened wide in horror. He must have been recalling the extensive cleaning that had taken place the day everyone moved in. He opened his mouth, perhaps to complain, but soon closed it. "Yes, absolutely. I'll do that first thing in the morning," he said.

Morgan crossed her arms over her chest and stared at him. She remembered when she had done something wrong as a teenager. Her mom never yelled at her but simply looked disappointed. Somehow, that was always a thousand times worse. Morgan channeled her mom and made her most disappointed face, lips curved down as far as possible.

Gavin slowly seemed to get a clue. A light went on in his eyes. "Or right now. Yes, I can clean up right now. That's not a problem," he said.

Morgan smiled slightly. "Thanks, Gavin. I really appreciate it, and I want to thank you again for everything you've done. I know it's not easy having us here and disrupting your life."

"You know I care a lot about you guys and baby MJ! I couldn't forgive myself if anything happened to you," said Gavin. He leaned forward as if to hug Morgan, but she blocked him with a hand out in front of her. He still had germs on him from the stranger, and Morgan didn't want him anywhere near her.

Gavin took a step back and made an air high five gesture. It wasn't the same as a hug, but it was something. Morgan and Nate gave him air high fives, too.

Morgan was amazed at how easily she was able to confront Gavin and stand up for what she needed to keep her family safe. She felt that she had matured by decades over the last few weeks—having a baby and losing a husband in such rapid succession had deeply changed her. Months or even weeks ago, a confrontation like this would have left her shaking and crying. Now, it was just another task that needed to be done.

Morgan and Nate went back to their own beds to pass another night, waiting for the moment when Nate could finally take the antibody test. As Morgan slipped into bed, she realized that he hadn't had any adverse reactions yet, which was at least one good sign.

CHAPTER 62

. . .

The phone rang, jarring Morgan awake. It was her neighbor, Sarah. Morgan had been in the midst of the most wonderful dream. She and Jonas were at a beach, relaxing on a blanket with little MJ, now a toddler, between them, building a beautiful sandcastle big enough for them and all their friends to live in.

"Hi, Sarah," she said groggily when she picked up. Something unusual must have happened for Sarah to call so early in the morning. Morgan hadn't been in touch with Sarah at all since packing up and leaving her house. The last time she had talked to her had been a quick call to let her know that MJ had been born and that they were both healthy. A few days later, Morgan had found a tuna casserole and a bouquet of flowers on her porch with a lovely note from Sarah. She wondered if her neighbor had noticed she had been gone.

"Hi, Morgan. Sorry to call you so early, but there are a lot of women wearing all black, swarming around your house right now. I thought you would want to know. They look like they're military or police." *Oh no.* Just what she needed. They were probably from the government. It was only a matter of time before they figured out where she was.

"Thanks for calling, Sarah. I appreciate it." Morgan missed Sarah. She had always valued their friendship. There was something special about having a good friend who lived nearby, someone you could stop by to see without making elaborate plans. She wished they had time for a nice, long chat right now, but Morgan knew that was not possible.

"I haven't seen you around lately. Where are you?" Sarah asked. Morgan definitely didn't want Sarah or anyone else to know her location. She wondered about the government's ability to track her by her phone activity. She had better shut this down.

"I can't talk about it, Sarah," Morgan said quickly. "In fact, I should get off the phone."

"All right, take care of yourself, Morgan," said Sarah, a question mark in her voice.

Morgan hung up without saying goodbye. She realized that she hadn't told Sarah anything about what had been happening in her life, not even that Jonas had passed away. Morgan wanted so much to share so they could cry together. Sarah would understand how she was feeling. Morgan wondered briefly if Robert's health was failing, too. She promised herself that she would call Sarah as soon as it was safe to do so.

The sound of Gena doing her stair exercises interrupted her thoughts. As long as she was up, Morgan might as well tell her what was happening. She slipped out of her room and walked through the living room.

"Gena, stop doing the stairs for a minute," said Morgan.

Gena stopped at the bottom of the stairs, bouncing from one foot to another and staring at her watch. She was monitoring her heart rate on her fitness device, which she had declined to update with a newer model that could produce snazzy holograms, because she was attached to the old one. "What?" she asked.

"I got a call from Sarah, my neighbor. There are government people poking around my house."

"Shit," said Gena. "Well, it was only a matter of time." She adjusted her ponytail, sweeping sweaty curls out of her face.

"What do you think we should do?" Morgan wished Gena would stop moving around so much. It was distracting.

"We could test Nate now and see if we pick up any antibodies."

"It's only been a few days. It's too early. It's unlikely that anything will show up."

"It doesn't hurt to try. It would be amazing if we could show results," said Gena, a gleam in her eyes.

"I don't know if Nate would be up for it." Morgan chewed her lip.

"It won't hurt to ask him."

"I guess you're right. We might as well—it's not like we have anything else to do," said Morgan. She wrapped her arms around herself as she felt goosebumps prickle her skin. "I'll get everything set up for when Nate wakes up."

CHAPTER 63

...

When Nate came into the kitchen for breakfast, Morgan and Gena already had everything they needed to conduct the antibody test laid out. Gavin and Patty were hanging out and entertaining baby MJ. Gavin ran through a surprisingly large repertoire of ridiculous faces. Patty had fashioned a sock puppet and was putting on an elaborate play, probably more to amuse herself than the baby, who seemed only mildly attentive.

"What's going on?" asked Nate as he poured himself a bowl of cereal, added milk, and sat on a stool.

"My neighbor called," said Morgan. "There are people at my house looking for us. Gena and I thought it would be a good idea to test now, even though it's early, to see if the vaccine worked. We don't know how long we have until they find us."

Gena nodded. "Once they find out where we are, all bets are off."

"Do you mind giving it a try now, Nate?" asked Morgan hopefully. "Please be aware that it's still very early and we might not find anything yet."

"Sure, go ahead. It would be amazing if it'd already worked. Might as well see," said Nate in between slurps of cereal. Morgan and Gena paced around the kitchen, waiting for Nate to finish his breakfast.

Gavin held the baby propped up so he could see, one arm across his tiny chest. MJ didn't look very comfortable, but neither was he crying. Gavin bounced up and down, either from excitement or to keep the baby happy. Patty went over and sat on the couch, picking up her journal and getting ready to take notes. She had been documenting their experience.

Nate finally finished eating, placed his bowl in the sink, and sat back down on the stool. Gena put on gloves and got a needle ready. She had Nate make a fist and plunged the needle into the bulging vein in his arm. She drew the sample, filling a test tube with his blood and then placed a Band-Aid on Nate's arm.

Gena took a white test strip marked with a single blue line, carefully lowered it into the test tube, and set a timer for three minutes. Morgan took one of Nate's hands in her own. It felt cold and sweaty, but Morgan still noticed the long, elegant fingers and remembered how they had touched her so intimately. The minutes dragged on. Gena paced around the living room, still wearing gloves. All was silent except for the sound of Patty's pen scratching against the paper. Morgan stroked her baby's head. Gavin couldn't even come up with a wisecrack to lighten the mood.

What seemed like weeks later, the timer dinged. Everyone rushed over to the kitchen island, even Patty. Gena picked up a pair of tweezers from among the sterilized supplies and used them to pluck the test strip out of the vial. There were now two blue lines on the white test strip, one very faint.

All heads swiveled toward Morgan.

"Oh." She sighed, then covered her mouth with her hand.

"What does it mean?" asked Nate.

"It's inconclusive," said Gena. "You seem to have some

antibodies, but not enough to guarantee that you're immune to the virus. We need to wait another few days or a week and repeat the test. Then we'll probably have a better idea."

"Wait a week?" asked Nate. "And then you'll *probably* have a better idea! I don't think so."

"Please be patient, Nate. It would have been quick for antibodies to form. It was wishful thinking that we'd have a result by now. It's good news that there are some antibodies developing. I feel pretty confident that, by next week, you'll be fully immune," said Morgan, patting Nate's arm.

Nate wrenched his arm free, got up and walked into the beach bedroom, closing the door behind him.

"I think this result is super exciting. The vaccine's working. We just don't totally know for sure yet." Gena drew Morgan aside to a corner of the room where they could speak more privately.

"I know, but I don't think Nate can handle it. He wants a yes or no so he can move on with his life. The uncertainty is so painful," said Morgan. "It's understandable."

"Morgan, I think we should vaccinate the baby. It's only a matter of time before someone from the government figures out where we are, and what'll we do then? Even if they don't find us, we can't stay here forever, we're all going to go crazy. We have to go back to our lives at some point. Give the baby the vaccine—it'll probably work— and we can go public with it."

"Gena, I can't use my baby as a guinea pig. We don't know if the vaccine is safe." Morgan bit her lip. Her chest tightened, and she felt like she wasn't getting enough air in her lungs.

"Nate had no adverse reaction yet, and that's the best evidence we have right now."

"'Yet' is not good enough! I have to protect my child. What if something happens to him? I've already lost my parents, my brother, and my husband. This child is all I have left. I can't risk his life."

"Morgan, all of our lives are at risk right now. The government could find us at any moment, and who knows how far they'll go to destroy this vaccine? If they put us in jail, or worse, what's going to happen to Mark Jing? Even a policewoman coming in here would put him at a huge risk. We've got to give him the vaccine now."

"I need time to think about it." Morgan looked over at her baby, Gavin and Patty still playing sweetly with him. She felt the threat of tears. Her whole heart lived in that one tiny body. She couldn't fathom anyone or anything hurting him.

"You don't have time! Remember that the body may require more than a week to produce sufficient antibodies, especially for a baby. How long do you think it will take before they find us? One week? Two? Think about this place being stormed by government agents. Really think about it. Imagine them carrying manflu germs and potentially infecting MJ."

"I wish we had a conclusive result on Nate now. That would make everything easier." Morgan looked at the floor.

"Well, we don't."

"I'm not ready, Gena."

"I've said what I had to say. It's up to you, Morgan. You're his mother." She shook her head.

"Well, we'll test Nate again in a few days. There's nothing else we can do right now."

CHAPTER 64

...

Gena went upstairs to her room. Morgan returned to the group in the kitchen.

"What do we do now?" asked Gavin, playing peekaboo with the baby, who was in Patty's arms.

"We wait until we can test Nate again," said Morgan calmly.

"And if we get the results we're hoping for?" asked Gavin.

"Once we have that data to release publicly, the government will lose its power," said Morgan. "They won't be able to 'put the genie back in the bottle.' And it would be very suspicious if anything happened to the scientists who successfully developed the first manflu vaccine. So we should be able to go back to our normal lives. At least, that's the plan."

She approached Patty and the baby. She reached out and gently poked one of his hands, which immediately closed over her finger in a tight baby fist.

"Can you imagine what will happen when this vaccine is out there?" said Patty, "It's going to change everything." She looked into MJ's eyes as she spoke.

"I've been waiting so long for this day to come," said Morgan, "And now I have even more reason. When Mark Jing gets this vaccine, he will be able to live a totally normal life. I'll be able to take him to playdates, daycare, school, the zoo! Imagine him on a swing at the park, splashing in a pool. He's going to love being outside. And he'll have friends." She swung his little fist around with her finger still trapped inside.

"Babies will be born. So many male babies. I guess I'll have some competition," said Gavin, "in about twenty years!" He laughed.

"There's still a chance that it won't work, right?" said Patty. "Maybe you shouldn't get your hopes up yet."

"It's going to work. I know it," said Morgan. "A few more days and we'll have proof."

"All right. What should we do while we're stuck here waiting?" asked Gavin. "Another pool tournament?" He pretended to shoot pool in the air, which Morgan thought made him look both extremely cute and a little dorky simultaneously.

"How about a Scrabble tournament?" suggested Patty.

"Watch out for her, she's a Scrabble wiz," said Morgan, lifting a finger in warning.

"Game on!" said Gavin, lifting up on the balls of his feet as if about to jump up and down with excitement.

Morgan's mood suddenly shifted as memories flooded in. "Jonas loved Scrabble," she said, sighing. She closed her eyes and brought her hands to her chest. For a moment, she was in another world, one that she'd shared with Jonas. It was a world of weekend afternoons spent drinking strong coffee, listening to the sound of Scrabble tiles clanking against each other in their velvet sack, and taking breaks in between rounds to read their favorite poems aloud to one another. She slowly opened her eyes and said, "I'm in. I want to play. Jonas would have wanted me to."

"Great, I'll set up the tournament," said Gavin. "You all better take today to study up on those two-letter and 'q' words. The games begin tomorrow morning."

CHAPTER 65

• • •

The next morning, Gavin, Morgan, Gena, and Patty gathered around the kitchen island. Gena cradled the baby while Morgan munched on a bagel. Patty and Gavin sipped coffee.

"Are you guys ready for the tourney?" asked Gavin. "Who's been studying? Quick—is 'qe' a word?"

"Not a word," said Patty. "Wait a minute, did anyone ask Nate if he wants to play?"

"I'll go check on him," said Morgan.

She returned a minute later. "He didn't answer the door."

Gena said, "Where else could he be?"

Morgan shook her head. She hadn't seen Nate leave his room. Patty shrugged. Gavin didn't say anything.

"This little guy and I are going to take a walk around the house and check," said Gena, hoisting MJ up. "We'll take the upstairs. Patty—how about you look around on this floor?"

Gena and Patty went off, leaving Morgan and Gavin in the kitchen. Morgan's chest tightened. *Where could he be?* Gavin chewed his lip, which did not help Morgan's nerves. She drummed her fingers against the kitchen counter. Patty soon came back to the kitchen, shaking her head. "I didn't find him," she said. Gena came downstairs with the baby. "He's not upstairs," she said.

"Has anyone seen him since yesterday morning?" asked Gena.

Gavin and Patty shook their heads. They all looked at Morgan.

"Mark Jing and I slept in the other room."

"Did you actually go into his room, Patty?" Gena asked.

"No, I just checked the rest of the floor."

"I'm going in," said Gavin. He strode toward the beach bedroom with Morgan and the rest of the crew following close behind.

"Hey Nate, open up, man!" said Gavin, knocking loudly. There was no response.

Gavin opened the door slowly and poked his head into the room. He threw the door open all the way. Nate was gone.

CHAPTER 66

...

"Where could he be?" asked Gavin, his voice raised. "Could he really have left the house?"

"He knows how dangerous that would be!" said Gena.

Morgan felt frozen in shock. She tried to think about where he could have gone, but her mind remained stuck on the image of the inconclusive antibody test result, and she couldn't think about anything else.

"Did he take his things?" asked Patty. "Morgan?"

Morgan shook herself out of her stupor and focused on what Patty had said. Nate's things. She could check his room and see if they were still there. If he was coming back, his things might still be there. Everyone else stayed in the hallway while she walked into the room, ignoring the surf decor. She crossed to the walk-in closet and opened the door. Empty. She turned to the others and shook her head.

"I can't believe he's really gone!" said Gena.

Morgan and the others went back to the living room and sat down. She reached out to Gena for Mark Jing and shifted him into her lap, finding comfort in his small, warm body. She couldn't even begin to imagine where Nate might be. She was terrified at the thought of him out in the world, exposed to manflu.

"Morgan, why don't you try calling him?" Gena stood and started to pace around the living room.

Morgan dug in her pocket for her phone and called him. To no one's surprise, there was no answer.

"I'm so scared for him," said Morgan softly.

"He wanted to live his life, have adventures," said Patty. "He didn't want to wait anymore."

Adventures? Is that what he was doing? What if he had been seized by the government? No, Patty was right, he must have left so he could move on with his life. If the government had taken him, there would have been a scuffle, and the rest of them would have been apprehended as well. But how could he have left before he knew if he was actually immune to manflu?

"This is terrifying. He's not fully immune yet, and he may never be. We just don't know," said Morgan. "He could become seriously ill, and he would be all alone."

"I can't believe he did this when we're so close to finding out if the vaccine worked!" said Gena. "Now we won't have his results."

"What are we going to do about Mark Jing?" said Morgan, looking down at her son. "We won't know if the vaccine is effective or even safe to give him. How could he do this knowing his son's life is hanging in the balance?" She started to cry.

"This is so immature! Unbelievable." Gena stomped around the house, swearing under her breath.

"Maybe he'll come back," said Gavin, getting up and taking the baby from Morgan. "Maybe he just needed a break from this house. It's been pretty intense."

"He's not coming back," said Patty. "I saw the look on his face after you said the test was inconclusive. He couldn't stand to have his hopes and dreams put on hold for a moment longer. He's gone."

"What an asshole!" swore Gena. "He abandoned his son."

Morgan quietly sobbed. After a few moments, she dragged herself to her bedroom where she could collapse privately. She was sprawled on her bed, her whole body shaking with rage and sadness, tears soaking the sheets, when she heard a loud noise.

CHAPTER 67

...

"There's a helicopter circling the house!" Gavin shouted from the living room.

She roused herself over to join the others. She heard a dozen car doors slamming one after the other like dominoes falling. Everyone ran to the window. Morgan peered out at an all-female SWAT team dressed in black, armed to the teeth, and surrounding the house.

Gavin handed her the baby and quickly hit a button on his phone, activating a powerful set of outdoor privacy blinds all over the house. The living room went dark. Mark Jing started to cry. Gavin hit another button, and the lights came on inside. Morgan embraced the baby, quieting him.

Gavin spoke first. "What do we do?" His voice had a desperate, pleading tone.

Gena said, "We need to stay calm."

"Let's think. What do they want?" said Morgan, swaying with the baby.

"They want the vaccine gone," said Patty.

"She's right," said Gena. "If we can convince them that no one will ever find out about the vaccine, maybe they'll let us go."

A familiar woman's voice commanded over a bullhorn, "Come out with your hands up!"

Gavin chewed on a hangnail. "Should we go outside?"

Morgan looked at Gena and Patty. They simultaneously turned to Gavin and said, "No!"

"We'll communicate on the phone. I'll pass a piece of paper outside with Morgan's cell phone number on it. They can call us," said Gena.

Patty walked over and picked up her journal from an end table and ripped out a page. She handed it to Gena along with her pen. Gena wrote down Morgan's phone number, folded up the piece of paper, and slid it out through the mail slot in the front door. She quickly stepped back to the living room where everyone else was gathered.

Footsteps could be heard outside as one of the officers picked up the paper. A few moments later, Morgan's phone rang. She pressed the button to answer the call, tapped another button to put it on speakerphone, and then placed the phone on the coffee table. Everyone stared at it.

CHAPTER 68

. . .

"Hello?" said the woman on the other end of the phone. Morgan recognized the voice. Andrea. While she had known Andrea was involved in the plot to stop the vaccine, she was surprised that she had actually shown up with the SWAT team. She looked at Gena, who nodded to indicate she also realized with whom they were dealing.

"I'm here," said Morgan.

"We're going to need you to come with us so no one gets hurt."

"We're not going anywhere, Andrea!" said Morgan. She hit the button to end the call.

"Power move. I like it," said Patty.

"Why did you hang up?" Gavin squeaked.

"I just needed a minute to think," said Morgan, "I wasn't expecting Andrea to show up!"

"You know her?" asked Gavin.

"Yes, she's the office manager at work. Gena and I suspected for a while that she was involved in this."

Gavin whistled. "This really goes deep, doesn't it?"

"Gena, we have to vaccinate Mark Jing right now," said Morgan. "Then we can give them the rest of the samples." She clutched the baby to her chest.

To her credit, Gena nodded in agreement without saying, "I told you so."

"You're going to give them the samples?" asked Gavin, his shock apparent.

"Don't worry, we have records of everything in a safe place. We can recreate it. We'll have to promise not to publish it, but we'll find a way. Just go along with whatever we say," said Gena.

"Sure, going along with everything you guys have said has worked out great for me so far," said Gavin sarcastically.

Someone pounded on the front door. "Open up! Now!"

"We should be recording this," said Patty, taking out her phone.

"That's your concern right now?" asked Gavin. "Why, do you want to use the footage in one of your philosophy lectures?" His voice sounded high and squeaky.

"No, she's right, Gavin. We need a record so they don't try anything," said Morgan. "We need to be broadcasting this live. Gena, get the vaccine set up, and Patty, get a livestream going."

The phone rang again. Morgan again answered the call and put it on speakerphone.

"Can you please stop the pounding and the helicopter so we can have a reasonable conversation?" said Morgan. She ended the call.

Patty came back into the living room with her cell phone. She had a feed set up. "Are you ready, Morgan?"

Morgan took a steadying breath and let it out. "I am."

Patty pressed a button and pointed her phone at Morgan.

CHAPTER 69

...

Morgan stared directly into the phone as she held the baby on her lap. "My name is Dr. Morgan Digby. This is my son, Mark Jing. I am a vaccine researcher, who has spent the last decade, alongside several colleagues, researching a vaccine for manflu. We have developed a potential vaccine. It was being readied for human trials when a fire was set deliberately in our lab. We believe the government is trying to prevent us from releasing this vaccine."

Pounding could be heard in the background.

"I am in hiding at the home of a friend. The government is literally at our door. We have committed no crime. They are going to destroy this vaccine. A vaccine that could potentially save the lives of all the Vulnies out there. A vaccine that could allow the world to safely have male babies again, which is what the government does not want."

The helicopter circled overhead.

Andrea shouted via the bullhorn, "Come out with your hands up!"

Gena approached Morgan with the needle ready in one hand and a cotton swab soaked in alcohol waiting in the other. Morgan held

Mark Jing in her lap tightly, binding his arms and legs. Gena found a spot on the baby's thigh, wiped it with alcohol, and took one last quick look at Morgan. She nodded. She was more scared than she had ever been about anything in her life, but she intended to stay calm for the sake of her son.

Gena quickly stabbed the leg with the needle, pushing in the liquid that might give the baby a chance at a normal life. Mark Jing wailed, unaware of his role in a larger conflict, feeling only pain. As soon as Gena finished, Morgan picked up the baby and placed him on her breast to nurse, still broadcasting on the livestream. The baby quieted quickly and fell asleep in her arms. Morgan trembled on the inside but held herself steady.

Her phone rang again. The baby startled in his sleep but did not wake up. She again took the call on speakerphone. Morgan noticed that the helicopter was quiet and the pounding on the door had stopped.

"Morgan?" said Andrea.

"Yes," said Morgan. She wondered if Andrea had seen the livestream.

"Are you ready to talk now?"

"I am. You should be aware that we are livestreaming everything that's happening."

"We are aware. We're monitoring all digital activity occurring in the home. We're sure all three of Dr. Patricia Heartwig's PhD students are very much enjoying the show."

"She has notified the entire university. The number watching will be increasing momentarily," said Morgan confidently. She motioned to Gena, who grabbed her own phone and began scrolling through, clearly trying to generate a larger following for the livestream.

"We are going to need you to return the property you stole from the lab," said Andrea.

"To what property are you referring?" asked Morgan.

"You know exactly what you have."

"I believe you are referring to samples of a potential vaccine that we have evidence may prevent manflu infections."

"That vaccine is the property of a government-funded laboratory. It is still in the development phase. Unapproved uses of the materials may be extremely dangerous. Theft and use of government property carries the penalty of fines and jail time."

"As you know, the samples were removed to prevent destruction by government agents."

"We need you to return the samples." Andrea's voice betrayed no emotion.

"If we return them, will we be free to go?"

"There is a concern that if we let you go, you may share confidential information with the public."

"You mean tell everyone what's in the vaccine?"

"That is a concern."

"As if it is so easy to recreate a vaccine! It's not like baking cookies. Very few people in the world have the expertise to manufacture this. Or do you mean tell everyone about your relationship with Ximena Álvarez and the debt collectors who have been hounding you?"

There was an audible gasp on the other end of the phone. Morgan realized Andrea hadn't known the full extent of their intel. She delighted in being able to jab at Andrea after all the pain the woman had inflicted on her.

"Why are you both so determined to prevent this vaccine from reaching the public anyway?" Morgan's curiosity had gotten the better of her, and she felt compelled to ask, although she didn't really expect an answer.

"There are things you don't understand about the world, Morgan."

"What if it gets out to the public that Ximena Álvarez is working against public health like this? Aren't you concerned that it will destroy her chances for re-election? We've already broadcast on the livestream, and there's nothing to stop us from going to the media."

From the speakerphone, Morgan heard loud cackling. She hadn't intended to make a joke.

After several moments, Andrea finally stopped laughing. "First of all, you overestimate the concern women have for men's wellbeing. A lot of us are pretty sick of a lot of them. And second, you underestimate Ximena's popularity. Women love her, and a little thing like this is not going to stand in her way."

"Where do we go from here, Andrea?"

"Well, we expect you to abide by your contract as an employee of a government-funded lab and keep all research information confidential. And any *incidental* information you might have discovered as well." Andrea's voice had dropped an octave, and she pronounced each word deliberately.

"Fine. We agree. We will leave the samples outside the house. We expect the SWAT team to disperse after receipt." Morgan held her breath to see if that would satisfy Andrea's demands.

"We will disperse the team after we confirm that all of the samples are there."

Gena made a face at Morgan that said, "Uh oh!"

"I'm going to be honest with you. There are two samples missing," said Morgan.

Now it was Morgan's turn to be hung up on.

CHAPTER 70

...

Morgan motioned for Gena to cut the recording.

"Morgan, why did you tell them that two samples were missing?" asked Gena, looking confused.

"Don't you think they would have figured it out? I'm sure they know how much was in the lab. They've been monitoring us for a while."

"Couldn't we just fill up those little bottles with water or something?" asked Gavin.

"This is not like that time in high school when you topped up your parents' vodka with water, Gavin," said Morgan. "This is serious. They're going to test it."

Incredibly, baby MJ remained asleep in her lap despite the whisper-shouting.

"How much do they already know?" asked Patty, wringing her hands.

"I broadcasted Mark Jing getting the vaccine, so they know about him," said Morgan.

"They must know about Nate, too, since they had someone

poking around his aunt's house," said Gena.

"But they don't know we vaccinated him. If we tell them we vaccinated Nate and he disappeared, what are they going to do?" Morgan asked, thinking out loud.

"I'm in over my head. I'm calling my lawyer," said Gavin. "I don't want to go to jail for harboring fugitives!" He took out his phone.

"Calm down, Gavin," said Patty. "If we're going to jail, it's probably for illegal disposal of a body. Remember Jonas in the backyard?"

"Oh, no, what if they ask where he is?" Gavin bit off another nail.

"Wait, I've got it!" said Morgan. "We tell them we tested the vaccine on Jonas, he died, and we buried him in the backyard. We don't mention Nate."

"That makes no sense, Morgan," said Gena. "Why would we give Mark Jing a vaccine that killed Jonas?"

"Good point, Gena," said Patty, nodding.

Gavin speed-dialed his lawyer and began talking rapidly to her while he paced. Everyone else stared at him until he finally hung up.

"What did she say?" asked Morgan.

"She said not to tell them anything," said Gavin.

"Easy for you! You're not accused of anything." Gena ran a hand through her curls.

"Well, get your own lawyer!" said Gavin.

"I'm going to come clean with them," said Morgan.

"Are you sure that's a good idea?" asked Gena.

"I don't know what else to do." Morgan hit a button on her phone to return the last call.

CHAPTER 71

...

The phone rang several times until Andrea finally answered.

"Look, we want to be transparent," said Morgan.

"I'm listening," said Andrea. She lingered on the "s" sound as if hissing.

"We tested the vaccine on a Vulny. We didn't get any conclusive results, and he ran off. We don't know where he is. And then we gave a dose to my son. That's it. You can have the rest of the samples. Please let us go. We want to go back to our lives." Her voice held a pleading note.

"Leave the samples outside." Andrea spoke coldly.

"Do you give your word that you won't storm in?"

"We will have no need to enter the home or disturb any of you further if the missing property is returned and the confidentiality agreement is respected."

Gena took the samples out of the fridge and dashed outside to leave them by the front door. Morgan stayed by the phone. Gena returned and sat beside Morgan on the couch.

A commotion ensued outside as the SWAT team picked up the samples.

"We have received the samples. You're free to go *for now*. Please respect the conditions of your employment contracts. If not, there will be consequences. We will be contacting you again to follow up regarding the Vulny you mentioned. We expect full cooperation at all times. Don't forget that you're being carefully monitored."

Morgan let out a sigh of relief. Gavin raised a fist in the air in a silent cheer. Gena squeezed Patty's hand and turned to hug Morgan. Was this really it?

Morgan clicked a button to end the call. Boots stomped outside as SWAT team members returned to their vehicles. Doors opened and closed. Gravel crunched under tires. And finally, silence.

CHAPTER 72

...

Could it be possible that this ordeal was over? Would Andrea leave them alone now that she had the vaccine samples and their promise not to speak out? Morgan hoped and prayed so. She thought about returning to her home and life and smiled for the first time in ages. She couldn't move quite yet, though, because the baby was still sleeping on her lap. The baby. She looked at him. Soon, Gavin and Patty stared at him, too. How would he react to the vaccine?

"What are you looking at, Gena?" Morgan asked.

Gena appeared to be transfixed by her phone. Morgan could tell she had found something interesting.

"I just did a search on Andrea's former husband."

"Why didn't I think of that earlier?" said Morgan.

"I don't know, but listen to what I found," said Gena.

"I can't wait!" said Gavin.

"Andrea comes from a wealthy Argentine family. They built a very successful restaurant business in the U.S., selling everything from empanadas to steak accompanied by expert wine pairings. Andrea's ex was a charmer who targeted the daughters of prominent families, married them, and got his in-laws to invest in his shady business dealings. This was long before manflu, obviously. He used different names so no one could track him down, but he was eventually found out and sent to prison for fraud. Unfortunately, this came too late for Andrea, because he walked away with a large portion of her family's fortune and left her and their daughter penniless."

"Oh my goodness. That's horrible!" said Morgan.

"I can understand why she's disenchanted with men," said Patty.

"That really sucks," said Gavin. "What an ass."

"Between her husband and Ximena's husband with the secret family, no wonder they're not keen on men," added Gena. "And I can understand why she was so cranky at work—she probably never expected to have to work a boring office job, coming from such a wealthy family."

"Ximena and Andrea are quite the pair. It makes sense that they're not fans of a vaccine," said Morgan. "All this time we were working so hard, and they were working against us. So much wasted effort."

"Well, it wasn't all wasted, we got where we wanted to go eventually," said Gena, looking at the baby again.

"I hope this works, Gena," said Morgan.

"Me, too," said Gavin.

Gena's phone dinged with an alert. Everyone's head snapped in her direction. "What was that?" asked Patty.

"News alert. Poll results are in. Ximena Álvarez is headed for a landslide victory in the election," said Gena.

"I can't say I'm surprised," said Morgan.

"Ugh, my taxes are going to go up," moaned Gavin.

"Apart from the whole vaccine thing, she did a pretty good job in her first term," said Gena.

Morgan glared at her. "Really?"

Gena shrugged. She glanced back at her phone. "President Álvarez just announced her new chief of staff." She looked up. "Any guesses?"

Morgan, Patty, and Gavin all said, "Andrea," simultaneously.

"Yup."

"Say, what are you all going to do now?" asked Gavin.

"I guess we'll all go home, don't you think?" said Gena, looking at Morgan.

"I'm going to miss you guys. You've become like family to me," said Morgan.

The four of them plus the baby gathered in an awkward group hug.

"I mean it. I didn't know what I would do without Jonas. But you've shown me that family is so much more. I love all of you so much." Morgan wiped a tear from her cheek.

Gavin coughed awkwardly, hurriedly wiping away a tear while making it look like he was covering his mouth.

"I'm going to miss baby MJ," said Patty. "Oh! I finished his baby blanket. You have to take it with you."

"That's so kind, Patty," said Morgan. "Thank you."

"I'm going to miss that pool table," said Gena. Everyone laughed. "I mean, I'll miss everyone, too, especially the baby."

Gavin cleared his throat. "While I am happy to get back to my, ahem, social life, I will miss all of you, too. I hope we can keep getting together. With Jonas having passed away and Nate gone, I feel a responsibility to be a father figure to this little guy," he said, softly rubbing the baby's back.

"I'm honored that you've all grown so attached to MJ! I would love to have you continue on in important roles in his life. He needs all the caring adults he can get. I consider all of you to be his bonus parents. He's so lucky to have you."

"When will you know if the vaccine worked?" asked Gavin.

"We can do an antibody test. This time we'll wait at least a week," said Gena.

"And if it worked?" asked Gavin.

"We will find a way to get the vaccine manufactured," said Gena.

"We're not going to let Andrea or anyone else stand in the way of a goal we have been striving toward for so long," said Morgan.

"What now?" asked Gavin.

"I guess I'll take MJ home and wait there with him until we know the results," said Morgan.

"It's not like either one of us is going back to work anytime soon," said Gena.

"I didn't even think about that! We're definitely going to need new jobs," said Morgan.

"Work sure is awkward when the office manager and the President of the United States are conspiring to prevent you from achieving your goals!" said Gena.

Everyone laughed, breaking the lingering tension. They had another little group hug, and Gena and Patty went off to pack their belongings so they could return to some semblance of their normal lives. Morgan paused for a moment, remembering the final days she had spent with Jonas in this house. She dismissed the memory, preferring to hold tight to images of a stronger, healthier Jonas from earlier in their marriage instead.

Meanwhile, Gavin started scrolling through his phone. Morgan had a pretty good idea of what he was up to. She sighed at the thought of Gavin as a father figure for the baby she held in her arms. He wasn't perfect, but no one was. This was her family now, and she loved it just as it was.

EPILOGUE

. . .

Two Years Later

Mark Jing, curly black hair flowing, toddled around the patio of the restaurant where Morgan, Gena, Patty, Gavin, Sarah, and Beth sat enjoying brunch on a perfect, sunny day. With MJ safely vaccinated against manflu, Morgan took him out all the time. He wasn't exactly well-behaved in restaurants, but she was so happy to have him among other people, she didn't mind handling the occasional tantrum. Gena lifted her mimosa and proposed a toast. "To Patty, whose book of poems has achieved record sales!"

"Cheers!" said everyone, raising their glasses.

"And to Morgan and Gena, who are doing such important work, researching treatments for menopause symptoms," said Patty. "Critical work. Cheers to you both!"

Everyone drank. Gavin looked around and gave a half smile in anticipation of someone toasting him.

"To Gavin!" said Morgan, raising her glass. "For taking us in when we needed somewhere to go."

"Cheers!" Everyone drank more of their mimosas. Gavin beamed. Sarah turned and gave him a kiss on the cheek. When Robert had died, Morgan had thought to set Sarah up with Gavin. They had been dating ever since. Sarah positively glowed. Gavin couldn't keep his hands off of her, and she clearly loved it.

"We should take a moment and toast to the German lab, too," said Morgan. "All that time we thought they were focused on developing a vaccine when they were more concerned with identifying therapeutics—and they were successful. Now, men won't have to suffer with post-manflu complications like Jonas did."

"Absolutely!" said Gena. "To the Germans!"

"Gena, don't be modest, I know your research laid the groundwork for the German team," said Morgan.

"That's my Gena!" said Patty as Gena smiled humbly.

"Actually, we have Gavin to thank. Or to be more precise, Gavin's mom. Those herbs she's been sending you all these years are powerful antivirals," Gena said to Gavin. She turned back to the group. "They are a huge part of the new treatment. The German team had already been working to understand why rates of transmission were lower in Asian countries. Some people assumed it was because of higher rates of mask-wearing, but many of us thought there was more to the story. After we realized the Germans were not the ones working against us, and I couldn't continue my work because the lab had burned down, I sent everything I'd learned to the German team so my findings wouldn't be lost. Fortunately, they were able to complete the process of developing effective therapeutics."

Gavin smiled modestly. "I'm glad I could help. My mom is over the moon that she has contributed to science. And she is totally vindicated on her herbal remedies. My dad's sure singing a different tune now, too. She probably saved his life with her magic teas all those years ago. And now on a more serious note . . ." He stood. "A toast to remember Jonas. May he rest in peace."

"Hear, hear!" said the chorus.

"And a toast to Nate, wherever he is," continued Gavin. "Hopefully, he's on a beach surrounded by friends and beautiful women."

Glasses were raised. About a year earlier, Morgan had received a single postcard in the mail, featuring a collage of pictures: a tropical beach, a crowded nightclub, and a gourmet meal. The back of the postcard was completely blank apart from her address. She had known instantly it was from Nate.

On one hand, she was happy he was experiencing life and enjoying his twenties as one should. But on the other hand, she was resentful he had abandoned her and their son. She still held out hope he would come back one day, if not for her, at least for MJ. She turned to Beth. They gave each other sad smiles, both missing Nate.

The group of friends ate and talked and chased Mark Jing around. And they flipped through a copy of Patty's best-selling poetry book, the last page of which contained some unusual text that looked like a secret code. Those who knew what they were looking for understood that it was a sort of recipe—the steps to produce the manflu vaccine disguised to avoid raising red flags. Who would look for medical information in a poetry book?

A couple sat at the table next to them. Two women, one clearly pregnant. As they settled into their chairs, the pregnant woman said to her partner, "I know we just sat down, but I have to go to the bathroom. The little guy is kicking me right in the bladder. We better get him on the list for soccer now!"

Morgan and Gena's ears perked up. "Did you hear that?" said Gena to the table.

"They're having a boy!" whispered Morgan loudly.

And they all toasted again.

Acknowledgments

. . .

I WOULD LIKE TO TAKE THIS OPPORTUNITY to thank the many people involved in getting this book into your hands.

First and foremost, thank you to Acorn Publishing for their willingness to take on *Manflu*, and for their creative and flexible approach to publishing overall. In particular, thank you to Holly Kammier and Jessica Therrien for walking me through each step of the process kindly and efficiently. I am grateful to the entire Acorn community for the support I have received.

Thank you to my editor Laura Taylor for making the book so much better than it otherwise would have been.

I am grateful to Savannah Gilbo, a fantastic book coach who helped me get unstuck when I was about to give up on novel-writing. I found her through Author Accelerator, a service I discovered by listening to the *#AmWriting* podcast, which has been a treasured resource throughout this process.

I owe a debt of gratitude to the Southern California Writers' Conference, where I learned enough in one weekend to make my head explode many times over. The organizers and attendees are a deeply knowledgeable, welcoming community.

A huge thank you to Shira Lee, a talented writer and editor and a fabulous friend without whom this book would not exist. She patiently gave me insightful feedback so many times, I have lost count. Every writer should have a writing buddy like Shira.

I am grateful to Dr. Veronica Lois, who has been a dear friend for half of my life (thus far) and who taught me all I ever wanted to know about viruses, real and make-believe. Many thanks to Wei Tang and Matthew Briones, who each read an early draft and were kind enough to say they liked it. For their late-stage reviews, I am grateful to Anita Grossman and Thomas Wing.

Thank you to my parents, Richard and Shelley Berkowitz, for inspiring my love of reading and encouraging my writing. Thank you to my brother, aunt, uncle, and in-laws who have all been incredibly supportive, especially my talented sisters-in-law, Josefina Muñoz Torres and Constanza Muñoz Torres.

Last but not least, infinite gratitude to my husband Enrique Muñoz Torres and my sons Alex and Daniel, who have been extremely patient with my writing. I hope that watching their mom write and publish a book has taught my children the power of sticking with something, even when it gets hard, and ultimately achieving one's goals.

About the Author

. . .

Simone de Muñoz writes dystopian, or perhaps *utopian,* fiction, depending on your perspective, where women drive the story and sometimes even run the world. She holds a master's degree in public policy from UC Berkeley and a bachelor's degree in economics from MIT, which she uses in her day job as a data analyst at a nonprofit. Based in Silicon Valley, she lives with her patient husband, their two young sons, and a grumpy dog named Fish. *Manflu is her debut novel.*